i never knew love 'til You

STEFANIE JENKINS

This is a work of fiction. Names, characters, places, and incidents either are the product of the author's imagination or are used fictitiously. Any resemblance to actual persons, living or dead, events, or locales is entirely coincidental.

Copyright © 2022 by Stefanie Jenkins

Editing by *One Love Editing*

Cover Design by *Ya'll That Graphic*

Interior Book Formatting by *Stefanie Jenkins*

Cover Photograph by *Lindee Robinson Photography*

Cover Models: *Alyse Madej & Andrew Kruczynski*

All rights reserved. No portion of this book may be reproduced in any form without written permission from the publisher or author, except as permitted by U.S. copyright law.

To Jameson + Tucker,
Almost every moment with Andy in this series has been inspired by the
two of you. But if you are reading this, you're grounded if you turn the
page.

"Love is the only force capable of transitioning an enemy into a friend."

– Martin Luther King Jr.

Prologue

Jaxon

"All right, baby, you're doing great."

I wipe the sweat dripping from my wife's brow with one hand while the other remains tight in her grasp.

It had been almost four hours since Courtney began pushing. Everything has been a blur as things progressed slowly, even though her contractions began yesterday. The doctors discussed preparing for an emergency C-section, but Court just wasn't having it. She wanted to do it this way for as long as she could—my brave girl.

Andrew, the name we picked out for our son, isn't even in the world yet and already showing he's stubborn as hell, waiting a week past our due date for labor to start. He clearly takes after his mother—not that I'm much better.

"Jax, I can't. I'm so tired." Her voice is soft and full of exhaustion. She rests her head against the pillow and briefly closes her eyes. Her breaths are harsh and ragged. How the hell a woman can go through this and then some even more than once is beyond me. My wife is a superhero for doing this.

I brush the drenched hair off her forehead and press my lips to her flushed skin.

"You are amazing. We are so close to meeting our baby boy. He's almost here, Court—just a few more pushes. Remember what your mom said—'once he's here, we will forget all about the labor.' I'm right here, baby." I give her hand a gentle, reassuring squeeze. "You and me. Ready to meet the little man that has been keeping you up at night with his kickboxing?"

A small smile appears on her face as she nods, and her blue eyes peer into mine. The last few weeks, it seems like Andy was only awake when Courtney was resting or, well, attempting to. Once we felt that first kick, it was like he never wanted to stop moving to make sure we didn't forget about him or that he always had our attention. *Trust me, little guy, there is no way we could.* I'm pretty sure since that first positive pregnancy test, it's all either of us has talked or thought about.

I wish I could say that once he is born, she will finally be able to rest, but I'm not dumb enough to fall for it. Sleep will be a mere dream that we will have to wait eighteen years for—longer if we decide to have another one.

"I love you, Jaxon."

Pressing my lips to hers, I try to channel all of my strength into her. We're both exhausted, but she can do this just a little longer. I know she can. "I love you, too."

"Okay, Courtney, here comes another contraction, and I want you to push, okay? Just a few more, and he will be out," Dr. Goodwin says from where she is between Court's legs, which are perched in the stirrups. If I didn't fear Court punching me in the balls, I would have made a joke that this is a similar position to how we got into this situation.

With one last squeeze of my hand, Courtney takes a deep breath. "I'm ready."

The sounds of our son's cries as he takes his first breath in this world soon replace his mother's screams and grunts. And boy, what a set of lungs he has. Again, something he got from his mother.

"It's a boy," Dr. Goodwin confirms, holding him up for us to see. He is beautiful. That is now two times I fell in love at first sight. First with Courtney and now our son, Andrew Colton McAdams.

I rest my forehead against my wife's, who is heavily panting beside me. Her strength is awe-inspiring. "I'm so proud of you, sweetheart. You did so good." I press my lips to hers, lingering for a moment before Dr. Goodwin interrupts us.

"Sir, would you like to cut the cord?"

I release our joined hands and step over to Dr. Goodwin to cut the cord. The nurse takes Andy to the station to clean him up and take his vitals while the doctor and other nurses tend to Courtney. Who knew birthing a baby was so intense with the number of people in the room? I'm glad that we opted out of allowing her mother in the room, too. I'm not sure that anyone else would have fit between the staff and equipment.

I glance back and forth between where the nurse took my son and where my wife lies, torn as to whose side to be beside.

"Jax," Courtney says just above a whisper, "stay with him. Stay with our boy." It's as if she knows the internal argument playing out in my head. Although it should be no surprise, most days, she knows me better than I know myself.

I walk the few feet to the nurses' station. Andy looks up at me as if he sensed his daddy was nearby. *My son, my world.* I can't stop the tears falling down my cheeks as we stare at each other, and I take in how perfect he is. I focus on him as the nurse takes his height and weight measurements—seven pounds and twelve ounces and twenty-one inches long.

"Hey, little guy. I'm your daddy." As I hold my pinky finger out in front of him, my heart skips a beat when he latches onto it. I know it's really because he is so amazed at the world he was just brought into and he doesn't know what else to do. I feel like I'm floating on cloud nine, and nothing could bring me down. I can't wait for Courtney to hold him.

The nurse is just about to place Andy in my arms when a loud beeping noise fills the room. I look up to see that it is coming from the monitor beside the bed. It doesn't only grab my attention but the doctors' and nurses' as well. Before I can even blink, bodies are moving into action as the beeping continues.

My eyes drift from the monitor to my wife, lying in the bed, her head drooped to one side with her eyes closed. "Court?"

One nurse rushes to her side—exactly where I should have been. *Why did I leave?*

"Baby?" I call out again, but no response.

"Someone get him out of here," Dr. Goodwin shouts as I try to make my way over to Courtney's side.

A nurse approaches me, placing her palms on my chest. "Sir, we need you to step out of the room so that our team can work on your wife." She attempts to push me backward, but I am twice her size and barely budge. I made the mistake once of leaving her side; I'm not doing it again. There is sensory overload in this room, and my head spins as voices shout in medical terms, my son screams, and that damn machine continues to make noise.

I begin to panic, taking quick, shallow breaths. "No," I bark. "I need you to tell me what's going on." I need to get to Andy and to Court and keep them safe.

Using all her strength and taking advantage of my focus being elsewhere, the nurse pushes me back enough to the doorway. "Sir," she pleads, "please let us do our job."

I am escorted out of the room, abandoning them both. My heart is racing and my palms sweating as the wooden door in front of me clicks, creating a barrier between me and the two most important people in my life. There are only faint sounds of the commotion on the other side. I feel helpless and completely cut off from the world.

It has already been two long days, and now I'm forced out of the room without even a word about what is going on and if Courtney is okay. The fog in my brain clears as I realize the monitor going off was her heart monitor.

She is in perfect health. Why was it going off like that? I don't know which is worse, knowing or the unknown? Who am I kidding? It is definitely the unknown.

Rubbing my hand across the back of my neck, I will the tears threatening to fall to go away. *How could this happen?* My heart is pounding in my chest as I filter through the worst-case scenarios. It could have been a faulty machine. They could rush her to emergency surgery; maybe she fell into a coma. She could even—*fuck*, I can't even bring myself to say it.

The tears freely fall now. I can't lose her. My life would be nothing without her. How could I move on?

Realizing that pacing the floor in front of her room isn't only not helping but making me more anxious, I lean back against the wall and look up at the ceiling panels. I close my eyes and say a silent prayer for my family. I should go to the waiting room, where my in-laws and best friend, Finn, have waited patiently for updates, but I can't be around anyone now.

I need to know that she is okay. She just has to be. I can't do this without her. We just brought a son into this world. We need to raise him together and go on all the family vacations she has spent months talking about.

How am I supposed to do that on my own? Why am I even thinking about things like that? What the hell is wrong with me?

What was supposed to be the happiest day of our lives has turned into the scariest. My legs give out on me, and I fall to the floor with a thump. Resting with my elbows propped up on my knees and my head in my hands, I wait for the doctors to come out with any sort of information. I will take anything at this point. *Tell me my wife is okay. Let me hold my son.* I can hear his muffled cries through the door, overpowering the commotion. All I want to do is bust through that door and go to him. Hold him in my arms and assure him that his mother will be fine—that we all will be fine. This is all just a nightmare that we will wake up from, and soon we can all go home and be the happy family we've always dreamed of.

The image of my son staring at me in my mind is the only thing getting me through this very moment while I wait for something—anything.

Chapter 1

Kate

"Mmm," I moan as the hot coffee assaults my taste buds—a combination of sweet cream, salted caramel, and heaven.

I crane my neck from side to side as the caffeine runs through my veins. Mornings aren't really my thing, but with a cup or two or three, I think I can handle anything thrown at me.

I bring the mug down as I lean against the pillar of my front porch. It may be a simple one compared to my brother Kyler's in-laws' home in Annapolis, but this is perfect. When I first pulled up to the address on the listing, I instantly fell in love with the front porch.

My mind takes me back in time to when I dragged my twin sister, Lauren, to see the house for the very first time.

"Why would you want to live here? It's so big. You realize you have to clean this by yourself. Mom won't clean up after you anymore," Lauren said as she took in the large empty house.

A house I planned to make my home.

I threw my head back in laughter. "Mom hasn't cleaned up after me in years." I looked around and sighed. "Can't you see it? I could have a bookcase over there with all the books you buy me but I never intend to read. A couch against this wall with the television hanging there." I pointed to the wall opposite where we stood. "When the lighting is right, I could set up my easel here and paint the neighborhood. If not, then I have a whole room upstairs that I plan to set up as a studio. It has a window facing the west so I can paint the sunsets. With the large backyard, I could have everyone over and have room for the kids to play. It's perfect."

I watched my sister as she wrapped her arms around her waist and nibbled her bottom lip. Was she seeing the same vision I did?

"Woah, kids? Have you given it more thought since—"

I waved my hand to cut her off. "No." I shrugged. "But one day, Kyler might meet someone he wants to settle down with. Or who knows, maybe you will have little bookworms running around."

Lauren smiled, however, it didn't reach her eyes anymore. She might not admit it, but I knew she was still healing her broken heart. Closing the distance between us, she threw her arm around my shoulder and rested her head against mine. "I think it's perfect, sissy."

Shaking myself out of the memory, I can't help but smile, realizing that it will all become a reality soon since my brother and his wife are expecting twins—the Lawson Twins 2.0, as I've nicknamed them. He is the first of us to start a family, but I'm sure Lauren won't be far behind now that she and her high school sweetheart, Finn, reunited after spending ten years apart and recently tied the knot.

And then there's me, the cool Aunt Kate, ready to spoil her nieces and nephews with presents, never tell them no, and sugar them up before sending them home to their parents.

Notice how I said *their* kids. I've known from an early age that family life wasn't for me. It's not like I haven't met a man I could see myself settling down with. Okay, maybe that is true. I have quite a dating history—it's often a topic of my siblings' conversations—but all that history contains is a bunch of fuddy-duddies not worthy of a second date. Maybe a man for me is out there, but I enjoy having fun with no strings and leave the falling in love to my siblings.

I adjust the sleeves of my hoodie. The closer we get to fall, the brisker the mornings are. Between my oversized hoodie, my hat, and the aviators blocking the sun from my eyes, I could easily be mistaken for the Unabomber.

I'm mentally going over my to-do list for the day before going over to my sister's house for a cook-out when movement across the street catches my attention.

New neighbors just moved in yesterday. I haven't met them yet but can only hope they are just as nice as the previous neighbors, the Lassiters. They were the sweetest couple, who recently moved to be closer to their grandkids.

What a great first impression I'm going to make—looking like hell under this hat and in dire need of a shower. I lean down and catch a whiff of myself. Well, at least I don't smell like I've been hanging out in a dumpster, and the sunglasses hide the terrible bags under my eyes. Between helping pull off my sister's surprise wedding and, well, just life in general, I've been working my ass off.

However, when I look up for the first glance of the new neighbors, it's not an adult I'm greeted with on the front porch but a little boy wearing pajamas. He can't be older than five. For sure, he is younger than the kids my sister teaches. He's looking around, and I follow his gaze, hoping I see his parents. Maybe I just missed them walking out before, but I come up empty.

He grabs the railing and walks down the steps to the front yard. A million different scenarios are running through my brain. Maybe he came out to look for someone to help because there's something wrong. Maybe his parents are having a medical emergency and he doesn't know how to dial 911. Even worse, what if they forgot the kid at home alone? Hey, it happens. The father thinks the mother is taking the kid to day care. Next thing you know, they're all over the news because the kid died. Okay, so maybe that's an extreme scenario, but I have seen *Home Alone* plenty of times.

By the time the boy reaches the bottom step, I've already set my coffee down. My mind is in a frenzy as I make my way down my sidewalk to make sure he's okay.

I freeze midstep and gasp, "Holy shit," under my breath. He's pulling his pajama pants and underwear down and peeing against a small tree in his front yard.

What in the actual fuck?
I grew up with a younger brother, but I don't remember Kyler ever walking outside to pee. Peeing outside to avoid having to go back inside, sure, but not specifically walking out to do so.

I freeze and slide my aviators down my nose to make sure I'm seeing what I'm seeing for sure and it's not just my mind playing tricks on me. If it is my mind, the least it could do is make me believe Chris Hemsworth is professing his love toward me and not a child that may be in danger. I wait for a moment for his parents to walk out, but once again, there's no one.

The little boy has finally finished his business and pulled his pajama pants back up by the time I make it to the edge of the sidewalk. He rushes back inside without a second glance.

I grip the back of my neck, stuck at a crossroads. Do I ignore it, or should I at least let his parents know that he just walked out the front door? I mean, unless he's being raised by a bunch of Neanderthals who purposely teach him to do that, they should be made aware. After all, he was lucky that it was just me out here and not some creeper driving by. Yeah, that settles it. I continue my walk toward the house.

It's a shame that I'm meeting the new neighbors under these circumstances.

When I'm halfway up his front yard, a tall man emerges from the front door, carrying a large trash bag in his hand. Forget Chris Hemsworth—he has nothing on this man. *Yep, I'm definitely regretting introducing myself now.*

It should be illegal to be that gorgeous. I'd say he's around six feet of deliciousness wearing dark jeans, black work boots, and a black fitted T-shirt that wraps around his bulging biceps. I'm close enough to notice a light coating of stubble lining his jaw, and I just want to run my fingers over it to feel the roughness on my skin… or on my thighs.

Get your act together, Kate. I need to stop thinking these thoughts. For all I know, he could be a married man, for fuck's sake. And I haven't had enough caffeine yet today, nor do I have my sassy pants on to take on his wife if she comes running out to stake her claim.

He finally looks up, and he jolts. His dark eyes meet mine, and I nearly melt. "Umm, can I help you?"

Wow, even his voice is sexy—deep and rough. *Lord help me.* My mind instantly wonders what his voice would sound like saying my name as I make him come. *Shit, I've been off the cock for too long.* I need to get laid and stop thinking dirty thoughts about my new neighbor.

He clears his throat, breaking me from my thoughts.

"Hi, sorry. I'm Kate. I live across the street." I point over my shoulder toward my house behind us. He raises a brow in confusion, wondering what that has to do with anything to him. I continue. "I was just outside on my porch, and your little boy ran out the front door and peed in your front yard. I wasn't sure if you were aware of him doing this, or maybe it's something new."

We stand off in silence. He huffs out a breath and grabs the back of his neck, clearly irritated by the information I just gave him. I try to steady my expression so as to not give it away that I notice just how his T-shirt clings to his sculpted arms.

He finally speaks. "I'm sorry, what was your name again?" *Jesus, does he have the memory of a goldfish?*

"Kate." I extend my hand to shake his, expecting him to introduce himself. However, he just looks down at my hand as if it's diseased. It may be a little dirty with paint, but that's about all.

"Right… Miss," he says curtly.

"No, it's just Kate." This time, I cut him off. Two can play this game, buddy. If I had known I was going to have a standoff this morning before I even finished my coffee, I might have put a little something extra in my mug.

"Do you have kids?" *What the hell does that have anything to do with this?*

"Well, no, I—"

"Then don't tell me how to raise mine," he interrupts. I may not have any kids, but I have fucking common sense.

"I didn't mean anything by it. I just didn't want him to walk into the road or walk away."

"Are you some neighborhood patrol or something?"

"Are you always this rude to people you've just met?" Maybe I should just ask to speak to the boy's mother. Hopefully, she is a lot friendlier than him. I try to catch a glimpse of his left hand to see if I spot a ring, but he's not making it easy for me.

"When they come over to *my house* and attack *my* parenting skills, I do." His nostrils flare, and the vein in the side of his neck pulses.

I throw my hands up in the air in frustration. *Sassy-pants Kate Lawson, it is.* "You were the one not watching your kid," I shout. "I'm not attacking you or judging you. I was just trying to be a friendly neighbor, for fuck's sake! Clearly, I was wrong for giving a damn."

His hard features soften for just a moment before he puts the facade back up, and anger swirls in his beautiful dark eyes.

"Look, Kate." He enunciates my name as if I'm a young child getting reprimanded. "Thanks for your concern, but like I said, I don't need your help to raise my son. I'm doing just fine on my own."

Well, I guess that might answer the question about the wife—for whatever reason, she's not in the picture. Maybe she got wind of his stellar personality. Pretty sure this dickhead *wasn't* voted Mr. Congeniality in high school.

Mr. Who I Never Caught His Name crosses his arms, signifying he has nothing more to say to me. I think of the first thing that comes to my head, and instead of it being an overly sarcastic response I would typically go for, I settle on, "Well, okay then." Okay, so I went for a bit of sarcasm.

I spin on my feet without even saying goodbye and head back home.

I let my vagina do the talking over my brain and nonchalantly peek over my shoulder to find him still looking at me. His jaw is tense, and his eyes are smoldering. I twist my head back around as my panties instantly dampen at the sight of him. In hopes he is still staring at me, I add a little extra sway of my hips to my steps. I'm just stepping up on my front porch when I hear the trash can lid slam. It's not until I hear his front door slam a little too dramatically that I finally feel like I can breathe.

Well, so much for friendly neighbors moving in. *Welcome to the neighborhood, asshole.*

Chapter 2

Jaxon

"**I**n a quarter of a mile, turn left onto Sherman Way," the GPS says through the speakers of my vehicle.

I sigh heavily and grip the steering wheel tightly as I follow the instructions and maneuver my way through the neighborhood. To say this move cross-country has been stressful as fuck would be the understatement of the year.

First, the house we were supposed to move into fell through a week and a half before moving, so it left me last-minute house shopping. Thankfully, this rental had just become available, and I took it sight unseen. Well, at least I had seen a photo that the Realtor had emailed. When Andy and I pulled up yesterday, I let out a breath of relief that the house looked just like the photo, and we hadn't been catfished. In fact, the house was beautiful. The type of house Courtney and I had always talked about owning one day.

From the little we've seen, I can already tell that it's a great neighborhood that we moved into. Which brings the next thing taking over my mind.

My new neighbor.

Squabbling with her first thing in the morning wasn't exactly how I pictured my morning going.

Did I overreact? Yes.

I shouldn't have bitten her head off, especially when her intentions were nothing but pure. But as a single parent, I'm doing the best I can. Andy has done nothing like that before.

Was she right? Absolutely.

I had been in the kitchen making breakfast after being on the phone with the moving company to complain about some of our shit being damaged on arrival, and I hadn't even noticed that Andy had walked right out the front door.

While Andy got dressed, we had a long talk that he can't just walk outside—out front, especially without me or at least letting me know.

My biggest issue with her wasn't that she cared enough to walk over to a complete stranger. Nope, that's not what plagued me since we departed. It was my reaction to her.

I haven't reacted like that since I met Courtney. The way her hips swayed side to side as she walked away. It was like they were hypnotizing me. I should have been nicer. Told her thank you for looking out. Instead, I panicked. How could I have these feelings for another woman? Courtney was the love of my life. The guilt is overwhelming. It's been almost five years since Courtney passed. I shouldn't still feel like I'm cheating, yet somehow, that lingering guilt is eating me up inside.

God, I miss her.

I've found other women attractive and have attempted a date here and there over the years, but dating and the single dad don't exactly go together like peanut butter and jelly. This time, though, shit, it felt different. It felt like wanting more.

While outwardly, I reacted like an asshole, scaring the poor woman away, inwardly, my body was burning. A hunger I thought was long since buried reared up, making its presence known. It was the thought of what she might hide under that oversized hoodie that attracted my hand to my cock like a goddamn magnet while I took my shower.

I should have walked over after I calmed down and apologized, but thankfully, Andy and I had a cook-out to get to at my best friend Finn's house. At least, that will hopefully give me a moment to breathe and *not* think of my new neighbor and all the ways I thought of punishing her for her sassy mouth.

"You have reached your destination," the GPS announces.

I park my truck behind a half dozen cars I don't recognize in front of a two-story colonial house.

This neighborhood has similar vibes to the one we just moved into—which once again makes me think of that spitfire. *Fuck me!*

For a moment, I think about putting my truck back in drive, speeding off, and never looking back, but then I remember the look on my best friend's face when he flew back out to Seattle to ask me to pick up my life and move my son and me cross-country to help him.

Finn and I had met when he moved to Seattle ten years ago after taking a job with Nathanial and Michelson, one of the top architecture firms in Seattle. Earlier this year, he returned to Pennsylvania after his father passed away suddenly to take over his father's company, Reynolds Contracting.

While it may have been tragic circumstances that led him to coming home, there was a plus side. He reunited with his high school sweetheart, Lauren. They ended up getting back together and tied the knot this summer. Sadly, with the timing of our move, I wasn't able to make it out to stand beside him as his best man as he had me. Finn had been there through it all with me. He stood by me as my best man when Courtney and I got married, was at the hospital when Andy was born, watched as they lowered her casket into the ground, and all the moments in between until his abrupt move back east.

I didn't really need much to think about when he asked me to move to come be the vice president and his right-hand man at the company. They were expanding, and he needed someone he trusted to help run things. I was ready for the new opportunity. It's not like there was much keeping us on the West Coast anyway. The only family I have left is Courtney's parents, who had retired to Florida; they encouraged us to make this change, and it got us closer to them.

I look out the windshield and chuckle at the roses lining the front porch. All that's missing is the white picket fence lining the yard. This style of house better suits him than the apartment life in Seattle, but maybe it's also that I know he is much happier here.

"Daddy! Daddy! Are we here? Are we here?" Andy chants from the back seat. He is so excited to live near his godfather. He and Finn have a special bond—sometimes, it makes me a little envious. Finn gets to be the cool guy, always spoiling the shit out of him, while I have to not only be the fun parent but the one who scolds him and puts him in time-out.

"Yeah, buddy. Just give me a second and we'll go, okay?"

In the rearview mirror, I watch Andy squirm in his seat impatiently. I grab my phone from the cup holder and reread the last conversation with Finn just before we left the house.

Finn: *Hope you guys are hungry. Lo has gone all out.*
Me: *I told you guys not to make a big deal out of this.*
Finn: *I promise we didn't do this for you. That's just a perk. We always get together like this. You'll get used to it.*

Me: *If you say so. Leaving soon.*

Finn: *Can't wait to see you guys. We'll be out back, so just come around through the side gate.*

I take a deep breath and give myself a pep talk. *You got this.*

"Dad," Andy whines. "Come on, Uncle Finn's waiting for me." I chuckle to myself as I unbuckle my seat belt.

"All right, all right." I give my best Matthew McConaughey impression that goes over Andy's head. "Let's go."

I grab my keys and phone, pocketing them as I exit the truck and walk around to the other side of the truck to get Andy out of his booster seat.

After helping him down, which, thanks to his squirming, took a little longer than expected, we make our way toward the backyard. I feel like a dick for showing up to a cook-out empty-handed, but if Finn tries to give me shit, I'll just say I brought Andy and that's good enough.

Andy and I are halfway to the gate when a familiar voice calls out, "Hey, man."

I look up to see Finn's brother-in-law, Chase, walking toward us, holding his son, Liam, in his arms. Holy shit, Liam grew up. I feel like it was just yesterday that Finn was beaming after he learned he was going to be an uncle for the first time.

"Hey, Chase, good to see you." We shake hands, and Andy clears his throat beside me. *Smart-ass.*

"Woah, Andy. Sorry, I almost didn't recognize you. What, are you heading off to college soon?" Chase jokes. Fuck, it sure feels like time is going that fast. He was born, and then I blinked, and here we are. Somehow, I've managed to enjoy the moments in between.

"No," Andy laughs, shaking his head. "I'm only four. I will go to kidorgarten next year."

Chase and I both laugh at his mispronunciation.

Andy tugs on my arm, trying to pull me toward the gate again. Patience is clearly not a virtue my son was blessed with.

We continue our walk before Andy goes into meltdown mode.

"How was the move?" Chase asks, and all I can manage is a grunt. He laughs loudly. "That good, huh?"

"All that matters is we're here." I let out a sigh of relief. It feels like it took forever to get here, though. And there's still plenty of unpacking left to do when we get home. And when I say plenty, I mean basically everything.

Chase slaps my back as we enter the backyard. "I know it means a lot to Finn and Kels that you're here." Finn's sister is the CFO of Reynolds Contracting, and it was her suggestion that they needed to bring someone on so Finn didn't run himself ragged.

"Well, look what the cat dragged in," Finn shouts as he sets a plate of food near the grill. *Speak of the devil.*

"Uncle Finn!" Andy runs and nearly knocks Finn over with the speed he was going.

"Ahh, Andy. I've missed you." Finn scoops him up and hugs him tightly.

"Jeez, way to make a guy feel like chopped liver over here," I joke.

Finn sets Andy down and pulls me into a manly hug, slapping my back dramatically.

Two other guys I don't recognize come up to join us.

Finn introduces me to Kyler and Zach.

"Andy, I was going to show Liam the little pond Uncle Finn has set up in the backyard. I think he just put fish in there. You want to check it out with me?" Chase asks, and I feel a sense of relief at the slight break. Does that make me a shit parent?

Andy looks up at me for permission, and I nod. I can still see him from where I stand, but my eyes move off him for a second when a little girl rushes over, and Zach scoops her up in his arms. *Holy sparkling blue eyes, Batman.* She is adorable, and judging by the way she buries her face in his neck, I'd bet good money she has him wrapped around her finger.

"And this crazy girl is my daughter, Emme. Don't let the shyness fool you. I think we're getting on to nap time." Andy never really had that shy phase. He has a bit of his mother's outgoing personality. "Maybe we can have a playdate one day."

"Thanks, I'm sure Andy would like that." I've known this man all of five minutes and already he's offering playdates. No wonder Finn loves this group. They're extremely welcoming. I feel like I've known them for years.

"Babies everywhere." Finn's brother-in-law, Kyler, laughs with a huge smile on his face. He and his wife are expecting twins soon. "Finn, when are you and Lauren going to start a family?" Ky pauses and then cringes. "Not that I need to think about my sister like that."

"Hey, welcome to my world, man," Zach teases, slapping Kyler on the shoulder. I really hope there isn't going to be a quiz after all these introductions. I had trouble keeping up with how everyone is connected in the introductions. But Kyler is married to Zach's sister, Dani. And Zach's wife is also his sister's best friend. It's moments like this that I miss Courtney even more because whenever I couldn't remember someone's name, which was often, I was forever grateful when she would be the buffer and swoop in and introduce herself.

"Someday." Finn glances over his shoulder. "Speaking of my girl…" He leans over to me. "Jax, there's someone I want you to meet."

Finn is going to be a great dad one day. He's had plenty of practice with Andy, his nephew, and I assume Emme based on how close this group is. I follow Finn away from the guys, but loud giggles from the other side of the yard turn my attention back to where Chase is playing with Andy and Liam.

I look up just in time to see two women approaching. Not just two women, but one is none other than—

"You," the same brunette that scolded me this morning shouts.

"You," I snap back.

She crosses her arms defensively. "What the hell are you doing here?" I glance around the group of people to find everyone's eyes on us.

It's then I notice the similarities between her and the woman Finn has since pulled into his arms and is having a hushed conversation with.

Holy shit. No fucking way.

The women are identical, minus the faded pink streaks in Kate's hair.

"Okay, pause on whatever the hell this is." Finn waves his hand back and forth between our standoff. "But you better believe we will come back to it in a moment. Jax, this is Lauren. Lo, this is Jax."

I hold out my hand in front, but she pulls me into a hug. I stumble into her arms, not expecting it. "It's great to meet you in person." She pulls back, and I run my hands down the front of my shirt and catch Finn chuckling beside us as Lauren takes her place back in his arms. "I'm sorry. It's just that I've heard so much about you. I feel like I've known you as long as Finn has."

"No, it's no problem at all. I feel the same. Thank you for welcoming me and Andy into your home."

A grumble under Kate's breath brings everyone's attention to her. She stands there still like a statue. Unlike Lauren's warm welcome, Kate's scowl is as cold as a winter tundra.

Did she know who I was this morning? "And this is my twin sister, Kate. But it seems you two already know each other. Umm, which is how again?" She glances back at her husband, and he shrugs.

"He's my dickhead neighbor I was just telling you about." I don't miss the emphasis on *dickhead.*

"Dickhead?" I arch a brow and cross my arms. It appears we both made quite an impression this morning if, hours later, she is talking to her sister about me. I clench my jaw to keep the smile from forming on my lips.

She scoffs and rolls her eyes. "Hey, if the shoe fits, buddy." I can feel the venom laced through her voice. *So maybe I was a little harsh this morning, but what the fuck is her deal now?* "I'd call you worse, but there's kids around."

I snicker. Before I can respond to not let that stop her, Finn cuts in.

"Woah, woah. Hold up, what do you mean, neighbor? I thought you were moving into Bankhead Landing."

I sigh and run a hand over my face. I forgot I hadn't mentioned any of this to Finn yet. Like I said, it was all fucking last-minute and a nightmare.

"No, that fell through. It's a long story." One that I don't need to tell in front of her. I don't need her continued judgment right now. "I'll tell you later. We ended up over on Birchwood. Right across the street from your…" I make direct eye contact as I sarcastically say, "Lovely sister-in-law here. She really knows how to welcome someone with open arms." I nearly choke on my sarcasm.

Finn whistles. "Well, fuck me, this surely got interesting." Yeah, no kidding. It's bad enough this gorgeous woman is going to be right across the street, but now she's always going to be around. Is this some sort of karma?

She opens her mouth to retort, but Andy comes running up, yelling my name. "Daddy! Daddy!"

I swoop him into my arms, and instantly, the frustration I've felt the last few moments falls away. "Daddy! Mr. Chase says I can come visit the firehouse and see the big rig. Isn't that cool?" Before we left Seattle, Andy's grandparents sent him a giant book of trucks, and he became obsessed with firetrucks on the drive to the East Coast. He pointed out every single one he saw—there were eighty-seven.

"Can we go? Can we go?" Andy squirms in my arms in excitement, and I tighten my grip to keep him from falling.

Chase approaches us, holding a sweaty Liam in his arms.

"I'm sure we can go soon if it's not too much trouble." I glance up to Chase for confirmation that my son isn't telling little white lies.

"Nah, it's no trouble at all. We can chat later and pick a day that works. I gotta get going, though. Welcome, Jax." He slaps me on the back. "Let us know if you guys need anything."

I nod. "Thanks, will do."

Chase turns to the others and waves goodbye. "Sorry to run, guys, but duty calls." Chase is a firefighter. He actually met his wife on a call, but that's a whole other story. I watch as he heads over to Kelsey to hand off their son and kiss her goodbye.

A slight pain in my chest rips through me as I watch their interaction as a family. Moments like that were stolen from me. Courtney never even got to hold her son and smile at him lovingly, like Kelsey is with Liam. I completely block out the conversation around me as I intrude on their picture-perfect moment. I spent years angry that I didn't even have just one photo of Court holding Andy. A part of me will always carry some form of anger—not only did I lose my wife, but Andy lost his mother. There are so many things that he didn't get to experience because of that.

"Wow, you're pretty," Andy says, pulling me from my inner demons, his attention now on Lauren and Kate. "Isn't she pretty?" His eyes are bouncing back and forth between the twins like a ping-pong match. Besides a show he watches on Disney Plus, I think this is his first experience with twins.

"Sure, buddy," I say nonchalantly as I set him back down on the ground. But that's the problem—Kate is pretty. I thought she was this morning hiding behind the hat and sunglasses, but now, fuck me sideways.

"Andy, you remember talking with Uncle Finn's wife, Lauren, right?"

"Yep." He buries his head in my leg, which is so out of character. "Daddy." His blue eyes meet mine. "I need to go potty."

I look up to find Kate staring, and I know there is a smart remark waiting on the tip of her tongue. Finn must sense it, too.

"Come on inside. I'll show you the bathroom." Finn extends his arm toward the house, and we follow him.

A not-so-hushed conversation begins over my shoulder between Lauren and Kate, but I try to ignore it. I huff out a long breath. *What did I get myself into moving out here?*

Chapter 3

Jaxon

I shove my hands in the pockets of my jeans as I wait outside the bathroom for Andy to finish up, trying to wrap my brain around this plot twist. My new neighbor is Finn's sister-in-law? How the fuck didn't I pick up on that? I think I'll add that to my speech when I receive the worst-best-friend-ever award.

When I hear the toilet flush, I lean closer to the door. "Hey, make sure you wash your hands."

"I know, Daddy," his little voice shouts, but it's muffled over the running water. I'm still not used to him growing up so fast. But I'm thankful to be out of the diapers phase of life.

Moments later, the door opens, and Andy walks out with a smile on his face—completely oblivious to the shitstorm around us.

"All set?"

"Yup." He takes my hand, and I scrunch my nose at his still-wet hand in mine. At least there's my proof that he did, in fact, wash his hands.

We follow the hallway back to Finn and find him and Lauren speaking in quietly in the kitchen. Lauren is the first to notice us.

"Hey, guys," she greets us with a big smile, and I can't help but return it.

Finn turns around with a matching smile but hesitation in his eyes. He quickly blinks it away, but I know his brain is going a mile a minute, wanting answers.

"Uncle Finn, I love your house."

"Thanks, little dude." He ruffles the top of Andy's head. "I'm glad you think so."

"It has the best-smelling soap." He brings his hands to his face and inhales loudly. "Ah," he exhales contently, and we all laugh at his dramatics.

"Well, that is this lady all right here." Finn tilts his head toward his wife.

"Daddy just buys the boring stuff, and I don't like the way it smells, so sometimes…" He glances at me before bringing his hand up to cup his mouth. "I don't wash my hands." He attempts to whisper, but I'm pretty sure his volume is louder. I smirk at his honesty. "We have a new house, you know, that has three bathrooms. Maybe you can buy some of those for our house?" Andy turns his focus from Lauren to me as if asking if that's okay.

I nod, and he smiles.

"Of course. Maybe one day you can come to Target with me, and we can pick some out. What do you say?"

"Awesome." He beams and throws his hands in the air. "I want that cupcake one."

Lauren crouches down to Andy's height. "Speaking of cupcakes, what do you say we go get one outside and let your dad and Uncle Finn catch up?" There's an ease and calmness about her that I'm pretty sure she could convince anyone to do anything.

All eyes are on me. "Sure thing. Make sure you listen."

She pushes to stand. "You two have a lot to catch up on. I'll have Ky manage the grill, and I'll let you know when food's ready." She leans in to kiss Finn's cheek, but he pulls her to his lips.

I clear my throat so they remember they have an audience at the same time Andy says, "Yuck! Kissing is gross."

Lauren and Finn quickly break apart and chuckle. He wraps his arm around her shoulder and kisses her temple quickly.

"One day, you might change your mind." Finn smiles as Lauren holds her hand out in front of Andy, and he takes it without a second thought. She looks over her shoulder with one last smile before they exit the kitchen and head back to the backyard.

"Wanna sit in the living room?" Finn's voice breaks my gaze from where I watch him bond with Lauren effortlessly. Andy's never had a constant female influence in his life. This move will be good for him.

"Sure."

He extends his hand toward the other room. "Go ahead, and I'll grab us some beers."

I head into the living room, but before I reach the couch, photos on the mantle catch my eye—well, two in particular. The first is a photo of a younger Lauren and Finn from what I assume is high school. They're wearing football and cheerleading uniforms. I can't help but laugh at how young they look—yet they still look exactly the same as they do now.

The second image that draws my attention is from their wedding day, not that long ago.

Finn had planned a sort of spur-of-the-moment proposal. Well, no, not spur of the moment. It was ten years in the making, and he put a lot of work into it. However, the day he proposed, he had also planned for them to be married that evening. He rented a beach house for them and their whole family and turned it into the perfect oasis. Or so I'm told. I would have given anything to be there.

"That was a good day," Finn says from behind me. I look over my shoulder and find him approaching with two beers.

"I can't believe you're married and that I wasn't there beside you as your best man."

Finn places his hand on my shoulder. "How many times do I have to tell you it's okay? You were there in spirit. So much was happening at once—me getting married, you uprooting your life to here. Which, speaking of, why didn't you tell me about the house?"

I take a swig of the cool liquid and move over to the couch.

"I don't know. I didn't want to burden you with my shit. I remember what newlywed life was like."

"That's bullshit. We're here to help anytime. It's why I asked you out here, Jax. You help me, I help you. Just like when I flew out to see you and Andy, I meant what I said. We're all here to help—me and Lo and all those crazy fuckers out there. They're good people."

"They seem like it."

"I guess at least I don't have to ask what the house is like. I've seen it plenty of times when at Kate's. I hadn't realized it was available, but it's perfect for you guys."

"Yeah." I snort. "Even comes with super-nosy neighbors." I try to hide my rising irritation by taking a quick sip of my beer.

Finn bellows out a boisterous laugh. It's good to hear him laugh. Finn has overcome some dark times, so seeing him like this makes me happy.

"Kate is, well…" He twists his lips, searching for the word as he takes a sip of his drink. "Kate."

I was thinking annoying, bitchy, or beautiful. I tense at the thought of speaking the last one aloud. If Finn senses something off with me, he doesn't mention it.

I explain the events of this morning, and Finn listens intently, throwing in a few laughs. Of course, I leave out the whole jerking off to thoughts of her like a goddamn teenage boy.

"I can't believe I didn't realize who she was. She and your wife are identical twins, for fuck's sake!"

"Yeah, I don't know either," he laughs. "But you're under a lot of stress and exhaustion." It didn't help that she was dressed like a homeless person, not resembling the sexy vixen currently a couple of hundred feet away. I think I almost preferred her that way. At least then she was all covered up and things were only left to my imagination.

Now her long legs are on display, covered by only a sorry excuse for shorts. The material of her black fitted tank clings to her chest. Her breasts may be on the smaller size, but I can tell they would fill my hands perfectly. The dips of her collarbone beg to be explored. Would she shiver under my touch as I dance my fingers along her throat? Maybe I can somehow convince her to wear a parka from now on.

I shift in my seat. The last thing I fucking need is a hard-on right now.

"I guess. Can I ask you a question?"

He nods. "Always. What's up?"

"Since they're twins, were you attracted to them both?"

"Nope," he chuckles. I wonder if this is something he's asked often. "It was more than just looks. They have totally different personalities. Lo and I just clicked. Kate and I are more like siblings. That banter hasn't changed even after all these years."

"Hmm," I hum. I guess that makes sense. I was attracted to Kate the moment I met her, but not Lauren—weird. That could make for some taboo love story—falling for your best friend's wife.

"I'm sure you don't think so, but under that rough exterior, Kate's a sweetheart. But shh, don't tell her I said that."

"Trust me, after our interactions today, I'm not sure there will be much conversation between us."

Finn's eyebrows shoot up curiously as he pulls the bottle to his mouth.

I slap his arm with the back of my hand, and he fumbles. "Not like that, asshole."

"What? Just saying." He holds up his hands innocently. "Double dates could be fun. We go out now with Lauren's brother and his wife. Now we could add the other two important people in our lives."

"You know I don't date." My voice is grim and matter-of-fact. My son is my priority.

"That was the old you. We're all about change this year. I'm always happy to hang out with my godson if you ever want to, you know… get your dick wet."

"Jesus, fuck! What is wrong with you?" Damn, I've missed my best friend, even with the stupid shit he says.

"Just looking out for my best friend and little Jax."

I don't need anyone looking out for me, not to mention, "little" isn't a word that should ever be associated with my dick. It has feelings and already isn't a fan that it sees more action from my hand than actual pussy. I've had sex with two women since Court—once, I was drunk out of my mind and instantly regretted it. The second, we met up a few times, but she wanted more, and I didn't. So, it was easy to cut things off, although I think my dick is holding a grudge.

"Enough with the dick talk. My dick is off-limits—to you or to anyone." Especially to brunettes with lips I'd love to have wrapped around my cock. That's one way to shut her up.

I rise from the couch. I should go out there and check on Andy. I don't want anyone to think I'm here to take advantage of someone else watching my son. "I'm going to tell your wife she made a mistake and to run far away."

He follows suit. "Good luck with that. She loves me."

"Who loves you?" Speak of the devil or, well, the angel of the Lawson twins appears in the doorway from the kitchen.

"You do, babe." He walks over and swoops her into his arms.

"Most days," she laughs and winks. "I was just letting you know food's ready. Oh, and Jax, Andy is cleaning everyone out with money for his swear jar. I think he's racked up over five dollars in that brief span of time. I'm not sure who's paid more—Zach or Kate. I'm pretty sure Zach hates the idea of the jar, and Haylee is ready to make one for Emme."

"We'll be right there, babe." Finn kisses her temple and releases her. She turns and walks out of the room.

"So, are you still gonna have my mom watch Andy even though you're on the other side of town now?" Finn's mom, Denise, offered to help me with childcare—one, it's expensive as hell, and two, I'm not sure how I feel about dropping him off somewhere I don't know. She watches her grandson, Liam, so he will have a friend, even if he's just a toddler. But that was when I had planned on moving into a place just down the road from her place. But my options are limited, so I can make do.

"Yeah, Andy knows her, and even though it's further away, the office is in the middle."

Finn and I walk side by side out to the backyard. "Well, you know we can make arrangements for whatever you need, right? That's the cool thing about this—we're the bosses." That's still so weird to think about. I'll be helping him run his company.

When we walk outside, Andy comes running up like a kid on a mission. "Daddy! Daddy! Look, I'm rich."

I glance into the red Solo cup he's holding up and see it's full of change, as if he was taking donations for charity. I laugh. I think we'll fit in with these folks just fine. Now others besides just me can contribute to his college fund.

"Daddy, did you see the room that Uncle Finn said can be mine?" Andy asks as I assist him into pajamas. Somehow, he caught a second wind on the ride home from the cook-out and hasn't stopped talking since we left. He's so excited to have a sleepover eventually at his godfather's house.

"I saw it. It's nice." It's really just their guest room, but Lauren had apparently bought a *Toy Story* blanket and a few things for him to help him feel at ease there.

"And he said that I could bring some toys over and leave them there. Which toys do you think I should take?" He finally climbs into bed.

"All right, champ, how about we table that conversation for another time? It's been a long day, and we have a lot to do tomorrow before Daddy starts work on Monday." The number of boxes left to unpack has my brain and muscles ready to explode.

"Do you need to leave me?" His voice is soft, and his bottom lip trembles. The unshed tears in his eyes make my shoulders deflate and my chest ache.

"I'll be back, I promise. And you know Uncle Finn's mom, Ms. Denise, and your friend Liam will also be there."

"Yeah, she gives me yummy treats. I'm sad Mr. Griffin went to keep Mommy company." *Me too, buddy.*

I lean down and press my lips to his forehead. "Good night, buddy. I'm right down the hall if you need me."

He nods and settles under the covers, getting comfortable. I turn to walk away, but his soft voice forces me to stop midway to the door.

"Daddy, do you kiss someone like Uncle Finn does?"

I close my eyes and curse under my breath at my best friend for planting shit like this in my child's head. "Umm, I used to kiss your mommy like that. Her kisses always made me feel better."

"Like when you kiss my booboos?" He looks down at the scrape on his arm that he got earlier today when chasing Emme around.

"Exactly."

He remains quiet, so I assume the conversation is over.

"Do you think Mommy has cupcakes where she is?"

I'm surprised by his question. I grip the back of my neck, unsure what to say or where that is even coming from. It's not uncommon for him to bring up his mom. As painful as it might be, I want him to know his mother since that chance was taken from us. I'm always open when he asks questions about her or wants me to tell him stories about her. I close the distance between us and sit on the edge of his bed.

"Umm, I don't know. Why do you ask?"

"Well, Uncle Finn called those cupcakes today heavenly, and I was wondering if maybe angels made them where Mommy is." He shrugs, and my heart squeezes at the innocence in his eyes.

I'm rendered speechless. The older Andy gets, the more I'm at a loss for words on some of the things he asks. It's not as simple as "where is Mommy?" He's so smart for his age, and honestly, how can I answer this question when I don't understand it myself?

Why was Courtney ripped from our lives before she ever got to hold our son? My voice catches in my throat for a moment, and I swallow it down. I can keep it together until I am out of his view.

"I'm sure they have them." Andy smiles, satisfied with my simple answer, and I let out a harsh breath of relief.

He rolls over to face the framed photo of Courtney on the nightstand. It was one of the first things he wanted to unpack in his room.

"Good night, Mommy. I hope you have those cupcakes because they were so yummy."

He then rolls back over and hugs his Buzz Lightyear stuffed toy tighter.

"Good night, Daddy. Love you," he singsongs.

"Good night, Andy. Sweet dreams."

I flick the light off and partially close the door, just enough to block out the light from the hallway. I head to my bedroom and maneuver around the piles of boxes to sit on the edge of the bed, resting my head in my hands. Today has been physically exhausting, but that small conversation was emotionally exhausting to last a lifetime. I wonder when or if those conversations will ever get easier.

It's when the silence surrounds me that I'm reminded of the pain. It's these moments that I allow myself to wallow in the grief I let no one else see.

I fall back on the bed, completely drained, and cover my eyes with my forearm.

I miss you. I picture her lying beside me. Whenever I would have a bad day, this is what we would do. I would tell her my problems, and then her response would be *It's okay. You survived another day.* What I wouldn't give to hear her voice say those words.

After a few calming breaths, I rise and get to work to set up the life I've set for my son.

Chapter 4

Kate

I'm just shutting my front door when I hear a car pull into my driveway. I turn around to see my sister's SUV pulling in next to my vehicle.

I walk down the sidewalk to meet her and approach her just as she's opening the back door and retrieving a box.

"Ooh, did you bring leftovers? Best sister ever," I singsong, but the smile on her face drops when she spins to face me.

I totally left her house yesterday and forgot to grab leftovers. I figured I would stop by after I hit up the batting cages and grab some to avoid going grocery shopping again.

"Umm, these aren't for you." Redness coats her cheeks as she drops her gaze in shame, which only leaves me confused.

"Okay," I draw out. "Then why are you in my driveway with a box full of food containers?"

She glances over her shoulder toward—oh no, don't fucking say it. I shake my head in disbelief.

"These are for Jax and Andy." There's a hint of guilt in Lauren's tone.

Of fucking course.

"What, do his cooking skills match his shitty attitude?" Maybe he and Haylee could start Shitty Cooks Anonymous.

"Who pissed in your Cheerios this morning?" Lauren huffs.

I roll my eyes at her comment. "No one. I don't even like Cheerios."

"Finn came over this morning to help unpack." I glance up at Jaxon's house and see Finn's truck parked in the driveway.

I cross my arms and humph. "I hadn't noticed."

She shakes her head at me, clearly knowing I'm lying. She knows I like to have my morning coffee on the front porch, so of course I would have seen him there.

"Whatever. Don't make it a habit of using my driveway if you're going over there." I tip my head toward his house.

"Why don't you come over? The more hands, the quicker it'll go. It could give you and Jaxon some time to get to know each other."

I throw my head back and laugh. "Yeah, no, thanks. I might not be a proctologist, but I can spot an asshole just fine."

I'm honestly not sure what my sister is trying to accomplish here. Does she think that this is going to turn out like one of those romance novels she loves so much where siblings end up with best friends?

"I can't with you." She rolls her eyes. "Where are you headed, anyway?" she asks as she transfers the box of food from one hip to the other.

"You know I don't tell you everything." *Lie.* I probably share more than my sister ever wanted or needed to know.

She tosses her head back, laughing. "If only that were true."

"Have fun," I say but don't mean actually mean it. "Also, watch out. I hear he likes to bite people's heads off on the front porch. Make sure you don't offer an opinion."

"Goodbye, Katherine," she huffs, annoyed.

"Ooh, full-name status," I tease as I get in the car and toss my bag onto the passenger seat.

I watch Lauren cross the street in the rearview mirror. She's walking up the front steps as I back up out of the driveway.

I pause, hoping to see a replay of our interaction yesterday. However, Jaxon opens the front door with a smile on his face and ushers her inside.

"Stupid fucker," I mumble as I drive off.

My phone rings through the Bluetooth of my car as I pull out of the neighborhood.

I press the Answer button on the dashboard screen. "Hey, Mom."

"Hi, dear, rough day? You sound stressed." Liz Lawson is a damn ninja for being able to sense that with only two words. When you become a mother, you must get superpowers or something. The same way Haylee can tell Emme is up to something when she's not even looking at her.

"How can you tell?"

"You forget that as your mother, I know everything. Plus, I not only carried you for nine months, but I raised your stubborn ass."

I laugh. *Thanks, Mom.*

"Does it have anything to do with your showdown yesterday?"

I groan, and she laughs in response. "Lauren?" *Which of my siblings told her?*

"Ky."

"That rat bastard," I mumble. I knew we should have sold him at that lemonade stand years ago. After watching one of the many Mary-Kate and Ashley Olsen videos as kids, we tried to put Kyler up for sale, but Mom came running out and said that's how kidnapping happens.

"Oh, be nice to your brother. He's in his own world right now." Oh, hell no, we are not using that as an excuse for him to enjoy gossiping like a mom at the school pickup line.

"Yeah, yeah. Or it's that he's the baby of the family and could get away with murder."

"So, tell me more about this guy. The one who seems to have gotten under your skin."

"He's not under my skin." It's a good thing my name is Kate Lawson and not Pinocchio because with the number of lies I've told this morning, my nose would be a mile long.

"Sure, sweetheart, whatever you say," my mom teases, and I roll my eyes. "If that's not the case, then you should have no problem talking about him."

"If you want to know about him, ask your son-in-law. He's his best friend." Why is she so pushy on this subject?

"And I will, but I want to hear about him from you."

"Maybe I just don't want to talk about him," I mutter, gripping the steering wheel tighter.

"Katherine Renee, what do I always say?" Jeez, Louise, called by my full name twice in one morning. This has to be a record for me lately.

"Talking it out with an outsider can often put things into perspective," we say in unison, although my tone is more sarcastic.

I press on the brake as I approach a red light and sigh back against the headrest.

"Fine," I huff. I explain what happened yesterday from watching Andy walk outside to leaving my sister's cook-out annoyed. Of course, I give her a rather watered-down version.

"Oh, honey, you have such a big heart. You weren't wrong about bringing it to his attention, but I know you, and sometimes you're hot-tempered and go about doing things in your own way."

"Mom," I shout. "Are you taking his side?"

She sighs. "Of course not, sweetheart, but I'm just trying to understand how things went sour so quickly." *Umm, because he's a fucking prick, duh.*

I grit my teeth. "He basically said because I have no children of my own, I couldn't possibly understand what being a parent is like. I wasn't trying to parent his kid or criticize him. I only wanted to make sure the kid was safe."

"He's a single father, right?" Her voice softens. I know she must be able to relate with him on some level, being a single parent.

"Yeah. So?" *Single parent or not, it doesn't give anyone the right to act like that.*

"You remember how I juggled everything with three kids after your dad left? I had my hands full. Well, imagine if you had been much younger and that life was all he ever knew. I at least had your father's help in the beginning. Now he is living in a brand-new place where he doesn't know anyone."

"It doesn't excuse him for being a dick." I know my statement is about Jaxon, but there's a bitterness to my voice that always comes up at the mention of my father. It's been nineteen years since he walked out the door and didn't look back.

"And you are one hundred percent correct, but maybe just cut him some slack. I got plenty of unsolicited advice over the years, but I'm sure as single dads, they get it even more. Sometimes dads can be viewed as the babysitter. It wouldn't be a far stretch to believe that everyone who tries to tell him how to parent his child would make him feel like he wasn't doing a good job."

I rub the crease between my brows. It's before lunch and already I'm mentally exhausted.

I pull into an open parking space at the batting cages, thankful to escape any more talk about *him.* "Well, Mom, I gotta go."

Over the past few years, whenever Lauren and I had a bad day, we'd go to the batting cages and "whack some balls." And I think it's safe to say that yesterday was the epitome of a bad day.

"I'll stop by this week."

"Good. I miss my baby," she says.

I roll my eyes. "I saw you just the other day."

"And?" *I see right through you, Liz Lawson.* I can read between the lines here. When she saw me a few days ago, it was before she had some gossip.

I would bet my life savings that the first thing she asks when I walk into her house will be an update.

I laugh. "All right, Mom, love you."

I hang up after she returns the sentiment and toss my phone in my bag.

The bell rings when I walk through the front door, alerting the owner, Trevor, of my arrival. He sets down his newspaper. "Well, good morning, beautiful," he says with a big smile when he sees me walking toward him. "Shit day already?"

"You have no idea, Trev. Who knows, I might just need to rent a lane by the month." With Jaxon and his shitty attitude invading aspects of my life, I have a feeling that if our interactions are anything like yesterday, then I can just start writing Trevor's rent checks directly.

"Won't see me complain. Your crappy days are good for my business, plus you're not too hard on the eyes."

I laugh as I hand over the cash to pay for the lane.

"I'm out of your league, old man." I'm pretty sure Trevor is old enough to be my grandfather.

Grabbing my bat and helmet, I head toward the back door that leads out to the cages. "Not in my dreams, you're not."

I can always count on this place to make me feel better, even if it's just remarks like that from a pervy old man.

Chapter 5

Finn and Lauren coming over today was a godsend. The house has transformed into a home—it's more than just four walls and a roof.

They offered to stay at the house with Andy and continue working on unpacking his room while I ran to the grocery store. I needed to stock up for the week and get something to say thank you for their help, especially for Lauren. The way she's taken to Andy is as if she's known him for years. She even ran to Target this morning and picked up some of the soap that Andy was talking about yesterday. He was a little disappointed he hadn't gotten to go with her, but she promised to take him next time.

I stroll down the wine aisle and browse the New Zealand wine section. I barely know anything about wine, and Court always picked bottles based on whether she thought the label was pretty. But I asked Finn what Lauren's favorite type is, and he said Kim Crawford pinot noir. I look up each row and pass sauvignon blancs, pinot grigios, cabernets, and—*aha*! There it is. *Yes, and there's only one bottle left.* It's gotta be a sign. Placing it gently in my cart, I head over to the bakery.

I know Andy was all about those cupcakes yesterday, and while these won't be the same, I figure we can have a special treat for dessert to go with the food Lauren brought over. I grab a ticket before stepping back out of the way. The line seems to move at a decent speed, but there are still five numbers ahead of me. I've never seen a bakery line so busy before. I pull my phone out and decide to check in with Finn to make sure everything is going okay and see if I need to grab anything else.

Me: *Just checking in.*

A response comes right away. It's not a message, though, but a photo of Lauren and Andy sitting on the floor, organizing his bookshelf.

Finn: *I think Lauren may never leave. She's a book nerd through and through and be careful. If you let her and Andy hang out long enough, I'm pretty sure you'll be adding a second bookshelf soon. She's gone into children's book heaven. LOL*

Me: *Well, I could think of worse things for someone to be addicted to.*

Finn: *Says the man whose bank account doesn't have at least $200 a month spent on new books.*

Me: **shrug emoji**

Finn: *Whatever, happy wife. Happy life.*

Me: *That's what they say. Everything good?*

Finn: *Yes, stop being a fucking helicopter parent and enjoy the peace and quiet.*

Me: *I'm in a fucking grocery store. What's peaceful and quiet about that?*

Finn: *There's no kids.*

I look up and see a woman with six kids hanging off her cart. She looks just about dead on her feet. I dip my chin to my chest to hide my chuckle.

Me: *No shortage of kids here. Pretty sure they might sell them in aisle 8.*

Finn: *Nah, I'm pretty sure it's aisle 6.*

Me: *I'm just grabbing one last thing. Anything else I need to grab?*

Finn: *Nah, man, all good.*

Me: *Great, see you soon.*

I'm pocketing my phone just as the guy behind the counter calls, "Number sixty-eight."

I step forward, holding the ticket up at the same time a familiar female voice calls out, "Right here."

Wait, did I just imagine her voice? I glance over to find the one and only Kate Lawson standing just a few feet away. My body tenses. I know that this is a small town and all, but can't a guy catch a break?

I look down at the small white ticket in my hand and verify the number.

"Oh no, wait your turn. He called sixty-eight. That's me." I hold up the ticket with the red block lettering clearly showing "68."

"No," Kate drags out and pops out her hip. "My ticket says sixty-eight." She holds up an identical number.

We spin to face the employee, who can't be more than maybe seventeen, and he looks scared shitless. His gaze bounces back and forth between Kate and me. She looks like she's about to shoot lasers out of her eyes at him.

"I guess I should let you go first, right? You seem to think you're more important than the rest of the world," she scoffs.

"Well, normally I'd say ladies first, but you're not acting much like a lady. Besides, I have a kid to get home to. What's so important in your life to get home to? A cat?"

Am I being unreasonable right now? Sure. But she knows exactly how to rile me up.

"Having a child doesn't make your life more important than someone else's. You don't know anything about me. Don't pretend you do." Her skin flushes, and I feel as though maybe I've struck a nerve and gone too far, yet I can't seem to take my eyes off her. The hairs on the back of my neck rise as I feel everyone else surrounding us.

"You know what? You're right." Her eyes widen in shock. I extend my hand in front of me. "You go first."

She shakes her head. "Oh no, Mister I'm the center of the world. I insist." She mocks my movement with her hand. "I insist. You go first." She settles back, sinking into one hip with her arms crossed in front of her, her rigid stance telling me she's done with this conversation. *Fine, be that way.* We could easily go round and round for hours, so I take her out.

I huff out a breath and turn to face the counter again. The poor employee literally looks unsure of himself. I give him a weak smile, but it does nothing to ease the awkwardness and tension.

"Yeah, can I get a half dozen assorted cupcakes?"

The employee nods and turns to grab them. I can feel her heated gaze on me, but instead of acknowledging her, I watch her with my peripheral vision. I straighten my spine and bring my cart to block the front of my pants. Going toe to toe with her, watching her chest heave up and down, has my cock standing at half-mast in my jeans.

She looks down at my cart and growls—like I'm pretty sure an actual fucking growl left her pouty lips.

"Looks like it's your lucky day, sir. These are the last of the cupcakes." He hands me the package just as Kate huffs under her breath, "Are you fucking kidding me?"

"You have a nice day, ma'am." I tip my imaginary hat just to taunt her as I turn and walk toward the checkout.

Chapter 6

Kate

I open the door to Momento and instantly feel my body relax. While my family and I get together often for dinner or to hang out, it became a tradition years ago to come to this restaurant once a week. Although as our lives have gotten busier over the years with work, marriages, and babies on the way, sometimes it's only once or twice a month. Family dinner is the one place I don't have to worry about running into *him*. Jaxon McAdams is the bane of my existence.

He puts me in a sour mood without even trying. It must be a skill at the top of his resume. He's been here a week and a half already, and every morning, I've been rudely awoken by the sound of his truck starting at a god-awful hour. Like seriously, who needs a truck *that* loud, and who needs to start it *that fucking early*?

It's like he's everywhere—at home, at the grocery store, buying the last bottle of my favorite wine and the cupcakes I was willing to take as a consolation prize. I had to settle for some blueberry scones, and it just wasn't the same. Worst of all, he's made his way into my dreams almost every night. It's like all I have to do is think of him and he magically appears. So tonight, it's simple—I'm not going to think about him.

I wave to the hostess as I pass and head toward the large table in the corner, where I see my family seated.

"Sorry I'm late," I say to no one in particular as I shuck off my jacket and put it on the back of the empty chair before taking a seat. I glance down and see a beverage in front of me and smile. "Oh great, you already ordered me a drink."

My sister goes to open her mouth to speak as I take a large swig and gag. "Ew, what the fuck is this?" My family knows me well enough to know what I drink and what I don't, and *this* is definitely on the top of the list as something I *don't*.

"It's an Arnold Palmer. But, more importantly, it's mine," a gruff voice says behind me.

My shoulders tense. *You've got to be fucking kidding me. Seriously?* I wasn't even thinking about him. What sort of voodoo magic is this?

"Who the hell invited you?" I fumed.

"Not that it matters, but I did," Finn announces as he carries Andy in like an airplane and sets him down next to the table.

"I thought these dinners were for family," I spit harshly and stress the word *family*.

"They *are* for family." I know Finn considers them his family, but not exactly what I meant.

"And if I remember correctly, I wasn't family when I was first invited," Dani adds from her seat at the end of the table. "By *you*, actually." If it weren't for the fact she's carrying my niece and nephew, I'd slap that smug smile right off her face.

"That was different," I admit. My sister and I insisted Kyler invite Dani to a family dinner before they were dating because we wanted to meet the girl who had flipped my brother's world upside down.

"Hey, we can go. I can sense where we're not welcome," Jax says softly enough for Andy to not overhear him.

Great. Bye, Felicia.

My sister nudges my leg under the table with her foot. Okay, so it wasn't a nudge; it was a full-blown kick to the shin. She gives me "the look" to step up and do something as I lean down and rub the sore spot.

Jaxon walks around to where Andy stands and crouches down to his eye level. "Hey, Andy, I just remembered," he begins.

Wonderful, he's going to lie to his kid because of me.

"He just remembered we hadn't ordered appetizers," I interrupt. "Is there anything you like?"

I can feel my skin heating from everyone's eyes focused on me while my eyes are on Andy's. His eyes are a brighter blue, whereas his father's are almost like the midnight sky. All that's missing are twinkling stars.

"Cheese sticks," he mutters in a deep, demonic-like voice. *Woah, where the fuck did that come from?* My brows raise to my hairline in surprise. It causes everyone, including me, to laugh to lighten up the mood.

I wonder if he does that voice often, or did he sense the tension in the air, needing some reprieve? Sometimes children are like dogs. They can smell fear.

When our laughter dies down, I lean forward on my elbows and give him a genuine warm smile. "What do you know? Those are my favorite."

"I love them, too," Dani shouts before turning to my brother. "Oh, can we order a plate, too? Babies love the idea of cheese." In the years I've known Dani, there's one thing she loves more than my brother, and that's cheese.

He kisses her temple. "Anything for you, babe."

I catch Jaxon staring at them, not in a Creeper Mccreeperson way, but almost like he's trapped in his mind of memories. I don't know much about what happened with his wife, just that she died when Andy was born. When Finn and Lauren talked about it, I didn't pay much attention.

He finally notices me watching him and tenses. The softness that was just present washes away, and the hard exterior is back in place.

"So, when are you due?" Jaxon asks as he pulls out the chair directly across from me and Andy climbs up in it.

"About six and a half more weeks," Kyler says and presses his hand on her growing belly.

"Ugh, my due date can't get here soon enough," Dani whines.

"Soon, sweetheart. Soon," he coos. I smile at how sweet he is with her. I am truly happy for them.

"Well, enjoy it now. Before you know it, they'll be older, soaking up everything people say around them and asking a million questions like about kissing and such." Jax narrows his eyes at Finn, and Finn chuckles with a shrug.

"Oops."

"Hey, I know you." Andy's voice draws my attention to him. "You were at Uncle Finn's, and you live in the house with the big tree."

I nod. "Yep, Uncle Finn is my family."

"Cool. He's my family, too." Andy picks up a crayon from the cup in front of him that the server must have placed before I arrived and starts to color the place mat—a kid after my own heart.

"I think you should hang a tire swing on that tree," he says, keeping his focus on the place mat.

"You do, huh?" I grab a crayon and begin doodling along with him. I could totally get used to having kids around. In all the years we've been coming here, it's the first time we got crayons.

"Yup, my daddy said before we moved, we would have a real big yard and could build a swing set or a tree house, but I think I want a tire swing."

I find inspiration from our conversation and grab a brown and green crayon from the cup.

"I think a tree house is pretty cool. We had one growing up." I find talking to this kid easier than talking to most adults these days.

Andy pauses and tilts his head to the side. "What did you do in it?"

"Well, I know what Kyler did in it," Finn mumbles, and Ky chokes on his drink. I'm not sure what that's all about, but I have a feeling it's not appropriate for little ears, so I turn to focus my conversation back on Andy.

I swap out the brown crayon for a black one. "Umm, well, we played hide-and-seek and even camped out once. It was fun." I don't mention that as a teenager, it was the perfect escape from the house when my parents would argue.

"That sounds cool." He glances over my drawing, but I pretend like I'm back in the third grade and cover my paper with my forearm. He giggles and sticks his tongue out before mimicking my move. But since I'm much taller than him, I can see right over his little arm, but I go along with it.

After a moment, he returns to his drawing. "I think I still want a tire swing."

"Yeah, how come?" I'm putting the final touches on the picture.

Andy looks at his dad, whose expression is hard to read as he focuses on us. "My mom had a tire swing when she was little."

Words catch in my throat at this little boy in front of me. Scared that I might say something stupid, I remain silent. Honestly, I don't even know how to respond to him.

He pushes his place mat forward to show what I guess, based on the coloring, is a fire truck.

"What did you draw?" He pushes up on his elbows to see better.

With one last look at my picture, I'm overcome with emotion. I'm suddenly torn over whether I should show it. When I started drawing it, I didn't know the meaning behind it.

I spin the place mat around to reveal a tree standing alone in a grassy field with a tire swing hanging from one of its extended branches. It's a simple drawing, having only a few basic crayons, but I could give the bark of the tree dimension with shading, and it's a stark contrast to the light blue sky background. It's all in the details.

"Look, Daddy! She drew a tire swing. Just like Mommy used to have." The side conversations going on at the table all halt. Andy holds it up close to Jaxon's face, probably too close for him to actually see it. I'm impressed he didn't smack his dad in the face with it with his excitement.

Jaxon places his hands on the place mat and pulls it down but never looks at the image. If Andy noticed, he doesn't let on, but I did. *Wow, fuck you, too.*

I look down at my lap and clear my throat, hoping that will keep the anger that begs to be unleashed on Jaxon. I do something nice for your son and you're still a dick? I seriously can't win.

"Can I keep it? Please," he pleads.

"Sure thing." I smile at him. It's amazing that something so simple puts such a smile on his face. I look around and flag the server down and request a new place mat, not wanting to ruin it when the food arrives.

After the waitress brings one to me, my eyes drift to Jaxon, whose jaw is so taut I feel like I should call his dentist to make an appointment to get his ground molars replaced. The pinch in his brows creates wrinkles in his forehead. Anger is coming off him in waves. *What the fuck is his problem?* A shiver goes up my spine, and I don't know if it's from the chill of his cold disposition or something else, but I'm not in the mood to find out.

I could easily make up an excuse to leave, but then I'd feel the wrath of my family, plus I'm fucking starving, and the Cajun chicken and sausage pasta is exactly what I need to make all right back in the world.

A short while later, the waitress delivers our meals, and it's quite impressive there's room for anything else.

The rest of dinner goes off… not exactly smooth. The tension rose back up after my drawing. Here I thought I could bond with his kid to make him not be a dick, but Jesús. I'm pretty sure the man murdered me seven ways from Sunday in his mind. I give my family a brief goodbye and ignore him as I all but run to my car, needing a reprieve.

Too bad it's short-lived because his brake lights flash behind me before I even get out of my car as Lord Dickhead himself pulls into his driveway.

Chapter 7

Jaxon

Kate Lawson—*I'm officially convinced this woman was put on this earth to torture me.*

Because that's exactly what sitting through a Lawson family dinner was—torture. When Finn popped into my office earlier in the afternoon and invited Andy and me to join the elusive sibling dinner that I've heard so much about, I was hesitant to accept. I didn't want to infringe on their family time, but after reassuring me it was okay with Lauren and pulling the "I want to spend time with my godson card," I gave in.

I expected her reaction to us crashing. However, when I learned that there had been previous guests not officially in the family to crash before, I knew the cause of her anger—us, or more specifically, me.

What I hadn't expected was her total one-eighty of an attitude just as I was about to break the news to Andy that we couldn't stay.

What I also didn't expect was the feeling that hit me like a ton of bricks when that smile that she shares with her siblings was constantly directed at my son. For a moment, I was jealous of him—jealous of a four-year-old. I wanted that smile to be for me. I wanted to reach across the table and kiss her as a thank-you for making my son feel special and including him.

Honestly, I'm not even sure how we got home. One minute we were pulling out of the parking lot at the restaurant, waving at Finn and Lauren, and the next, I was putting the truck in park. Thoughts of her swam around in my mind the entire drive.

The way I felt her dark eyes bore into me when she thought I didn't notice. But it's hard to miss, especially when I was already watching.

The little moans she let slip from her lips as she took almost every bite of her dinner.

The way she bonded with Andy. She could have easily ignored him after allowing us to stay. It would have broken my heart, but she made him feel welcome.

I open my eyes to find the red break lights still shining bright in the rearview mirror from her driveway. She had arrived home just before we did, but she hadn't gone inside yet. It may or may not be why I've been stalling myself. Whether it's my stubbornness or the fatherly instinct to protect that needs me to see her get safely inside her home, something inside me is telling me to wait. A few more minutes pass by, and I wonder if she is doing the same. If I've learned one thing about Kate Lawson, it's that she's just as fucking stubborn as I am.

If you looked up the word "stubborn" in a dictionary, you would see Jaxon McAdams, and at the bottom for synonyms: *see Kate Lawson.*

Finally, I release a breath of relief when I see the lights fade and she exits the car. My eyes follow her as she walks up the path and into her house. The light on her front porch flicks on as she closes the door behind her.

I glance over my shoulder to see Andy's head tipped down, resting against his chest, and his eyes closed. Of course he fell asleep. That explains the silence.

I've become a pro at transferring a sleeping child from the car to his bed over the years, especially when some nights I had to drive him around town to get him to fall asleep. I gently undo the seat belt harness, and Andy stirs. *Shit!*

"Daddy, don't forget the picture Miss Kate drew," he mumbles, not bothering to open his eyes as I lift him into my arms. He becomes dead weight against me.

That fucking picture—it was like a bowl of ice water dumped on my head.

"I will, buddy. I'll come back out after I get you settled."

The soft puffs of air against my neck tell me he passed right back out. I juggle him in my arms and unlock the front door.

After carefully carrying him up the stairs and into his room, I lay him down on his bed. I chuckle at the little orange fuzzies left between his toes after I slip off his shoes and socks. Thankfully, he wore sweatpants today, so I don't need to change him into pajamas. It's moments like this that I wish I didn't make his bed every morning because I struggle to get him tucked under the covers without jostling too much, but he doesn't even stir, so I think he's out cold. Not even a marching band practicing in his room could wake him up at this point.

I place a soft kiss on his forehead and whisper, "Good night," as I brush the blond hairs off his face.

I jog down the stairs and back out to the truck to grab my work bag, his backpack, and the drawing. I spot the place mat on the seat beside his booster seat, careful not to crinkle or tear it. The last thing I need is to feel the wrath of a four-year-old.

Dropping the bags by the door, I stalk to the kitchen and hang the drawing on the fridge. With my back resting against the counter, I stare at the piece of paper—the reminder of the collision of both of my worlds. The world that I lost when I lost Courtney and the world of possibilities for the future. When Kate had spun this place mat around to reveal that she had listened closely enough to Andy to understand the importance of the tire swing, I thought my world was going to implode for a moment. I refused to let the emotions slip, so I kept the hard facade up. Honestly, it may have just been better for us to have left before he opened up to her.

When Andy brings up his mom to people, I typically get looks of sadness and sympathy. Over the years, those were emotions I knew how to deal with, but tonight, I found neither in Kate's eyes when she glanced my way. Did she understand the loss we went through? I guess I honestly don't know much about her. I figure if she had, Finn would have mentioned it. It's much easier to not know all the things that make Kate Lawson tick. Was that something I could seriously consider exploring? When I'm around Kate, I feel on edge. The only way to combat the need to pull her into my arms is to grind my teeth and clench my fists because for every one thought I have of having more with Kate comes two more of guilt for moving on from Court. I know she would want us to, but it's not that simple.

Will the guilt of moving on and having thoughts about a woman that I once had about my wife ever go away, or will it eat me alive?

I flick the kitchen light off and head upstairs for a shower and leave those questions for future Jaxon to deal with.

Chapter 8

Kate

The incessant buzzing of my phone pulls my attention from the canvas in front of me. When I pull out my earbud, Alanis Morissette fills the space. A photo of my sister making a kissy face at the camera looks back at me when I glance down at the screen. I sigh heavily and press the red ignore button. *Sorry, sissy, not in the mood for you today.*

"Busted," my sister shouts from behind me, and I jump, causing my phone to slip from my hands and crash to the floor.

"Jesus fucking Christ, woman." I clutch my hand to my chest, willing my heart rate to drop to a rate not resembling the aftermath of running a triathlon—not that I would know. Lauren was always the athletic one between the two of us. I hop off the stool and retrieve my phone.

Phew—not a single crack. She's lucky because if there were, I would have made her replace it.

"Are you trying to fucking kill me?"

"Ha." My sister shrugged. "If only it were that easy."

I narrow my eyes at her and flash her the middle finger, which only makes her smile bigger.

"But maybe," she draws out, "if you would have answered my phone calls and texts, then you would have known I was planning to come over."

"I've responded to your texts," I admit, and it's not a complete lie.

"Yes, no, and single emojis are not actual responses. Maybe for some people, but not me."

I roll my eyes. I'm pretty sure those *are* actual responses.

"You've been avoiding me," she states matter-of-factly.

"Have not," I whine like a child. "I've been working." Again, not a total lie. I've had a few pieces left to finish up for clients.

Lauren places her hands on her hips and steps her foot out of the side. "Have, too. And further proof—" She holds up her phone, revealing our text conversation with a slew of unanswered texts from her. "—if you had read your latest messages, you would see that I said I was coming over after I set up my classroom."

Before I can ask her what she's doing here, her eyes catch onto the colorful canvas behind me.

"Ooh, this is new."

"Thank you. Just finished it." I step back beside her and admire the painting before us. I can't help but smile when I notice in my peripheral vision that Lauren and I are both tilting our heads to the side with our arms crossed.

"It's different from your usual."

I twist my lips. "Yeah, I guess it is." Art has always been a way for me to channel my emotions and escape the real world. I let my inner demons bleed onto the canvas with every stroke, allowing people to see the parts of me I keep buried deep. I guess that's why my pieces have always had darker undertones to them. My art is the only way I know to share my deep, dark secrets.

This piece is different—it's bold and vibrant. I hadn't even realized the difference as I was painting it. I nibble on my bottom lip while I try to think what the inspiration behind this piece could be. What's the difference between today and the last time I painted? Only one thing comes to mind… dinner last night, interacting with Andy.

No, it couldn't possibly be, right?

I shake the thoughts away and move over to gather my brushes to take them downstairs to clean them.

"So, not that I don't love it when you stop by unannounced, but what's the emergency?"

"I wanted to talk to you about dinner last night."

Why do I feel like I'm about to be scolded like a damn child?

"Look, I know that you and Jax"—my body goes rigid at the mention of his name—"had an intense first meeting."

I snicker. I don't know that "intense" is the word I would choose, but sure, we can go with it. "Are you here for you? Or are you here because your husband asked you to?" I point a paintbrush in her direction.

"Now, that's not fair. If Finn had something to say, he would—we both know that. I'm doing this because last night was awkward as fuck." Her voice raises, shocking us both. Lauren is the more levelheaded one out of the two of us, so when she loses her temper or raises her voice, you know she's fired up.

Is she seriously trying to pin this all on me? *Oh, hell no.* "And whose fault was that? I wasn't the one to crash a *family* dinner."

"Jaxon and Andy *are family*, whether you like it or not. Finn is the most important person in my life—"

I gasp dramatically, bringing my hand to my chest. "I am offended. And to think we shared a womb," I scoff.

Lauren rolls her eyes and lets out a harsh breath. "You know what I mean, Kate. And just like you are to me, Jax is important to Finn. Look, I know that shit happened, and you guys just seem to clash like oil and water."

I laugh at her analogy because there couldn't be a more perfect way to describe it.

"But—" Her eyes and voice soften. "—he's had a rough go of it. Maybe throw a little compassion his way, will ya? For me?"

First Mom, now Lauren. I can see the challenge shining in my sister's eyes. This isn't a topic she's going to let slide, so I concede.

"Fine, whatever," I huff, tired of talking about him.

"Thank you," she sighs. "I'm not asking you to be besties and paint each other's nails. Just be cordial."

"I already agreed. But just remember that it's not just me. I can't be held responsible if he pokes the bear." I hold my hands up like a bear in defense mode and growl.

"I get that, but I can at least feel better knowing that you won't be instigating it." I leave my hands by my side as she steps up and hugs me, then rushes out the door, shouting, "Love you." Talk about door dash.

Long after my sister leaves, I'm annoyed with her. Not even a long, hot shower relaxes me. Later, I'm lounging on my bed, still wrapped in a fluffy towel, flipping through Netflix, when a loud noise from outside startles me.

"What the fuck?" I hop off the bed, holding my towel tighter at the knot, and walk to the window.

"Holy motherfucking shit," I shout as soon as I flick the blind open.

The noise I should have recognized to be a lawn mower belongs to none other than my *lovely* neighbor.

But it's not the interruption to my towel time that has me feeling hot all over and damp between my legs. It's the view of Jaxon shirtless, pushing the lawn mower.

I have always laughed in my sister-in-law's face when she's made comments as to how hot it is seeing my brother doing chores around the house—one, because it's my brother, but two, I've never believed that for myself. But holy guac-a-freakin'-mole, that man is straight sex on a stick in front of me.

I lean further to get a better view. I think I'm far enough away that he won't see me creeping on him like a Peeping Tom. Although is it still a Peeping Tom if you're looking out of the house versus looking into the house?

Jaxon pauses and grabs the shirt that's hanging on the handle. He removes his sunglasses and wipes his face before placing the shades back on.

I imagine the sweat dripping down his chest, glistening and begging to be licked up with my tongue.

I close the blind back up and make my way back to my bed. The thrumming between my thighs continues to the same sound as the lawn mower outside.

I rub my thighs together to create some friction, however, it's not relieving the ache.

I lie back on my bed and open the knot on my towel, revealing nothing but skin. Reaching over into my nightstand, I grab my teal bestie, aka my favorite vibrator. Guys may come and go, but this has been a constant for a few years. When I need a quick but powerful orgasm—because hey, sometimes you only have a few minutes when the urge strikes—this clitoral simulator toy is my go-to. The V-shaped tip surrounds my clit and sends tickling vibrations that have always guaranteed mind-blowing pleasure. *Who needs a man when you have one of these?*

No lube needed because just the sight of him has my thighs slick with arousal.

I hold the vibrator so that the two prongs are just on the outside of my clit. The first vibration sends a jolt up my spine. I let out a sigh of relief and continue.

The lawn mower cuts off abruptly as the buzzing of the vibrator fills my room.

I'm so lost in the feeling that I don't hear the front door open or the footsteps up the stairs. My bedroom door slams open against the wall. My eyes widen in shock to see a shirtless Jaxon standing in my doorway, sweat fully dripping down his bare chest. What is he doing here? *I should stop what I'm doing and cover up, but it just feels so fucking good. I pull my bottom lip between my teeth and squirm against the toy.*

A coy smile tips his lips upward. "I was knocking on the door, but now I see why you didn't answer." *He stalks toward the bed. Pressing a knee on the edge of the bed, he looks at me as if he wants to devour me as his last meal.* "Fuck, baby, look at you touching yourself. Does it feel good?" *I nod.*

"Spread your legs further, baby." *He scoots up closer on the bed.* "I want to see how wet you are, how wet watching me made you." *His words send a fresh wave of wetness to coat my fingers. I listen and spread my legs a little more, but it's not enough for him because before I can even blink, his rough palms are gripping my thighs and pushing them so far open, I can feel my lower lips on display, wetness gathering at my opening.*

"Mmm," *we groan in unison.* "Just like that." *He hovers between my open thighs and trails soft kisses, starting from my belly button and moving up between my breasts.* "Seeing you like this has my cock so hard. Be a good girl and come for me, then maybe I'll give you my cock," *he says against my bare breast. His tongue teases the tip of my nipple before doing the same to the other. The slight burn of his facial hair against my skin has me begging for me.*

"Come for me, Kate."

I shake my head. "No, not yet," *I pant. I'm so close but don't want to give in to the pleasure yet. But the fire in his eyes tells me that his orgasm would just be the first of many.*

"Do you always have to fight me, baby? Would you rather I force it out of you?"

I bite my lip as I press the button to increase the speed, and my breath quickens. Writhing against the toy and pressing it deeper against my skin, I press my head further into the pillow, and a moan slips from my lips.

"I said, come for me," he commands.

I press the button to increase the toy to the highest speed, and my back arches off the bed. The orgasm barrels into me like a damn freight train, sending pulse waves of pleasure throughout my body. I couldn't stop it even if I wanted. I know my clit will be buzzing long after I turn the toy off. When I can't take it anymore, one name leaves my lips: "Jaxon."

I sink back in bed in a postorgasmic bliss—so what if I just jilled myself off to the image of my neighbor? People do it to the thought of celebrities all the time. Why can't I do it to the bane of my existence? If there's one positive for him living across the street, it can be content for my spank bank. Everything else is just meh.

Chapter 9

Jaxon

I sigh heavily as I approach Finn's office. I scrub my hands over my face and close my eyes for a moment. I could probably fall asleep standing up. *Oh, the joys of single parenting.* I make a mental note to grab some coffee on my way back to my office after this meeting.

Thankfully, Finn's assistant's desk is empty. Natasha is the last person I want to deal with right now. Her flirty advances are overkill. She might as well have a sign on her chest that says "will spread legs for anyone."

I tap my knuckles twice on the closed door.

"Come in," he shouts from the other side.

As I open the door, a female giggle echoes in the space.

Oh shit. I look up to see Finn sitting on the couch on the other side of his office with his wife in his lap.

"Finn, stop," Lauren laughs, squirming in his arms.

I miss that—obviously not with Lauren, though. I've told myself over the years that I was fine being just me and Andy, but after watching my best friend be happy and in love, something in me has shifted and has made me wonder—what if?

I always wonder, *What if Courtney hadn't died?* But lately, the what-if has turned into what if I had someone by my side, in my arms, in my bed? Would that be such a bad thing?

Suddenly, in front of me, I no longer see Lauren and Finn but a different Lawson twin sitting in my lap. Her dark hair thrown over one shoulder, exposing her skin for me to pepper kisses on as she laughs at my beard tickling her. The way her chocolate eyes would look up at me and lick her lips in anticipation of my lips claiming hers.

I blink rapidly, and that image disappears. Clearly, it's the mental and physical exhaustion getting to me.

"What?" He glances over at me. "It's just Jax."

"Yeah, it's just me," I chuckle. My, how the tables have turned. I lost count of the number of times over the years that Finn had interrupted Court and me. At least these two are fully clothed.

"But it could've been any of your employees," she added.

"But it's not, babe, so just relax." He presses a kiss to her temple, and she seems to relax. "Plus, three words—Conference. Room. Table." Finn turns his attention back to me with a devilish glint in his eye and an arched brow.

I place my hands in my pockets and shrug.

"Okay," Lauren draws out. "I don't know what that means and think it's better that way." She's probably right. Finn and I had been working late for weeks on a new project, and it felt like forever that I had spent time with Court. So she stopped by one evening wearing sexy lingerie, and we snuck off to the conference room for, well, *a moment*. Just as Court sank down on my cock, Finn walked into the room. No one said anything, but we all made eye contact before he bolted from the room.

"I can come back later. I should've called to make sure now was a good time."

Finn goes to speak, but Lauren cuts him off. "It's okay. I was just leaving. I have to meet Kate. We're grabbing some last-minute items for Dani's shower."

"Do you have to?" Finn whines and nuzzles his face into his wife's neck.

I cover my mouth with my fist to hide my laughter. My best friend is a damn lovesick puppy.

She pushes off him and stands. She brushes her hands down the front of her clothes, straightening her outfit. Lord knows what I would have walked into had I waited a few more minutes.

"Chill out, ya big baby. I'll see you home in a few hours."

"Fine," he pouts. He pushes to his feet, pulling her into his arms, and presses his lips to hers in a passionate kiss. *Get a room.* I spin around to give them a private moment and walk over to the built-in shelves in the far corner of his office. On one shelf, I notice a framed photo of Finn and me standing in front of one of the first buildings we ever designed together. That feels like a lifetime ago, especially because Courtney was the one who took the photo.

"Good to see you, Jax," Lauren says behind me.

I glance over my shoulder just as she's walking out the door. "Bye."

"So, what's going on, man?" Finn asks as he rounds his desk and takes a seat.

"Umm, you said you wanted to meet me and Kels to go over things today at one."

"Oh shit, you're right. Damn, is it one already?"

I sink into one of the chairs across from him, resting my head back and closing my eyes.

"You look tired, man."

His words force my attention back to him.

I let out a sadistic chuckle and adjust in the chair so I'm now leaning forward with my elbows resting on my knees. Tired doesn't even cover how I'm feeling.

"Court used to say that when someone says you look tired, it's the polite way of saying you look like shit."

Finn smirks. "I remember. I just thought I would be nicer by saying you look tired than you look like shit."

"Since when did you beat around the bush about anything? Well, minus your true feelings for Lauren."

He holds his finger out at me. "Touché."

Finn spent years pining over Lauren, and it wasn't until he lost his dad and came back to the East Coast that he got his head out of his ass and went after what he wanted. "No, it's just all the traveling back and forth." When I had agreed for Denise to watch Andy, we were supposed to be living closer, not on the other side of town. "I feel like I'm constantly on the road. I leave even earlier to get Andy to your mom's."

Finn remains silent as I talk.

"And please don't think I'm not grateful for your mom helping, because shit, I am." I run my hand through my hair and settle on the back of my neck, gripping it tightly, trying to ease the tension. "It's just getting to be a lot. Maybe I need to look into something closer. But the thought of shipping him off to a stranger makes me anxious as hell."

Finn steeples his fingers together, resting them on his lips. I can feel his thoughts turning from here. "Okay, hear me out. I have an idea."

I push off my elbows and sit up, matching his position. "This should be good," I say sarcastically.

"Kate is home. Why not just ask her to watch Andy? I'm sure she would say yes."

I hold my hand up. "Look, I'm gonna stop you right there. I know she's your sister-in-law and all, but I think I wouldn't trust her with a pet rock, let alone my child."

"Actually, she's great with kids. You should see her with Kyler's niece, Emme. She has a soft spot for her. Not to mention she always stops by Lo's class, and her students always seem to love her."

I remain silent. Just because she's good with other people's kids doesn't mean I'm willing to trust her with mine.

"Just keep that in the back of your mind in case of an emergency, 'kay? We're all here to help. I brought you here to help, but if you run yourself into the ground, you're not going to be much help now, are you?"

I sigh, knowing he's right.

"All right, let me call Kels."

He presses the speakerphone button on his office phone.

"This is Kelsey," she answers before it even rings.

"Hey, are you still good to meet me and Jaxon this afternoon?"

"Shit, is it one already?" She panics slightly, and we can hear the shuffling of paperwork on her desk.

I chuckle at how similar these two are.

'Yep," he says.

"Okay, I need about twenty minutes to finish these invoices, and then I can meet you guys. That work?"

Finn glances over to me, and I nod.

"Great, see you then."

The phone call disconnects.

Finn leans back in his chair again. "Why don't you go over to the coffee shop down the street, grab yourself some caffeine, and then meet back here? Kels should be ready by then."

Coffee actually sounds amazing right now. "Yeah, I think I'll do that." I rise from my chair. "Want anything?"

"Nah, I'm good." He turns to focus on his computer screen.

I'm just in the doorway when he calls out my name. "Hey, Jax?" I turn to face him, bracing my palm on the doorframe. "Just think about what I said. You know about Kate."

I shake my head. Yeah, that won't be happening, but I appease him. "Sure, whatever. I'll be back. I got my phone on me."

Fifteen minutes later, I've got a large black coffee in hand, and I'm focused on my phone, looking at the photo Denise just sent me of Andy and Liam, their faces covered in what looks to be chocolate. Andy has already been through so much and is finally settled after the move. He loves being at Denise's and has a blast with little Liam. As great as cutting back the travel time would be if I did even consider the idea of asking Kate, I couldn't do that to Andy to switch things up when things are going to change soon anyway.

Someone runs directly into me, and I hiss as the hot liquid burns my flesh. Thankfully, my shirt took the brunt of the impact.

"Jesus, maybe you should watch—"

That voice. I look up to find eyes that match the ones I just saw in Finn's office earlier.

"For fuck's sake. Did you run into me on purpose?" she barks.

Is she for fucking real? Yeah, I ran into you on purpose because I prefer to wear my coffee versus drinking it.

"You were the one that fucking ran into me," I snap back.

"Kate, are you—" Lauren approaches and gasps as she takes in the scene. "Oh, Jax." Lauren looks at my shirt. "Oh my God, are you okay?"

"Sure, ask him if he's okay, not your fucking blood."

I roll my eyes at her bitter tone. The barista comes over, bringing a stack of napkins that I use to clean up most of the liquid.

"I'm fine. Maybe your sister should watch where the fuck she's going." I pat my shirt, not that it does much good.

My phone buzzes in my hand. I look down to see Finn's name. He's probably wondering where I am.

"I gotta go. Lauren, nice to see you again." I give her a tight-lipped smile, now that the pain is subsiding. I turn to Kate, who is still glaring at me. Her eyes are baring daggers directly at my jugular. Finn is out of his ever-loving mind if he thinks I would ever trust her with my son.

I storm out of the coffee shop and am thankful that the weather is decent. Had it been a chilly day, it would have been an even more miserable walk back to the office. I ignore the stares as I enter the building and step off the elevator on our floor.

Kelsey looks over her shoulder and gasps when I walk back into Finn's office.

"What the fuck happened to you?" Finn barks when he looks up from the paper in his hands and takes in my appearance.

"Your fucking sister-in-law happened."

He gives me a look, needing more than that.

I hold my hand up. "Do. Not. Fucking. Ask." I take a seat beside him. "Let's just get this over with."

Kelsey hands me a stack of papers, clearly sensing I don't want to fucking talk about it. I feel Finn's gaze on me, and I look up from the paperwork.

"You know, when I told you to go get caffeine, I thought maybe you'd drink it, not pour it all over yourself. Is that what kids these days are doing?"

I take a page from my nemesis's playbook and glare at him.

"Yeah, sorry, that was my one and only joke."

If only I actually believed that.

Chapter 10

Kate

"**S**o, you want to admit it now?" My sister's question catches me off guard as I accept the tape from her hand to attach one of the baby shower decorations to the wall. I've been filling my sister about my latest run-in with Jaxon as we set up for Dani's baby shower.

It took every ounce of strength to not look up as I walked out to the mailbox. Instead, I counted the cracks in the pavement along my driveway. Once my back was to him, I exhaled a breath of relief, even as the soundtrack of the lawn mower continued behind me.

I knew I should head back inside. Yet I stalled, sorting through the various envelopes—nothing but junk and bills. When the mower abruptly cut off, my mind instantly went back to the fantasy that had played on repeat for days. I made the mistake of glancing over my shoulder at the exact moment Jaxon leaned over and moved some sticks that had been in his way. Even with the brief distance between us, I could see the defined corded muscles of his back. The slight pink hue to his skin told me he'd been out in the sun a while—probably a typical man, not wearing sunscreen.

I pulled my bottom lip between my teeth as I imagined massaging suntan lotion into his skin or aloe to treat the sunburn. Sweet fucking Jesus.

Before I could stop myself, I opened my mouth. "Put some clothes on, for the love of God! You're scaring the neighbors." *Or turning them the fuck on, and they don't have time to rub one out.*

Jaxon turned around at the sound of my voice. Fuck, the front is even better! *He crossed his arms so that the muscles in his biceps tensed, drawing my eyes directly to them. I followed the drops of sweat that dripped down his skin. Seriously, it was unfair that this man looked like a fucking god. When did he even have time to work out? If he wasn't home, he was typically at work or at my sister's—not that I knew his schedule or anything.*

My mouth went dry because every drop of moisture in my body went straight to my panties. I rubbed my thighs together, trying to relieve the ache that blossomed.

When my eyes lifted, I met his. He had the audacity to smirk at me as if asking if I liked what I saw. I just rolled my eyes. The man knew he was hot—no need to stroke his ego.

"You know, that's funny. I hear something quite different." He started walking closer to me, and my breath hitched. "I hear I have a little fan club that meets once a week over there." He pointed his finger at my house.

Fuck! I clenched my fists by my side, nearly crushing my mail, and gritted my teeth. "I'm going to kill my brother-in-law." I knew Finn had to be the reason he knew. There was no way that Lauren would have told him nor Tweedledee and Tweedledum, also known as Dani and Haylee. I'd made the mistake of mentioning it to the girls once, and they made it a point to stop by on Saturday mornings for the view. So that narrowed it down to one other person.

Jaxon threw his head back in laughter, and it only furthered my scowl at him.

"Does the sacred vow of marriage mean nothing," I exclaimed.

The laughter died down, and his brow furrowed in confusion. "I'm not sure I follow."

"You know, the sacred vow of marriage."

"Yeah, I'm familiar with it, thanks," he bit out. His confused expression shouldn't bother me, yet I explained further.

I placed my hands on my hips and continued. "Well, Lauren and I share DNA, so I'm included in that, too. Therefore, anything I tell Lauren or Lauren does, she may tell Finn. However, the buck stops there. He's supposed to become a vault."

He shook his head and mumbled something I couldn't quite make out. "And what, bro code means nothing?"

"Nope," I said, popping the p sound. "Twin card trumps that."

He rubbed his temples with his stretched thumb and middle finger. "Okay, whatever. You can take your crazy talk away so I can finish mowing. Some of us have shit to do."

I ignored the dig and turned, heading back to my house, when Jaxon shouted, "Oh, and Kate? If you're gonna stare, maybe next time you can bring me a lemonade. I don't put on a show for free."

I flung my middle finger in the air at him, and the sound of the mower soon drowned his smug laughter.

Hopefully, he ran over his foot or something.

I tilt my head to the side and purse my lips. Did I miss something? Did talking about Mr. Grumpy Pants make my brain mush and I blacked out?

"Admit what?" I accept the next item from Lauren's hand to hang.

"That you like him." Lauren says those four words as if it were a normal conversation, like talking about the weather.

"What?" I shout, dropping the decoration in my hand. "Are you insane?" My sister is downright certifiable if that's what she thinks.

"Are you?" Her brows raise to her hairline. "I've had to listen to you go on and on about him for the last twenty minutes."

"Yeah, but not in a good way." My chest tightens, and I can feel the thrum of my own pulse. I glance around the room to see if anyone else needs help and I can escape this conversation.

"No." She shakes her head. "You might think that, but if you didn't care, you wouldn't notice these things or constantly watch him. This has enemies to lovers written all over it."

"You have seriously lost it." Of course my sister compares my life to one of her romance novels. If there's one thing she loves more than Finn Reynolds, it's books. He even incorporated books into his proposal and got her favorite author involved.

"Say what you want"—she points her finger at me—"but I know the truth."

I step off the stool and cross my arms in defense. "Oh yeah? And what's that?"

"You. Like. Him." She enunciates each word. "And it scares you," she says in a softer tone. "It's okay to admit it. Remember how scared I was with Finn coming back?"

Scared is an understatement. My sister, who typically has a calm demeanor, was thrown for a fucking loop.

"This is nothing like that. You two had a history. Finn was the love of your life. Jaxon McAdams is just another asshole in my life."

She smirks and makes a clicking noise with her tongue. "If that's what you want to go with, fine. I'll let you believe that for now."

"Okay, I think you and Finn need to switch up your sex positions, because it's obvious he has fucked your head into the headboard one too many times. Maybe try taking him for a ride sometime." I swivel my hips, pretending to be riding a mechanical bull.

"Oh my God, please stop!" Lauren's cheeks turn as red as a tomato.

"I'll stop if you stop," I comment back with my eyes wide.

"Fine, fine." She holds up her hands in defeat and turns back to the table beside her, adjusting the plastic tablecloth. "Some days, you're worse than my students."

I pretend to wear a formal ball gown and curtsy. "Thank you. I'll take that as a compliment. Now, let's get back to setting up before the mom-to-be arrives."

"Thank you, girls, so much for hosting this shower," Dani's mom, Kelly, says, interrupting us.

She sets a tray down on the table. I look down and see the largest charcuterie board I've ever seen, and the assortment of meats and cheeses literally has my mouth watering.

"Of course." Lauren gives her a side hug. "Dani is one of us—there's no way we wouldn't."

"I'm thankful she has you both. I know those drives are getting hard on the girls at this stage in their pregnancy, so I'm glad we could host it here instead of my house." Dani's and Haylee's parents both live in Annapolis, which is about a two-hour drive from here.

I can't imagine what they're both going through, especially with Dani carrying two babies. She mentioned the other day that Ky had to paint her toenails because she hadn't been able to see her feet in a while. But I'm pretty sure all the back pain, heartburn, and constant potty breaks are all worth it in the end when you get to hold a little bundle of joy that you created.

Kelly turns to me. "So, Kate, what's new in your life? Any new men?"

Lauren snorts, and when I turn to glare at her, she pretends to focus on something in front of her. *I've got your number, Lauren Reynolds.*

I huff out an annoyed breath but ignore my sister and turn back to the conversation. "Not any recently, Kelly. You know I'm still holding out hope for me and your son." I can't even say the words with a straight face. Over the years, it's become a running joke about my love for Zach. I look at him only like a brother, but it's always fun to tease. When he and my brother first became friends in college, he was single and the biggest flirt around. Once things changed for him and Haylee, there's only one other girl that holds his attention besides her, and that's his daughter.

"Well, good luck with that, dear," she jokes before her eyes widen and jaw drops.

I follow her focus to the front door, where Jaxon just walked in, holding Andy in his arms. A scowl forms on my face. *What is he doing here?*

"Why, hello handsome, and who might that be?" Kelly mutters. She has no shame in eyeing him up and down. It's hard not to when every shirt in his wardrobe clings to him like they were tailor-made for his body.

I swat at her arm. "You are a married woman, missy."

"I might be married, but I'm not blind. A friend of yours?" Her gaze goes back to him.

I scoff. "Hardly."

"Hmm," she harrumphs. "Could have fooled me by the way he can't take his eyes off you since he walked in."

"What?" I snap my gaze to his, only to find him talking with my mom, and his eyes are on her, *not me.*

Kelly and Lauren snicker, and I realize I fell for their trap.

"You all set, babe? Need anything else while you have big, strong men around?" Finn says as he approaches and wraps his arms around Lauren from behind.

"I think we're all set."

"Great." He kisses her quickly. "I'm fleeing this estrogen-crazed house before I'm forced to turn in my man card."

Many pairs of eyes narrow at him, and Finn blows a whistle. "I mean…" He trails off and grips the back of his neck. Oooh, I'm going to enjoy watching him squirm. "Umm, yeah, I'm just going to go now before I need a shovel to dig myself out of this hole." He chuckles.

"Yeah, that's probably a good thing." Lauren caresses his cheek before lightly tapping it. She turns to Jaxon. "Be sure to keep my husband in line, please."

He laughs, and I hate that it sends butterflies to my stomach. "Sorry, Lauren. I can't make any promises about that. You ladies enjoy your day." He gives everyone a panty-melting smile—like yep, *poof!* My panties just burst into flames.

From the corner of my eye, I see Kelly watching me watching him as they walk out the front door.

"Uh-huh," she mumbles.

"What?" I shriek, my voice an octave higher than normal. I clear my throat.

"Nothing. It's nothing. He just seems very nice, that's all." She smiles and pats my shoulders before heading off to the kitchen.

Am I seriously the only one who knows Jaxon McAdams is a wolf in sheep's clothing?

Chapter 11

Kate

C lick. Click. Click.
     Click. Click. Click.

"Ugh, come on, baby, don't fail me now." I turn the key in the ignition again, and nothing, only clicking noises. When my phone buzzed with a text from my brother that it was finally baby time, I quickly grabbed my keys but haven't made it very far.

I slam my hands against the steering wheel in frustration and scream. Yeah, I know that we have time until the babies get here, but I want to be there for Dani and Ky. This is the first of the next generation of Lawsons—it's a big fucking deal. I rest my head against the wheel and pray for a miracle. *Maybe Lauren hasn't left yet.*

I'm leaning over the passenger seat, searching for my phone in my purse, when there is a knock on the window.

"Holy shit," I scream, clutching my chest as I find a shadow beside me. I open the door and come face-to-face with Mr. Asshole himself. *Great, when I said a miracle, I meant from an angel, not fucking Satan.* Fallen angel or not, I'm not in the mood to go another round with him today.

"Having trouble?"

I groan and roll my eyes as I run my hands over my face. "Look, I'm not really up for fighting with you right now. My niece and nephew are coming into this world, and my damn car decides now of all days to stop working." I hope he doesn't notice the break in my voice.

His blank expression gives nothing away. Does he just want to waste my time? I wish his dark eyes didn't pull me in, craving to know what's swirling behind them.

Jaxon jerks the door wider. "Get out. Let's go."

"Excuse me?" I jolt back, completely taken by surprise.

"I don't think I stuttered. Come on. Denise picked up Andy this morning, so I can drop you off on my way to work."

I am taken aback by the non-hostile action. I think for a moment of saying no, thanks, that I can just call AAA or something. But who am I kidding? That could take forever, and I don't want to miss this, so I don't fight him on it. I grab my purse and follow him to his truck. His eyes widen for a moment that I agreed so quickly. *Trust me, buddy. So am I.*

With a click of a button, the truck roars to life as we approach the doors. I snicker at the fucking monstrosity in front of me. It may be his vehicle, but to me, it's become my alarm clock every morning.

I cautiously watch Jaxon as he walks around the passenger side next to me. I reach for the handle at the same time he does—but he's a split second quicker.

"You know I can open the door myself. I'm not some damsel in distress," I say in a clipped tone. "I'm not some weak little girl needing a man to help me."

"Sure about that?" He quirks a brow with a smirk I want to slap off his face. Okay, so maybe I am a bit of a damsel at the moment, requiring his help.

He holds his hand out to help me up, but I push past it and step up on the running board, reaching up to grab the oh-shit bar, and climb in.

"Well, all righty then," he mutters under his breath as he slams the door shut. I hope that he's not planning on kidnapping and leaving me somewhere in the middle of nowhere. Then again, I'd be pretty foolish since I willingly got into his truck. Eventually, someone would come looking for me.

Jaxon runs around to the driver's side and hops in the truck with much more ease than I did. He buckles in and puts the truck in reverse. With his hand perched on the back of my headrest, he turns to face me. "For the record, I'm well aware you're not a damsel in distress. I was just trying to be a gentleman. Won't make that mistake again."

He backs out of the driveway without giving me a chance to respond.

The ride is silent, but surprisingly, it's not uncomfortable. Jaxon leans forward and turns the radio on, only to blare the final verse of a popular Alanis Morissette song.

"Going through an angry breakup as a teenage girl, huh," I tease while listening to every girl's breakup anthem from the late nineties. Even I'm guilty of playing this song and screaming it at the top of my lungs. "Do we need to stop to pick you up some rocky road ice cream?"

He throws his head back in laughter as he approaches a stop sign. "Nah, mint chocolate chip is my usual breakup food, and I have the freezer stocked, but thanks for your concern."

"Ooh, now you're speaking my language." Mint chocolate chip ice cream is delicious, too.

Woah, are we having a conversation without arguing and *in agreement on something?*

The next track begins to play, which is a more subdued track. I hum along with the chorus as I focus out the window.

"I don't know why I'm surprised that you like '90s grunge." His deep voice sends a shiver up my spine.

"Who says I actually like it and I'm not just trying to avoid further conversation?" My voice holds zero conviction.

"Hmm," he hums. "Well then, I guess you won't mind if I change it, then."

Jaxon reaches forward at the same time I do, and I smack his hand away from the knob. A jolt of electricity runs through my veins, and I pull my hand back quickly and rub my sweaty palms on my pants.

"Ouch," he hisses, shaking his hand. *Big baby. I didn't smack him that hard.* "Message received."

We sit in silence for the rest of the song, but the tension in the truck's cab is rising, threatening to suffocate us both. I try to keep my focus forward, but my curiosity gets the best of me, and I keep checking on him with my peripheral vision. Each time he grips the steering wheel tightly, I wonder what is going through his mind.

I recognize the opening chords of the next track right away and do a little happy dance in my seat. This radio station is amazing.

"You okay over there?" There's a playfulness in his voice that tells me he caught my dance.

"Yeah, sorry." I wave my hand in the air. "It's just my favorite." I spent many mornings on the ride to school annoying Finn and Lauren with my butchering of this song.

Jaxon leans forward, and I frown because I think he's going to change the song or turn it down, and I'm about to tear him a new one. I don't care if this is his car or not. However, he surprises me. Instead of doing either of those things, he turns the volume up a little higher.

When we arrive at the hospital, Jax makes a right toward the parking garage instead of a left to the front entrance drop-off.

I look over my shoulder out the back window to where he should have dropped me off, but it gets smaller the further we drive away. "Umm, where are we going?"

"Parking," he responds as if the reason is clear as day.

I stare at him blankly as he pulls up to the gate and grabs a parking ticket.

"I get that, but why? You just needed to drop me off."

He's quiet as he parks the truck in a corner spot. Whatever, I don't have time to wait for him to decide when he wants to talk to me. I hop out of the truck and start walking toward the elevator. Jaxon is hot on my heels. I add a sway to my hips to fuck with him. He wants to stalk me and go back to ignoring me—good for him. I'll give him the extra show.

The admin at the front desk administers guest passes and directs us to the labor and delivery waiting room on the third floor, which is where I find my family waiting. Of course, I'm the last to arrive. Even Dani's parents beat me.

I hope that Jaxon miraculously disappears from behind me before anyone sees him, but of course, my luck, that is not the case. My sister is the first to look up, and she adjusts in her chair, jolting upright as she smacks Finn's arm and nods in our direction. I'm sure Lauren meant to do it discreetly but fails miserably. I'm pretty sure the sound of her smack echoes throughout the entire floor.

I ignore the stares and drop in the seat next to her and pretend I didn't just arrive at the hospital with my archnemesis. I glance back over at him, and he's standing there with his hands in his pockets, looking unsure of what to do. Good—serves the asshole right. Maybe he should have just dropped me off.

"Any update? Are the babies here yet?" I hope my question can bring the attention off me.

Lauren looks back and forth between the two of us. *Okay, no such luck, I guess.*

"Hello, Earth to Mrs. Reynolds." She whips her head toward me and smiles. Yeah, she's so mushy like that. She always smiles at her new last name. *Gag me.*

"No update yet." She leans over, propping her arm on our shared armrest. "What's going on?" she asks in a hushed voice.

I look back over in Jaxon's direction to find Finn now chatting with him. I shrug, unsure how to explain it, so I go with the simple version and pray she doesn't ask why because I haven't figured that part out yet. "My car wouldn't start, and Jax offered me a ride."

Her eyes widen, and I'm pretty sure her mouth hits the floor in shock. "Oh, it's Jax now? Huh? You guys on a nickname basis now?" Her tone is teasing, and all I get the chance to do is flip her the middle finger before we're interrupted by Finn leading Jaxon over to the empty seats across from us.

It's been two hours, and Jaxon is *still* here. He even made a coffee run to the cafeteria so no one had to leave. Although it was a hard pass for me since that is *not* coffee and basically liquid sludge.

All conversations come to a halt when Kyler appears in the waiting room. It was so quiet as we waited with bated breath for news. His expression gives absolutely nothing away, and it's killing me.

Are the babies here?

Is everything okay?

Were there complications?

Everyone quickly stands. "It's official," he shouts. I've never seen my brother so happy; not even on his wedding day was his smile this big. Wow, my brother is officially a father. How the fuck did that happen? "They're here."

The room erupts in cheers, and tears trickle down my cheeks.

"Dani is getting settled, and then the nurses said I can bring you guys back, but Dani needs to rest, so you guys will have to cut your visit short."

There are a few boos in the crowd, mainly from Dani's father, Adam, who is sporting a "Proud Grandpa of Twins" shirt. I wonder if Christopher Lawson had been here or even still in our lives, would he share the same excitement? Does he even know or care that he's a grandfather? Now is not the time to ruin a happy moment thinking about him.

I walk up to where my brother is standing next to Finn and Jaxon, along with Dani's brother, Zach. I interrupt their conversation, pulling him into my arms. The hug is a tad awkward because of our height difference, but I don't care.

"I'm so happy for you, Kyler. I am going to spoil the shit out of those babies." He squeezes me tightly before letting me go. I have to wipe more tears using the corner of my sleeve.

He laughs. "I have no doubt about that." He puffs out his cheeks, blowing out a harsh breath as reality sets in. "I'm never sleeping again."

His father-in-law comes up behind him and slaps him on the shoulder. "You'll sleep again in eighteen years."

A look of fear appears on his face as he laughs awkwardly. Poor guy. I know he has a plethora of babysitters lined up to watch those babies, though, so that he and Dani can sleep or do whatever it is they choose to do. I prefer not to think about Kyler and how these babies got into this world.

"Everyone ready?" Ky asks, clearly eager to get back to his wife and children.

Our large group follows, and I bring up the rear. I stop when I see Jaxon hasn't moved and is glancing around the room like a lost puppy.

I turn back and walk over to him. "Not coming?" I mean, he's waited this long. Might as well go meet the babies.

He places his hands in his pockets and shakes his head. "Nah, I don't want to crowd the new mom. I should get going anyway." He pauses. "Unless you need me to stay and give you a ride home."

I give a soft smile. "No, that's okay. I'll catch a ride home with my sister."

"Right, of course." He grips the back of his neck and looks down at a spot on the floor. *Was that disappointment in his voice?*

"I'll be sure to let Dani know you were here and send your regards."

He looks up, nodding a nonverbal thank-you. *Why am I standing here, stalling?*

"And Jaxon, thank you for the ride."

He shrugs. "It was nothing. Just—"

"You being a gentleman again?" I tease, using his words from earlier.

"Now you get it." He smirks, and something inside me has me craving to reach out and touch his cheek. Instead, I push his bicep and cover my teeth with my lips to suppress the moan of feeling the muscle flex underneath my touch.

"Shut up," I tease.

"Kate, you coming?" Lauren shouts from behind me.

"Well, you better go," he says, tilting his head over my shoulder. "I'll see you later, Kate."

With a small wave, he turns and heads toward the elevator. I'm still frozen in place, so my eyes are still on him when he looks back over his shoulder and smiles. I clear my throat and shake off whatever that was. I ignore my sister's stares and goofy grin as I pass her to meet up with the rest of the crowd to meet the newest members of the Lawson family.

Chapter 12

Jaxon

"Jeez, do I pay you to work or stare out the window all day?"

My best friend's voice startles me, and I spin in my chair to find Finn standing in the doorway to my office, leaning against the doorframe with his arms crossed. Too bad the playful smirk on his face and the lack of conviction in his voice contradict his body's stance.

"You pay me to sit here and look hot in my business suit. Drives all the ladies crazy." He chuckles, knowing that's far from the truth. "What are you even doing here, anyway?"

He pushes off the doorframe and enters the office. "Well, it is my company and all."

I grumble at his comment. *Smart-ass.* "I meant, what are you doing here *now*? I told you I had a handle on things today. You could've stayed at the hospital longer."

He approaches my desk and hikes up his pant legs before sitting down in a chair across from me. "Nah, Dani needed her rest, so after a quickish visit, Ky shooed us all away. The girls went to get a late lunch before heading back to the hospital. So, they dropped me off. Figure I'd be more useful here."

"You need a ride home?"

"Since you seem to be playing taxi today, that would be great. Unless you only give rides to beautiful brunettes whose names rhyme with late." There are so many underlying questions in that one statement. I pinch the bridge of my nose, knowing this was going to happen. The only information I gave him at the hospital was that she needed a ride, so I offered. He didn't push for more information, not wanting to make a scene and take the attention from what was happening.

"I mean, I already have the beautiful brunet part down." He shakes his head, pretending he has long hair and posing like a model on a photo shoot.

"Fuck off," I tease.

Finn opens his mouth to say something, but I don't let him by changing the subject. I'm not sure I'm ready to answer his questions yet. Shit, I don't even have the answers to my own questions.

"So, everyone all good? Babies healthy? It was a boy and girl, right?"

He narrows his eyes, catching on to my avoidance, but then relaxes his expression and smiles.

"Yep. Levi Adam and Charlotte Rae, but they're gonna call her Charli. Hold on—" He retrieves his phone from his pocket. With a few swipes of his finger, he passes over the phone to me. "They're small, but fuck, oh so adorable," he sighs as if there were heart emojis in his eyes.

I take in the image in front of me—two little babies lie together in one of those hospital bassinet things. Levi is on the left, swaddled in a blue-and-white-striped blanket and navy hat. He's mid-yawn, his arms stretched up. His glove-covered hand is in his sister's face, but she can't seem to be bothered. Wrapped in a matching pink-and-white blanket and pink hat with a bow attached, she is sound asleep.

"I gotta say, with the number of people that were in the waiting room, I'm impressed there's a photo where someone isn't holding them."

He laughs. "Just you wait." He indicates with his finger for me to keep swiping.

The corners of my lips turn upward as I realize I spoke too soon as I swiped through photo after photo. There are ones with the happy parents and their new little ones and the proud grandparents. There's one of Kyler holding Levi like a football, blocking his Uncle Zach from holding him. I'm sure that moment went over well with Dani.

"Oh, boy." I hold up the phone to show him what photo I'm referring to. Lauren is holding Charli in her arms while Finn looks over her shoulder. Lauren is beaming up at her husband with tears in her eyes. "Looks like someone has baby fever."

"Oh yeah, the plan was to take our time starting a family, and if it happened, it happened. But as soon as that first baby was placed in her arms, I was ready to whip my dick out and make a baby right then."

I cackle at his abrasiveness. "Well, I can think of quite a few people who are probably glad you didn't." I shake my head, not needing that mental image, although that would make for a great story one day to tell your kids.

Finn continues talking about their visit, but I don't pay much attention. Pressing Play on the video, I watch Lauren pass Charli to Kate, who is sitting in a glider in the corner of the hospital room. Once she is situated, Kyler comes into view and does the same with Levi. Her gaze bounces back and forth between the two babies cradled in her arms. Her smile lights up her entire face and damn near takes my breath away. Like call 911 because I need some oxygen pumped into my veins. This woman somehow manages to look beautiful whatever she does, even when she looks like a bum, but this look—the pride in her eyes, love flowing directly from her pores. One day, she will look at her child with the same adoration. Making that first eye contact with your child, there's nothing that can top that moment ever. The bond between a mother and a child…

One thought barrels through the forefront of my mind—Courtney. She never got that moment with our son.

My pulse races, and I place my hand over the dull hollow ache in my chest.

I'm struggling to find my breath now.

"Jax? Jax, hey, what's wrong?" Finn says, rising from the chair, but his voice is muffled, as if it were far away.

The voice loud and clear in my mind and the vision as I close is my eyes is of Dr. Griffin approaching, removing her cap from her head. The distraught look on her face has my heart falling into the pit of my stomach.

"Mr. McAdams—"

"Where's Courtney? Let me see my wife," I barked, but I promise it was worse than my bite. I needed answers. I needed to know what was going on. I needed to get to my son.

"I'm sorry to tell you this, but—"

A hand clamps down on my shoulder, pulling me out of the darkness of my mind.

"Jaxon, breathe, man. Talk to me."

I hold my hand up, telling him to just give me a minute. *I'm fine. But am I?* My hand is trembling. I form a fist and press it to my mouth to keep the guttural scream from escaping. I close my eyes and lift my head to the sky, exhaling a loud breath.

"I don't have photos of Andy like this. I'll never have them." I pick up Finn's phone from where I must have dropped it. Shit, I don't even remember doing that. I inspect it to make sure there was no damage.

"Fuck. Shit." We swap the phone for a water bottle he is holding out. "I'm such an insensitive prick. I didn't even think about how all this would affect you today. I'm so sorry."

"Don't be." I guzzle half the bottle down. The cool water does nothing to the way my body is on fire, as if I'm burning at the stake.

I wipe the droplets off my mouth with the back of my hand.

"No, I shouldn't have encouraged you to stay when you arrived."

"You didn't." To be honest, he had very little to do with my decision to stay. Something transitioned with Kate and me today on the drive, and I wanted to savor that change as much as possible before things reverted to how things used to be between us. "It wasn't until just now that it all hit me." *Like a goddamned freight train.*

"Not when I offered Kate a ride, knowing where we were going. Not sitting in the waiting room with your crazy family. Not even when Kyler came in, grinning ear to ear. It was looking at the video of Kate that it hit me—holding the babies."

I run my fingers through my hair, tugging on the strands. "God, what is fucking wrong with me?"

"Jax, nothing is wrong with you."

"I spent all day not dwelling on the loss."

"That doesn't make you a bad person. It makes you human. You went through something traumatic. You lost the love of your life, the mother of your child. That will never leave you, but you don't need to carry the burden. You don't need to carry the guilt. Courtney knows how much you loved her."

"It's hard. It's so fucking hard, especially…" I trail off, resting my head in my hands.

"Especially what?" Finn bends down at eye level with me, and I look up. "When there's someone that makes you feel alive again?"

My brows rise, and he quirks his lips.

"Come on, asshole. I've got eyes, you know."

"I just don't know that I'm ready," I sigh.

"Look, I'm not saying you are—I'm not saying you aren't."

An awkward laugh slips from my lips. "Then what are you saying?"

"Go easy on yourself, or the guilt is going to consume you."

I think it's too late for that.

Against my better judgment, I dropped the vulnerability shield and let her in and look where it got me. Guilt slipped through the cracks, setting roots and leaching its teeth into my mind and heart.

I think the best thing for now is to keep my distance from her. Which obviously is easier said than done.

Chapter 13

"Hello, my darling sister," Lauren singsongs into the phone before I can even say hello when I answer her call. *Someone sure is chipper today.*

"What do you need?" I balance my phone on my shoulder while I continue wrapping the present in front of me. I can't believe Christmas is already here.

She gasps dramatically. "What? Can't I just be calling you to say hi?"

I know Lauren too well, and yes, she calls all the time just to chat, as do I. There have even been times when we FaceTime just to be near each other as we go about doing other things. We're weird, we know. But today is different—I can hear it in her voice that she wants something. My twintuition radar is flashing, telling me to be on alert.

"Of course you can, but the question is, are you?" I'm met with her silence, and a victorious smile spreads across my lips.

A heavy sigh comes through the phone. "Fine," she huffs. "So, Finn's company is hosting its annual Christmas party on Friday."

"Yeah, you've been talking about it since Thanksgiving." A perk of working for myself is that I don't have to deal with all that hoopla, but listening to her talk to our mom about details of the event, I can't help but be a little jealous and wish I was attending.

"Right. So remember all those times growing up I covered for you, no questions asked."

I knew that one day that would come back to bite me. I'm kicking my sixteen-year-old ass right now. Why do I have a feeling that I'm not going to like what she's about to say, but also, because she's Lauren, I'm not going to be able to say no? And worst of all, she knows that.

"Will you just spit it out already?" I snap. I'm pretty sure it will have come and gone by the time she says whatever she needs to say. I can't decide if her reluctance to ask is a good thing or not.

"I need you to go." She pauses. "As Jax's date." Her line goes silent, and I have to pull back the phone to make sure she didn't hang up. She's probably holding on with bated breath to hear my reaction.

I bark out a laugh, grateful that I didn't have anything to drink in my mouth because I would have spit it right out. "I'm sorry. It sounded like you just said you want me to go on a date with Jaxon."

After he helped me the day the twins were born, I thought we had made a truce, so to speak. But I must have just dreamed that because he's all but avoided me since. Which I have to say is quite impressive, living directly across from each other and being tied together through Lauren and Finn. I don't know why I've let it bother me, but Jaxon McAdams has wedged himself under my skin, and I'm just not sure how to handle that.

"I did. I mean, not a date date, just accompany him."

"Then hire a hooker," I snap. It was the first thing that popped into my head. Not necessarily the most logical idea, but sounds a lot better than me going on a date with him.

She must be out of her damn mind if she thinks this will do anything but blow up in her face.

"Kate, I'm serious," she scolds.

"So am I," I retort. I peel myself off the floor and head into the kitchen to grab a bottle of wine. Any more of this crazy talk and I'll need something to take off the edge.

"How do I know this isn't some ploy to get the two of us together? I already told you that was never going to happen, especially since he's back to having that stick up his ass." Did I, for a second, think after the hospital that it wouldn't be such a bad thing, at least having him as a friend? Yeah, and I blinked, and it went away.

"No, I promise." She pauses, and I'm tempted to switch the call to FaceTime so I can have a visual of her making that promise and not with her fingers crossed. Can't say that I fully believe her words. "Look, it's important to Finn for Jax to be there, but Christmases are tough for him. And I figured if we're there as a group, then he won't feel like a fifth wheel."

"Again, my idea of hiring a hooker feels pretty fitting here. It could even be a two-for-one deal—a date for the party and his Christmas present."

A wave of jealousy passes through my veins at the thought of another woman on his arm. I swallow it down and chase it with a swig of red wine.

"Come on, sissy. You know how what that's like." For years, I've been the odd man out, and it's not necessarily a bad thing. At least he's easy to look at. Now, if only he would keep his mouth shut. Besides, do I really want to sit at home wondering who he ended up taking?

I lean back against the counter and sigh. "That's a low blow." I push off the counter, and my body goes rigid. "And Jaxon just agreed to all this?" I swear I get whiplash from his mood swings. One minute he wants to pretend I don't exist, and now he wants me to be his date? "Why do I find that hard to believe?" I scoff. If he was going to want somebody by his side that night, I highly doubt I would even be in the running.

"He, umm…" She fades, and I picture her looking around, avoiding eye contact, even though we aren't physically together.

"Lauren Elizabeth Reynolds." I do my best impression of the one and only Liz Lawson—able to strike fear into anyone with the use of their full name.

"He doesn't know, okay?"

"What?" I screech, and I wonder if he heard the vibrations from my high pitch from across the street.

"Just hear me out, okay?" she pleads. "If you already agree to it, and we already have Denise agreed to watch Andy along with Liam, then he's out of excuses to say no."

I laugh awkwardly. This is unbelievable. "I don't think this is a good idea."

"Please," she whines, and without even seeing her face, I know she has puppy dog sad eyes and is pouting into the phone.

I'm just about to decline, not wanting the backlash this plan will cause, when Lauren adds, "There's an open bar."

Damnit. I'm no lush, but I would be certifiable to turn down a party with delicious food *and* free alcohol. It appears she's used the same tactic with me she and Finn are using with Jaxon. An answer for every excuse. *Well played, sister.*

Lauren knows she won with my heavy sigh, and I can picture her smiling big into the phone and doing a happy dance.

"Fine, but your husband is buying my dress."

"Deal," she agrees a little too quickly. I wonder how her husband will feel about that.

"And for my hair appointment."

"Whatever you want. Kelsey and I have spa appointments earlier that day, so you can join us."

"Fine," I huff. "For the record, I am only doing this for you. Don't get any funny ideas and pull something like this again. He better be on his best behavior."

"I'll make sure of it. I can't wait to tell Finn," she squeals with excitement.

The corners of my mouth can't help but tip upward as well. Less for the fact I'm being forced to be around *him* and more about the fun I'm going to have spending my brother-in-law's money.

"Love you, sissy."

I roll my eyes when I hear her smooching into the phone. "Yeah, yeah, love you, too. Come shopping tomorrow, and bring your hubby's credit card." I hang up before she can object. No going back now. It was part of our deal.

Looks like I've got a date with the devil at the end of the week. Then again, he hasn't agreed yet, so there's still time for hell to freeze over.

Chapter 14

Jaxon

Whoever came up with the saying "out of sight, out of mind" clearly never purposely avoided a woman for weeks, hoping the constant thoughts of her would waver. Because let me tell you, it does the complete opposite. Since I decided it was best to keep my distance, she's been at the forefront of my mind.

When Finn proposed this plan for us all to attend the company Christmas party together, more importantly, with Kate by my side, my dick was the first to accept. Finn had thought of every viable excuse I could come up with and prepared for it with a solution.

My dick was completely on board while it took my head and my heart time to catch on. Actually, no, my brain was next to be on board with this plan because it was over the vision of her in my mind and stolen glances. It needed the real deal.

What could one night do? It's just for a few hours, and it's important to Finn for us all to be in attendance. The annual Christmas party was a big deal to his father, Griffin Sr., who always made an enormous deal of this event, including the employees and their spouses, vendors, and some clients. Kelsey has worked hard the past few weeks to continue her father's tradition.

It's just one night. I can do it.

Well, one night can change everything—and it's amazing just how fast it can change. My heart nearly gave out the second I laid eyes on Kate when she arrived at Denise's, where we all met before we piled into the limo that Finn rented to bring us downtown.

I spent most of the ride purposely staring at the passing city to keep from staring at her. It was like there were magnets in each of the colorful sequins that lined that dress. My resolve has been slowly breaking all night.

I've had to keep my hands in my pockets all night to keep from touching her. Are her toned legs that are on display with the short length of that dress as soft as I think? If I slid my hands up to the apex of her thighs, would I find panties? Or is she completely bare under that material? The low dip of the back of the dress tells me she's not wearing a bra. Don't get me started on what my dick wanted to do as soon as I noticed this fact.

My coldness in the limo seems to have paid off because, since we arrived, she has kept her distance. I should apologize—hell, I should apologize for everything and start over, explain my issues, that it's not her, it's me. *Jesus, that sounds like something that might be said on an episode of* Friends.

She's kept to the dance floor with the girls for most of the evening while I grew roots at the corner of the bar. I've spent the evening schmoozing with everyone with a smile on my face and my eyes not far from watching her.

With a refilled drink in hand, I prop my elbows against the wood counter and glance around the room. Chase has Kelsey in his arms for a dance that's definitely not the correct pace for this holiday favorite. The two of them are so consumed with each other that I'm pretty sure a meteor could hit and they wouldn't notice. Next to them, Finn and Lauren are the complete opposite, with their heads both tipped back in laughter as they watch Kate dance in front of them. She doesn't seem to care that her dance partners have since abandoned her for their spouses.

She's a free spirit, dancing to the beat of her own drum, swaying side to side to the vocals of Mariah Carey, lip-syncing to her twin.

If I wasn't still struggling with my internal war, I could down my drink, push off the bar and join them, swooping Kate into my arms and allowing the festive music to sweep us away.

Would she let me pull her against my chest?

Would she push me away and put up a fight?

I wouldn't blame her for the latter after the way I've acted, especially tonight. She didn't have to say yes to her sister for this plan, yet she did. The least I could do was be pleasant. But if I give an inch, it might take a mile. So instead, I'm letting my fear and guilt impede happiness. But with each passing hour, I feel the restraint splinter like a piece of cracked glass, ready to shatter.

My name is Jaxon McAdams, and I'm my own worst enemy, I think as I take a long pull from my beer.

From a distance, I can enjoy the view, torturing myself. With each sway of her hips, that sorry excuse of a dress rises higher and higher. My inner caveman is screaming to rush to her and keep her covered so that only I get to enjoy the view. I'm so lost in her that I don't notice anyone has stepped up beside me until a distinct throat clearing causes me to startle.

I turn to find Natasha, Finn's secretary, standing in my personal space. With her arms resting on the bar, the satin fabric at the top of her dress dips, revealing her large breasts. Clearly, she's not wearing a bra either, but I'm sure it's for a completely different reason than Kate.

She smirks when she realizes my eyes dropped to her chest. Hey, I'm still a man, and it's hard not to, but my eyes don't linger long.

"You don't seem to be having fun, Mr. McAdams." She says my name seductively.

I scoff and spin to face the bar and bring the bottle to my lips. "You're very observant," I say flatly.

She steps up closer to me, and the overabundance of her perfume threatens to choke me, reeking of desperation. She smells as if she just walked through the perfume aisle in the mall. "You know, Jaxon." The way she says my full name sends a shiver up my spine, and not in the same way when Kate does it. Even when Kate spits out my name like it's poison on her lips, it sends a straight shot right to my dick. But hearing it on Natasha's lips has my balls ready to shrivel away to nothing. "I can be a lot of things. I was wondering if you've been naughty or nice this year."

I don't miss the innuendos in there. Even if I was interested in anyone, it definitely would not be an employee. That's a damn lawsuit waiting to happen. Does she also think I'm dumb and don't know that before Lauren and Finn got back together, she was trying to sink her claws into him? She continued until one day, Lauren showed up at the office and staked her claim, all but pissing on him like a dog. That seems like something her sister would do more so than her, but then again, love makes you do crazy shit.

Before I can tell Natasha that I'm not interested and that it will never, *ever* happen between us, the hairs on the back of my neck rise. A small hand wraps around my waist, and I catch a whiff of her perfume. "Hey, baby, I thought you were going to join me out on the dance floor."

Turning, I find Kate with a huge smile on her painted red lips and a mischievous glint in her eyes screaming, *Play along, dumbass.*

I cough into my fist. "Oh, sorry, I got held up," I say, hugging her tighter against my chest. With adoration in my gaze, I slip into the comfortableness of this facade and allow myself to pretend that all this is real. I watch her throat bob as she visibly swallows. Our chests rise and fall in unison.

It's then I feel it—the pieces of my resolve imploding with a loud crash, knowing that I wouldn't be able to give this woman up even if I tried.

Natasha clears her throat, breaking our staring contest.

"Natasha, right?" Kate extends her hand to her. "I've heard so much about you," she says with a cheesy smile on her lips. I don't know if that's true or not, but judging by how much Lauren hates her, I would say it's definitely possible, and I would imagine there weren't many good things attached to them.

"Yes, hi. You're Lauren's sister." Kate nods. Natasha's eyes bounce back and forth between Kate and me, honing on the way my fingers move up and down on Kate's shoulder. "I'm sorry. I didn't realize you two were together."

Kate rests her head against my chest and places her hand over my heart. Can she feel it beating like I just ran the Boston Marathon in record time? Keeping up appearances, I press a kiss to the top of her head.

"Yep," Kate responds with a loud pop.

The tension and awkwardness increase the longer we go with no one saying anything. Thankfully, though, for once, it's not between Kate and me.

I decide to be the first one to speak up. Natasha hasn't gotten the hint that she can scurry along to find her next victim. "Well, babe, how about that dance? I've kept my girl waiting long enough to spin me around."

I look down to see Kate still focused on Natasha. "Kate?"

She shakes her head as if trying to forget whatever thoughts are flowing through her mind.

"Sorry, baby." She dances her fingers up my tie. "I was just imagining you bending me over the bar top. My bad."

Fuck me.

She spins to face me and links her arms around my neck. "Let's go dance."

Can she feel my dick straining against my dress pants? Because it is definitely saluting her with a *hello, gorgeous.*

Kate drags me out to the dance floor just as the song changes to a slow Christmas classic. Dancing was never my thing. Court always had to drag me out onto the dance floor. But tonight, I would dance all night long if it meant I could keep touching Kate or that it kept a certain party away.

She links her fingers behind my neck again like she had at the bar.

"Sorry, I saw you over there, and you looked extremely uncomfortable," she says as we begin to move to the music.

"Thank you." I'm still in a bit of a shock that after everything, she came to my rescue and didn't just feed me to the wolves.

"If you want that bitch to believe our story, you probably have to pretend to actually like me and not reminisce about being at a middle school dance and slow dancing for the first time."

She pushes her lips together in a smug smile. The only reason I'm not is because I'm still trying to will my dick down. He appreciates her being in my arms.

"Yeah, you're probably right." I pull her closer to me so we are toe to toe and chest to chest. My fingers spread and firmly plant themselves into her back.

Silence fills what little space remains between us.

"The irony isn't lost on me that the one song I actually dance with my *date* to is 'Silent Night'—you know, since you haven't said one word to me all night till that conversation there. It's fine. I didn't agree with this for you."

"I'm sorry."

"I said I didn't agree—" she repeats herself, but that's not what I meant. I shake my head, cutting her off.

"No, I heard you. I meant—" I swallow thickly. "I meant I'm sorry. I owe you an apology for the shitty evening."

"That's all you wanna apologize for after months of being a dick?" A perfect curve forms in her arched brow.

"Yeah, that, too."

"Wow," she draws out. "You know you really suck at this whole apologizing thing."

Tell me something I don't know. I bark out a laugh. "So I'm told. My wife used to say the same thing."

I feel her stiffen at the mention of Court. I watch her throat bob, and I'm curious as to whether she's going to respond. "Well, she sounds like a smart woman. I mean, no one's perfect." She pauses. "She married you, after all."

"Ouch, Lawson." I slam a palm to my chest and wince as if her words hurt me, but then I pull her back against me after my jolt put space between us. "That's what made her perfect. She saw right through my grumpy ass and loved me anyway."

Kate only nods. Pretty sure talking about your dead spouse is not on the top ten list of things you should talk about on a date. Not that this is an actual date. She said so herself—she's not here for me.

"I'm sorry for your loss. I don't think I've ever expressed that before," she says softly before resting her head on my chest and begins playing with the strands of hair at the nape of my neck. Does she even realize she's doing it? I can feel my heartbeat in my ears. There's no way she can't feel it. This is what her touch does to me.

"Thank you," I manage just above a whisper. I look up to see Natasha finally storming away. I'm not ready for Kate to push away, so I spin us a little so her back is now to the bar.

We stay like that until I feel an elbow dig into my back. I stumble forward and push Kate back a little. I turn around to find Chase and Kelsey slow dancing right beside us.

"What the hell, man," I scold.

I turn around to ask Kate if she's okay, but Chase speaks up again.

"You gonna kiss her or not?" Color me confused. Chase senses it and nods above us, and Kate and I both follow the line of sight. "You're standing under the mistletoe, dumbass. Everyone knows you have to kiss the person you're standing with, or it's ten years' bad luck."

"Umm, isn't that what happens when you break a mirror?" Kate questions.

"Hmm, you're right. Maybe it's that you'll have whiskey dick for the year."

I flinch, and Kate must feel it because she giggles. When I throw a glance her way, which is obviously only encouraging his drunk ass, she pushes her lips together to hide her laugh.

"I don't know. Either way, are you willing to chance it? Because I'm sure as shit not," Chase says.

Even though Chase and Kelsey aren't directly under the mistletoe, he whisks her back and kisses her. She is flushed by the time he pulls her upright, and then they go back to slow dancing. "See? It's easy."

I turn around and try to ignore him, but he makes it a little difficult by chanting, "Kiss her, kiss her," under his breath but loud enough for us to hear it. He stops for a second, followed by a smack, I assume, from his wife and then goes back to it.

Kate has since pulled her plump, bright red lip between her teeth. When my eyes lift again to meet hers, it's clear that she caught me. I guess I didn't even try to hide it.

"What do you say, McAdams? Is that a risk you're willing to take?" I don't know if it's the alcohol flowing in her veins or she's just fucking with me, but there's definite arousal laced in her voice. Neither one of us wants to break the stare first, but I find our faces slowly drifting together. I freeze just a breath away from her lips. If Chase were to bump into me again, I would definitely be kissing her.

"Umm, excuse me." I pull away from her embrace and spin around, rushing toward the exit. I keep my head low to avoid the stares as I leave Kate in the middle of the dance floor before the song has even ended.

As soon as the cold air touches my skin, I let out a harsh breath. The last thing I needed was to have a panic attack in front of my employees.

The temperature has dropped a few more degrees since we arrived, and I can now see my breath in front of me as I exhale. I close my eyes and level out my breathing. *What is it with this damn woman? What sort of voodoo magic does she have over me?*

The door opens, and I wince as it slams against the brick exterior. I don't have to turn around to know that she followed me out here.

"Why do you hate me so much? What did I ever fucking do to you?" she shouts from behind me.

"I never said I hated you." I squeeze my eyes tighter.

She snorts—literally snorts. "Could've fooled me. Your body language and your shitty attitude toward me says it all for you."

"It's not that simple," I admit honestly.

"Actually, it is." The composure I've gathered in the few moments away from her snaps, and I spin around fast enough to give both of us whiplash. "You either do or you—"

I don't give her a chance to finish her sentence before I press her up against the brick, the rough surface possibly leaving scrapes on her exposed skin.

I devour her smart mouth with slow and steady strokes of my tongue against hers.

"You drive me fucking crazy, you know that, right?" I ask, pulling my lips away from her but not losing contact for too long.

I trail my lips down her neck, not giving a damn that we're currently in an alley. "I didn't kiss you back there because I knew if I kissed you, I might never stop." She thrusts against me when I nip the sensitive spot where her neck meets her shoulder. "I've avoided you because every time I'm with you, I feel your pull. I can't resist you. I don't want to anymore."

Her hands skim down my stomach, and the muscles tense under her touch, even with the material keeping her hands from branding my skin. When her fingers reach my cock, which is so hard it's ready to bust right through my pants, I grab her hands and pin her arms above her head. If she kept doing that, this would be over before it even began.

She gasps but doesn't push me away. I keep her in place with one hand and slide the other leg between her thighs and find damp material. Jesus, I've barely touched her, and she's already soaked.

"Fuck," I groan in her ear as I remove my hand from her panties and step between her spread legs. She grinds her pussy down on my knee, and I wonder if I can make her come without even touching her. The soft whimpers she lets out engrave themselves in my brain. They are better than any of the sounds that have played out in my fantasies.

"Jaxon," she whimpers when I graze my teeth over her exposed collarbone and lick away the sting. I kiss my way back up her neck and capture her lips again. She kisses back with such an urgency I know she is getting close.

A noise from behind us causes me to jump back.

"Shit. Fuck." I run my fingers through my hair, leaving the strands a mess. Before I can think better of it, I bring my gaze back to Kate, whose swollen lips and smeared lipstick look like a work of art. Her chest heaves up and down as she tries to catch her breath. The skin along her neck is flushed, either from her arousal or the burn of my facial hair brushing against it. Her chocolate-brown eyes shimmer in the light, I'm sure in shock—though I'm unsure if it's shock that we were just doing that or that I stopped.

"I'm sorry. That shouldn't have happened. I can't do this." I don't give her a chance to respond, and once again, I am rushing away from her, putting much-needed space between us.

Chapter 15

Kate

I run cold water on a paper towel and dab my face, careful not to mess up my makeup… even more. Jaxon did a decent job of all that on his own.

If it wasn't for the beard burn on my cheek and neck, swollen lips smeared with my lip stain, and the stickiness between my thighs, I would say I imagined it. Who knows, maybe the champagne got to me and it was all a figment of my imagination. It wouldn't be the first fantasy I've had of Jaxon, and now that I know what he tastes like and felt his erection against me—I can guaran-fucking-tee it won't be the last.

My mind is reeling over how his body overpowered mine when I reached for his cock—his very hard cock. Just thinking about it has my nipples standing at attention and my mouth watering. His hands were firm, but there was a gentleness to him, where I knew he wouldn't hurt me, only for pleasure. I was so close to falling apart in his arms when he pulled back. Why did he pull back? He said he was tired of fighting the pull he felt between us. Was it all just a ruse?

I adjust my dress and ignore the throbbing in my core. I think I've let enough time pass for everyone not to question what transpired in the alley when they see us returning together.

Tossing the paper towel in the trash, I reach for the handle of the restroom door. I take a few deep breaths and steady my shoulders before pulling on the handle, ready to face him.

Making my way back through the party, I grab a glass of champagne from one of the passing servers. I spot my sister standing at one of the cocktail tables off the dance floor.

"Hey, I was wondering where you went," she says as I step up beside her and set my restless hands on the table.

"The line for the bathroom was ridiculous. You know women always travel to pee in packs and take forever."

She giggles but buys my lie. I can't believe I just lied to her, but this is a conversation for sober us or, well, hungover us tomorrow. And I definitely can't discuss it with her before I talk about it with him. Speak of the devil. Where is he?

I crane my neck around, trying not to make it too obvious, but I don't see him. The crowd has thinned a little, so I can see better. I spot Kelsey and Chase still wrapped up in each other's arms on the dance floor.

I come up empty by the bar, too. *Where the fuck is he?* I smirk when I find Natasha at the other end of the bar, her tits leaving an imprint on some random schmuck's arm. *Poor guy never saw it coming.*

Out of the corner of my eye, Finn approaches the table, placing a drink in front of Lauren and pulling her into his arms.

"Well, shit," Finn mutters, drawing my attention back to him and his phone lit up in his hand.

"What is it?" Lauren questions.

"Jaxon just sent a text and said something came up and he had to go. Just left in an Uber."

He left? He just up and fucking left? Yeah, I'd say something came up—his dick. Jaxon took the cowardly way out. At least have the decency to face not only me but your supposed best friend to say goodbye.

"Oh no. Did he say what happened?" Lauren's perfectly manicured eyebrows draw together in concern.

"No," he responds, typing out a message and pocketing his phone. A frown settles on his face.

My inner Kate is screaming and enthusiastically raising her hand like one of my sister's students when she asks a simple question. *Me! It was me that happened! I'm the reason he bolted.*

A variety of emotions flow through my veins—embarrassment, shame, anger. I don't even know how or what to feel.

I ignore the conversation beside me as I attempt to calm the raging war inside my head. I could leave, go home, and bang on his door and demand answers. Instead, I throw back the rest of my drink and welcome the burning sensation down my throat.

Twice in one night, Jaxon ran away from me. *I got the message loud and clear, buddy.*

What's that phrase? Fool me once, shame on you. Fool me twice, shame on me? There most definitely won't be a third time.

"Are we going to eat or what?" my brother says as he rises and adjusts baby Charli in his arms.

"Shouldn't we wait for Jaxon and Andy?" The words slip free from my mouth before I stop myself. Tonight, I'm hosting my family for Christmas Eve dinner. It was technically Kyler's year to host, but with the new babies, I offered to host the second year in a row to take some of the stress off them.

You would think for all the trouble my sister went through to get me to say yes for the McAdamses to be included on the invite list, he would at least have the fucking decency to show up on time. Not like he had a fucking long commute or anything.

Finn steps up to the table and steals a piece of bread from the bowl. "Oh, right. No, he and Andy went to Florida for Christmas to visit Courtney's parents."

"Ahh, I see. Well, thanks for letting me know. I wouldn't have set the table for two additional plates, then." I try to cover up my annoyance with that, not the fact that he fucking ran away after nearly dry humping me to orgasm in a dark alley just a few days ago. Was that trip planned before? Maybe I can give him the benefit of the doubt that when Finn invited him tonight, he had said that he couldn't make it, but Finn forgot to pass the message along. *Yeah, I'll go with that.*

And here I thought fleeing was Finn's thing. Maybe it should be the new family motto—Kiss a Lawson, flee the state. Must be a twin thing since that's another thing Lauren and I have in common.

Everyone gathers around the table.

"I need a refill." I grab my wineglass and rush to the kitchen without another glance. I set my glass on the counter and press my palms into the granite. I press my chest down, stretching, and take a few moments to catch my breath.

"What's wrong?" my sister says from behind me, and I straighten up. I busy myself around the counter, trying to avoid her gaze.

"What makes you think something's wrong?" My voice is shaky that I'm not sure even I believe me, let alone someone who knows me better than I know myself.

Lauren approaches and leans against the counter with her arms and ankles crossed, matching my stance. "Well, for one, you don't need a refill." I follow her pointed finger to my full wineglass. "And two, there are three bottles of wine out on the table. So spill."

I close my eyes and compose myself. "Can I ask you something?" She nods. "Was Jaxon always planning to spend the holidays in Florida?"

Lauren purses her lips together. "Umm, I'm not sure. He called Finn this morning and asked for a ride to the airport. He wanted to save from airport parking during the holidays." Ahh, that explains his truck still being home all day—not that I was watching. But I'm glad that I didn't storm over there and bang on his door demanding we talk about it to ease the possible tension tonight. Then I would have made an even bigger fool because I would have thought he was just ignoring me.

"Where's this coming from?" she adds. "I figured you, of all people, wouldn't mind his absence." Of course she questions my curiosity. Normally, it wouldn't bother me. Why didn't I just shrug and roll my eyes and move on with the evening? *Fuck my life.*

I bring the glass to my lips and take a large gulp of liquid courage. "Ugh, I fucked up," I sigh as I set the glass back down.

"What do you mean?" Lauren spins and clings to the counter, as if bracing herself for whatever news I'm about to deliver.

"I kissed Jaxon," I admit.

Shock is all over her face as her mouth gapes and eyes bulge. She closes her mouth and holds her finger up as if she's trying to gather the words but settles on a simple question. "Where?"

"On the mouth," I tease, pressing my lips together to stifle a laugh.

She scowls. "I meant, where did you kiss him? When did you kiss him? Why am I now just hearing about it?"

All she's missing is the who and what of the interrogation, but then again, we've already established those.

"At the holiday party."

I watch the pieces all come to place in her mind. "Holy shit," she breathes and quickly covers her mouth with her hand.

"Lauren, Kate," my brother shouts, interrupting the conversation before we can talk any more. I've never wanted to hug my brother so badly.

"Mom says we can't dive in till you guys get back in here, and Emme is getting restless."

"Hey, don't bring my child into this," Zach follows up, chuckling.

We both laugh at the fact that Kyler just threw a toddler under the bus because he is so impatient. Hard to believe the man is a father when he acts like a child himself.

"Umm, we'll finish this conversation later. You know that, right?" Lauren loops her arm through mine and beings to pull me toward the other room.

"There's nothing to talk about. We kissed. It was a mistake. It's not like I haven't kissed plenty of other frogs before. And just like those, he didn't turn into a prince. Not all of us have that perfect happily ever after, sis." I steady my features, but I know of all people, she would be the one to see through my bullshit. *It was just a kiss—nothing more, nothing less. Just two people having a nonverbal conversation with their lips.* If I tell myself that enough times, it will come true, right?

Lauren gives a small smile when she realizes I'm done with the conversation and releases my arm and heads to her open seat beside her husband. I take in the surrounding room. The chatter may be loud, but there's no shortage of love.

Levi and Charli are asleep in swings set up beside the table where Kyler and Dani sit. Kyler's arm is wrapped around his wife, and she rests her head on his shoulder. Poor guys look like they're ready for a nap. Haylee is focused on a newborn baby Harper, who is wrapped against her body in one of those Mobi wrap things. According to Haylee, it's God's gift to creation, and I can't help but smile since I was the one who got her that. Emme is giggling from her chair between her parents as she watches her dad pour gravy lava down her mashed potatoes volcano.

Mom sits at the head of the table, resting her chin on her propped-up fists, a smile on her face as she observes her family.

My life might not be the happily ever after that others dreamed of, but life is damn good.

"All right, who's hungry?"

Chapter 16

Jaxon

There's a short list of things I shouldn't have done in my life.

In high school, I shouldn't have allowed my friends to convince me it was a good idea to be pulled on a skateboard by a tow rope attached to a golf cart. It resulted in a screw holding my broken wrist together.

I shouldn't have agreed to compete in the spicy tuna roll challenge with Finn. We had to eat ten spicy tuna rolls, each upping the heat level. I made it all the way to roll ten while Finn had tapped out at only number five. I got sick as fuck after that and even had to bail on attending Courtney's best friend's wedding with her. She was so pissed.

While kissing Kate in a dark alley isn't on the list, running away like a coward surely is. I've spent the last few days at Courtney's parents', escaping my feelings, thinking about the what-ifs if we weren't interrupted, and I allowed my doubt to crawl into my mind. Would I have fucked her right there in the alley? Absolutely. She deserves much more than a quick fuck against a brick wall, but that would have only been the beginning.

Adding to that list is accepting the invitation from my best friend when he picked Andy and me up from the airport this morning to come over to celebrate a "low-key" New Year. However, when their family is involved, that alone makes quite the crowd. Now I'm forced to stand here and watch Kate interact with some guy she showed up with.

In the months since I moved here, I have never actually seen her with someone before. Is this all a way to get back at me? If so, I deserve it—or even worse.

I'd rather have her anger than her silence. What's keeping her from making a scene right now? I want her to call me out on my bullshit. To tell me I was an ass. And I would tell her she is correct. I want to push her against the wall and finish what we started, not watch another man's hand draped all over her. She's barely thrown a glance my way all evening, but the few times I caught on to her, her gaze told me everything I needed to know—she wanted me to hurt like I hurt her.

"You know, you might want to take a picture. It might last longer." Finn clasps a hand on my shoulder. I tried to hide my shock at being caught by bringing my glass to my lips.

"I don't know what you're talking about."

With one last glance over his shoulder, Finn turns to face me with his arms crossed. "I know something happened, but I won't push for it now."

"I don't know what you're talking about." There's no conviction in my voice, though.

"Right. I'm here when you want to finally come to terms with it. I'll be here no matter what." One of the many things I love about my best friend is that he will wait for me to come to him. Maybe talking it out and getting an outsider's perspective is what I need. I don't know what to do, so I just nod.

"Look, I'm sorry for taking off like that without notice and needing a few days." I grip the back of my neck, hating that I did that to him.

"Jax, calm down. It's fine. We didn't have much going on with it being the holidays. And want to know a little secret?" He leans in closer but does not lower the volume of his voice. "We're the bosses. We can do what we want. Well…" He pauses and twists his lips before looking over his shoulder at where his sister sits on the floor with Liam in her lap. "Within reason, otherwise I'm pretty sure Kelsey will have our asses."

We both laugh, knowing that is totally true.

Finn clears his throat into his fist, and it draws my attention to Kate and her date walking toward us. I'm not ready for this. I can't guarantee I won't make a scene, so I take the cowardly way out.

"I'm going to step outside. Can you watch Andy?"

He nods, understanding that I need some space. He clearly knows more than he lets on.

When I step outside on the back patio, the cold air nips at my skin. Shit, it gets cold here. I regret not thinking this through and grabbing my coat.

A sniffling sound beside me causes me to jump. My eyes adjust to the darkness, and I turn to find Dani sitting alone at the patio table.

Dani looks up, noticing me, and stiffens. Her eyes are glazed over. She's either high as a kite or has been crying. I'm pretty sure it's not the former, so I tense. What could have caused her tears? I hate when women cry. I just never know what to do.

"Sorry, you must think I'm a hot mess." She wipes under her eyes.

"Oh, no, not at all."

"I just needed a minute."

"Trust me, I get it. Same reason I'm out here. I just needed a minute. I can go back inside. Sorry to disturb you." I turn to head back inside.

"Oh no." She rises from her chair. "You can sit. There's plenty of room for us both to have a moment." She gives me a soft smile.

I take a seat beside her.

"My hormones are still just all over the place still. Pregnancy is kind of like when you first transition into a vampire. All your emotions become heightened."

"Wait, what?" This conversation seems to have taken a turn off course, and I'm not sure I follow the analogy.

She laughs, sensing my confusion. "Sorry, during late-night feedings, I've been re-watching *The Vampire Diaries*. Kyler makes fun of me because I keep comparing things in real life to the show. I see I'm doing it again."

I'm not familiar with the show, so I don't understand the reference, but I do get the uncontrollable hormones, at least during pregnancy. Courtney once cried while watching a Michael Myers movie and cried because it was said that he was supposedly killed. The human body is quite strange.

The patio is silent, aside from the echo of laughter and music coming from the house. I'm not sure what Finn's definition of low-key is, but I would hate to see what going all out is.

I'm not fully familiar with Dani's past, but I have been given the CliffsNotes version. If anyone were to understand where my head is at, it would be her.

Dani used to be in a relationship with Haylee's brother, Emmett, but he was killed in a car accident in college. I can't imagine losing the love of your life at such a young age—at least I had a few more years with Court. I can't imagine trying to process grief then. Hell, I still don't understand it now.

I lean forward, resting my elbows on my knees. "Can I ask you a question? I don't want to upset you, so feel free to just tell me to fuck off."

She giggles softly. "Ask away."

"How do you do it? How do you forgive yourself enough to move on? You have a beautiful life, a wonderful husband that adores you, and two beautiful children. How do you do it and not let the grief consume you?"

She snickers. I bunch my brows. That wasn't exactly the response I expected. "Do you want the seventeen-year-old-Danielle answer or the today-Danielle answer because honestly, they are two completely different outcomes." She pauses and takes a deep breath. "The seventeen-year-old version of me would tell you to run. When I look back on the past, I'll admit it—I'm ashamed of how I acted. There are so many memories and moments that I missed out on because I let my grief and my guilt at having a future that Emmett was robbed of. I missed birthdays, holidays, watching my brother graduate college. When I came back, I wasn't even sure what life would look like or if my family could forgive me. I have to live with the choices I made for the rest of my life. What I also have to live with is the loss. It's never going to go away, but I carry him in here." She places her hand over her heart.

"When I first met Kyler, I was still deep in my grief, but slowly, he pulled me out of the darkness. Do I still have rough days? Sure." She holds her hands out, showing this very moment. "But I have Kyler by my side to guide me through it."

Would having Kate by my side ease my guilt?

"I don't know what it's like to lose a spouse or to be forced to parent alone." She blows out a loud breath. "I couldn't even fathom doing it without Ky. But you can keep yourself locked up and miss out on so many things and spend the one life you're given living in the past, or you can take a chance. I know it can be terrifying, but I can tell you from experience, it can turn out to be absolutely amazing."

A breeze blows past us, causing us both to shiver.

"We should probably head back inside. We might freeze out here if we wait any longer." We both rise at the same time.

"I hope I didn't overstep at all," Dani says as I usher her inside.

"No, it was actually very helpful. Thank you." I shut the sliding door behind us.

Dani catches me off guard by throwing her arms around me in a hug. "Sorry, we're huggers in this family." She giggles as she pulls back. "I'm here anytime you need to talk."

When we return to the crowd, I catch Kate heading to the bathroom. Dani's words replay in my mind. *"Or you can take a chance."* If I were to take that risk, I'd want it to be with Kate; however, before taking that plunge, I need to get her to talk to me first. This might be my only shot. I check on Andy, who is staring at the babies lying on the blanket on the floor. Both Andy's and Emme's expressions are like *what the fuck?* I slip away to the hallway and lean back against the wall and wait for her to come out. If I'm right here, blocking her way, she'll have no choice but to give me her attention.

The door swings open, and darkness consumes the hallway. I'm already standing in the shadows partially, so I don't draw attention to myself.

"Jaxon," Kate breathes. Her hand is clutching her chest. "What are you doing?"

I push off the wall and close the distance between us. "What I should have done the other night instead of running." I walk us back into the bathroom, turn on the light, and close the door, flicking the lock with a loud click.

Hauling her into my arms, I lift her until she sits on the counter of the sink. I step between her spread legs and thread my fingers into the curled strands of her silky hair.

The temperature rises at least twenty degrees in the small space as I lean forward and capture her lips with mine. At first, her body tenses in my grasp, but after a few swipes of my tongue, she deepens the kiss and pulls me closer, wrapping her legs around my waist.

"I believe I owe you an orgasm."

I quickly flip the button on her pants and instruct her to lift her hips. We don't have much time, so I need to make this quick.

With her pants and thong discarded to the side, I glide my hands up her thighs, spreading her legs to reveal her wet pussy and swollen clit, begging to be explored with my tongue. She places her hands behind her on the counter to brace herself as I lower my mouth and take a long lick of her sweet cunt. Fuck, she tastes addicting. *My dick has never been harder.*

"Jaxon, move."

"What?" I look up from between her thighs and meet her heated gaze, only it's anger there, not desire.

"Jaxon, I said move. You're in the way." Her voice is stone-cold.

I blink and let my eyes adjust to the darkness, realizing I had just been lost in my fantasy of how things would go if I followed her.

"Can we talk?"

"No, I don't think so. The time to talk has come and gone. The time to talk—" Her voice raises a little but not enough to draw attention to us in the hallway. Her nostrils flare as she closes the distance between us and pokes my chest with her manicured finger. "—was days ago, but you ran away like a fucking coward. You can hide behind your words, but I got the message fucking loud and clear, asshole."

I deserve those words.

She turns to leave, but I grip her wrist, stopping her. "I'm sorry."

"You know, you give out shitty apologies like the NFL gives Tom Brady Super Bowl rings."

Kate pulls her wrist from my grasp and turns to walk away. This time, I let her. I fall back against the wall and give myself a moment before returning.

"We can be 'decent' to each other, but we're not friends, and I sure as shit won't ever let *that* happen again."

I'm not really sure what I expected to happen. Kate isn't the type to just cave. She stands her ground and gives hell back. It's one of the many things I like about her. But clearly, I fucked up beyond repair this time.

Chapter 17

I'm just sneaking out of Andy's room after he fell asleep when my phone buzzes in my pocket. When I look at the screen, I see Denise's name. Worry fills my mind. *Is everything okay?* Why's she calling so late?

"Hello," I whisper as I close his bedroom door partially.

Coughing fills my ears, and I have to pull the phone back. "Denise?"

"Yes, I'm here. I'm so sorry about that." Her voice is hoarse, as if she had smoked two packs of cigarettes a day, which isn't true.

"That's all right. Are you okay?" Based on that coughing, I would say the obvious answer is no.

She coughs again. "No, actually. At some point from the time you picked up Andy on Friday, I came down with something." *Oh shit.* "It might just be a cold, but I've stopped vomiting long enough to call you. I'm so sorry for calling so late."

Last time I checked, I don't recall vomiting as a sign of a simple cold but more like the flu.

"I am so sorry to have to do this, but I can't watch Andy for the next few days till I'm better."

"Oh no, I totally understand. Please don't apologize. You need to get yourself better. Is there anything I can do or bring you?"

"You're so sweet." She coughs again, and I yank the phone away. "Sorry about that. But no, you don't have to do that. I have everything I need. Kelsey has already swung by with some soup, even though the thought of food… well—"

"Say no more. Please keep me posted if that changes. Feel better, Denise."

"Thank you. Again, I'm sorry to put you in such a bind."

"It's not a problem. I can figure it out. Talk soon."

After we hang up, I rest my head against the wall. "Well, shit," I mumble to no one. The joys of single parenting—you talk to yourself a lot. The scariest part is I even answer myself, too. Taking tomorrow off shouldn't be an issue. I pull up my calendar on my phone, and right there in big, bold letters is the reminder of a client meeting with the owner of Sedbrook Properties.

Fuck! I can't reschedule that since he's only in town on a limited schedule, and Finn is tied up with the outdoor learning project at Central Academy.

I enter my bedroom and pace the floor, trying to think of options. When I come up empty, I sit on the edge of my bed and hang my head in my hands.

Finn's words from what feels like a lifetime ago ring out in my head. *Kate is home. Why not just ask her? She's great with kids.*

What are my other options…? Nothing. I realize I don't have her number, and I feel like maybe it's too late to walk across the street and knock on her door. The way things have been so stressed between us, I wouldn't put it past her to hold a shotgun to my head, opening the door at this hour.

I respected her wishes and pushed my feelings aside because she made how she felt clear. We have remained amicable around Lauren and Finn, and she smiles and waves to Andy, but that smile does a total one-eighty when she directs it at me. I'm pretty sure in her mind I'm burning in hellfire.

I pull up Finn's number and shoot him a text.

Me: *Two things… I need a favor and for you to not ask questions.*
Finn: *A no questions asked favor, huh? Haven't heard that since your bachelor party.*

That fucker would bring that up now. This was a terrible idea.

Me: *You know what, never mind.*
Finn: *I'm kidding, and I'd do anything for you. So what do you need?*

I sigh heavily, dragging my palms over my face. This is a bad idea, but I can't reschedule this meeting, and there's no one else.

I type out four words before pressing Send and wish I could see Finn's expression as he reads my text.

Me: *I need Kate's number.*

A few moments pass, and I wonder if maybe I gave him a heart attack. My phone finally buzzes with a response.

Finn: *Kate Hudson? Kate Middleton? Because you couldn't possibly be asking for my sister-in-law Kate Lawson's number.*
Me: *What happened to no questions asked?*
Finn: *The last part technically wasn't a question, and the first part was to confirm which Kate you wanted to call.*
Me: *Lawson.*
Me: *I also highly doubt you have Hudson or Middleton's phone numbers.*
Finn: *That is very true—my wife would have my balls.*

I bellow out a deep chuckle. I'm pretty sure she would have more than just his balls. He might be six feet under.

Me: *Can we stop talking about your balls and just get the number?*

A new message pops up with her contact information.

Finn: *For the record, I'm pretty sure you have a better chance getting Kate Middleton than Kate Lawson.*
Me: *I'm not trying to GET ANYONE, but good to know. And thank you.*

I quickly save the information into my phone.

Finn: *No problem. I won't ask questions, but if I get yelled at for giving this to you, I'm kicking your ass.*
Me: *I expect nothing less, but I think I could take you.*
Finn: *Pssh. Fuck off. See you tomorrow.*
Me: *Later.*

Do I text her or call? I settle on an old-fashioned call. I bring up her contact and press Send. My leg bounces nervously, and I say a prayer that she answers strange numbers. I know many people don't, especially at this hour.

The phone rings and rings. Just as I'm about to hang up, she picks up. *Thank fuck.*

"Hello?" she questions, and her voice seems hesitant.

"Hi, Kate. Umm, this is Jaxon." I sound like a fucking teenager calling a girl for the first time after getting her number from a friend. *What the fuck is wrong with me?*

"Okay," she more so questions.

"McAdams." *Does she know more than one Jaxon?*

"I know."

"Oh. You just sounded unsure when you answered."

"Well, that's just because I'm wondering why you're calling me at—" She pauses. "—nine at night. This isn't a booty call, right? Because I thought we cleared that up at New Year's." Her tone grows angrier. Shit, I really don't want to fight with her right now.

"What?" I shriek, my voice cracking. "No! This isn't about that." But I can't help but allow my mind to go there. *Fuck.* I scrub my hands over my face and adjust my pant leg.

"All right," she drags out. "So if it's not that, then why are you calling me? Is everything okay?"

I exhale. "Yes. No. Maybe." I fumble over my words.

"Well, which is it," she snaps. "I can tell her patience is running thin with me.

"Look, I know things have been tense—"

"Since you kissed me, ghosted me, ran away, or were a dick since the very beginning," she interrupts, all in one breath.

I grip the back of my neck as the bitterness bleeds through the phone and all but smacks me in the face.

"Yeah. But I just got a call from Denise, and she's really sick. I have a really important client meeting I can't put off tomorrow, so I have no one to watch Andy. And while I love the movie *Home Alone*, I don't particularly want to live it. You're really my only option."

"Wow, you really know how to make a girl feel special."

"Fuck." I exhale under my breath and fall back on the bed, covering my eyes with my forearm. "You know what? Never mind, I'll figure something out."

"No, wait," she shouts just as I'm about to hang up.

Hope rushes through my veins.

"I'll do it. It's not a problem, but I need you to do one thing for me."

"Anything. You name it." I mean that, too. I would walk to the ends of the earth for whatever she needs since she's helping me out.

"I need to hear you say it."

"Please watch Andy." Can she hear the desperation in my voice?

She makes a clicking noise with her tongue. "No, not that."

"Then what?"

"I need to hear you say, Kate, I'm sorry and I need you."

Popping up from the bed, I hide my laughter with my fist. *Oh, she is good. I'll give that to her.*

I hesitate just to fuck with her, and after a moment—and I know her patience is thin—I clear my throat. "Kate Lawson, I am truly sorry, and I need you. Please," I plead.

"Okay, fine. I mean, I would've done it without all that, but since you asked nicely."

Oh, for fuck's sake. This woman is going to be the death of me.

"Thank you," I say sincerely, and I hope she really understands that. "You are a lifesaver."

I hear her settling in. I wonder what she's doing right now. How does she spend her nights? I shake the thoughts when her voice raises slightly.

"Jaxon, are you still there?"

"What? Sorry, I'm here. Just checking on Andy." The lie slips easily from my lips, but she doesn't question it, thankfully.

"I'll see you around like what, sixish?"

I blow out a breath and cock my head to the side. Wait, how does she know what time I leave in the morning? Shaking my head, I decide that's a question for another day.

"Umm, no, with heading straight to the office from here, I should be good to leave here like seven thirty. So like seven fifteen? Does that work?"

She makes a whistling sound that almost sounded like her saying phew. "Yup, that's fine."

"Great. I'll see you in the morning."

"Yup," she says, smacking her lips together. "See you then."

I disconnect the call and toss my phone on the bed beside me. Kate Lawson saves the day.

I can figure out the rest of the schedule for the week while I'm at the office tomorrow and make things work. I'm grateful that she didn't tell me to take a long walk off a short pier. We can put aside our own issues for my son. Maybe this is turning over a new leaf—only time will tell. I change the alarm on my phone for a later one, thankful that tomorrow we don't have to wake up *as early* and hoping my body clock enjoys the hour delay in our schedule.

Chapter 18

Kate

The sound of my Keurig is like music to my ears this morning. Even though Jaxon isn't leaving early for Denise's and I got to sleep in a little longer than usual, I still tossed and turned in anticipation for today.

When I answered the phone last night, he was the last person I expected to be on the other end. Things have been strained between us, but he hasn't tried to bring up the kiss anymore, for which I'm thankful. I worry that if he had, I would cave.

The desperation in his voice snapped something inside me, and I put aside our differences. The important thing here is Andy, and since he came into my life, I've found it hard to say no to him.

Once the coffee cup is full, I add a splash of vanilla creamer and caramel drizzle. I spin and rest against the counter, craning my neck from side to side.

I glance over at the time on the stove and see that Andy and Jaxon should be here shortly. I fight back a yawn. Somehow, I need to get my blood pumping.

An idea pops into my mind about how to wake up a bit more before they arrive.

"Alexa, play 'Boogie Shoes.'"

The corners of my lips turn upward as she repeats the name of the song and the first few notes ring through the speaker.

Starting with the tapping of my foot, I take a few more sips of my coffee, slowly letting the music take over and flow through my veins.

I am so in the zone as I do my fancy footwork to the chorus. When I spin around, shaking my hands in the air, I look up and scream. I quickly cover my mouth with my hands and will my heart rate to slow down. "Oh my God, you guys scared me," I gasp.

"For the record, we knocked, but you must not have heard," Jaxon explains.

I stop the music and join them in the foyer.

"Sorry, I didn't mean to, umm…" He pauses and purses his lips together. "Interrupt your practice for what? *Dancing with the Stars?*"

"Hardy har har," I mock. "No, my sister-in-law says sometimes you need to dance it out to get your blood pumping."

"Yeah, sure, okay. Well, your secret is safe with me." He waggles his brows, clearly making fun of me.

"You're an ass, you know that?"

"So I'm told. You keep reminding me often." He smirks, and I just can't decide if I want to kiss or smack that expression off his face.

"And you never deny it." Instead of this playful banter, I turn my attention to Andy. "Hey, little man," I ruffle the top of his head.

"Good morning, Miss Kate. You owe me a quarter for saying—" He cups his mouth and whispers, "Bad word."

I laugh, knowing that by the end of the day, I will owe him a lot more, I'm sure.

"Ms. Denise is sick and gross." He scrunches his nose. "Daddy says I get to hang out with you today."

I crouch down in front of him, steadying my hands on my knees.

"You bet. Is that okay with you?"

He enthusiastically nods his head. *Damn, can I channel even just the smallest amount of his energy without multiple cups of coffee?*

"I have some cartoons on TV if you wanna go climb up on the couch",—I point behind me—"while I finish up with your dad."

"Okay." He runs off, but Jaxon clears his throat.

"Umm, excuse me, sir, are you forgetting something?"

"Oopsy," he giggles. "Sorry, Daddy." Andy runs into Jaxon's open arms and *bousch*! My ovaries just exploded with cuteness overload when Jaxon lifts him into his arms.

"Be good, okay?" he says, placing a kiss on the top of his son's head before setting him down.

Andy's feet aren't even fully on the ground before he rushes off, shouting, "Okay."

Jaxon and I watch as Andy curls up on the couch and snuggles under my fleece blanket. The kid is just making himself at home.

"I hope you don't mind, but he's still wearing his pajamas. There's a change of clothes in his backpack." He holds up a *Toy Story* backpack, and I accept it.

"Not at all. I'm a tad bit jealous."

"Me too," Jaxon teases, and I rake my eyes over his dress shirt with rolled-up sleeves. Does he sleep in pajamas or possibly in the nude? *Jesus, Katherine. Get yourself together. It's too early for that shit. You are watching his kid, for God's sake.*

Jaxon looks down at the ground for a moment as if something is extremely fascinating. "So, do you do that often?"

My breath catches. Can he read my mind? Did he know I was thinking about him? Do I think about him often? All the fucking time. Folding my arms over my chest and sinking into my hip, I respond. "Do what?"

"Put on your boogie shoes." He snickers, pressing his lips together to suppress his laughter, and shakes his hips a little just as I had moments ago. I want to officially crawl into a hole and disappear. Great, this asshole is so never going to let me live that down.

We stare at each other for a moment, neither saying anything.

"If this is too much, I can just figure something else out." His eyes flick back and forth between his son and me, and he runs a hand over his stubbled jaw. He's clearly used to doing all this on his own and not used to asking for help. I hate that for him.

I reach out and wrap my fingers around his bicep. Both of our eyes trail to where my dainty fingers are touching his arm. After a moment of lingering, I pull back, and he sighs as if he's disappointed I pulled back. Honestly, so am I. But this is how it has to be. "It's fine. I've got this, okay? Now, go to work before you're late. Don't need the boss writing you up," I tease.

My breath hitches as he leans forward and presses his lips to my cheek. As he lingers a moment longer, I'm pretty sure my heart stops the entire time his lips are touching my skin. "Thank you."

If I moved, even with just an inhale, his lips would be on mine. Jaxon slowly pulls back, and desire swirls in his eyes, just like in the alley.

"Right, okay then." He runs his fingers through his hair. "Bye, buddy. Be good for Miss Kate."

"Jaxon," I call out once he's on the sidewalk. "Relax. He's going to be fine." I give him a reassuring smile.

He nods and jogs across the street to his truck. Once his truck has pulled away, I close the door and lock it, just as a precaution. I plop on the couch beside Andy. "So, are you hungry?"

"Daddy gave me some waffles, but I'm a little hungry." Just as he finishes his sentence, his little stomach growls.

"I can make you some more food." Hopefully, he's not too much of a picky eater and I actually have something that he likes.

"Can we sit in here and eat it?" He's hesitant, and I wonder if this is something Jaxon lets him do at home.

"Heck yeah," I exclaim. "I'll be right back."

Moments later, I return with two bowls of Reese's Puffs cereal.

"What's this?" Andy cautiously takes in the contents of the bowl. If he has never had this before, I'm going to scream at Jaxon for depriving his son of only the best cereal ever.

"Do you like peanut butter?" He nods. "What about chocolate?"

His little blue eyes widen, and a small gasp leaves his lips. "For breakfast?"

"Yup." I set the bowls on the coffee table and take a seat on the floor, patting the spot next to me for him to join, and he does. After he takes the first crunchy bite, he dives in for another and another.

"Stick with me, kid, and I'll show you the way of the dark side."

We both turn our focus back to the episode as we eat our breakfast, but the sound of crunching isn't the only sound filling the room for too long.

"Do you have kids, Miss Kate?" Andy asks with a mouth full of cereal.

I choke on the current mouthful of food. I take a moment to compose myself. "Nope."

"So why do you have this big house all by yourself, then?"

I chuckle at his question, the same one my sister asked all those years ago when I showed it to her.

"Well." I turn to face him, propping my elbow on the couch cushion. "I have a big family and a room for my art studio."

"What's that?" This kid is so inquisitive. I can see it in his eyes that he wants to be a sponge and soak up all the knowledge he can.

"I'm an artist. Do you know what that is?"

Andy nods. "You like to color."

I smile. "Something like that. My mom tells me I was younger than you were when I first started drawing, and then I got into painting after that and went to art school for college to fill my brain with everything I could learn about art."

"Could you teach me how to draw?" he asks, propping his head up on his fist, mimicking my body. I smile because it reminds me of playing copycat with my sister as a child.

"Sure. How about first we finish our breakfast and watch a little more cartoons? And then, after getting dressed, I'll take you up there. Sound good?"

I hold out my hand, and he places his tiny hand in mine, and we shake. "Deal."

Chapter 19

Jaxon

I forgot what it's like to arrive home at a decent hour—when the sun is still shining. I've been so used to the extra-long commutes, arriving home with enough time to feed Andy, bathe him, and get him into bed. I have to admit that it's quite nice as I pull into my driveway.

I get out of my truck and pocket my keys as I head across the street to Kate's house to pick up Andy.

"Daddy," Andy shouts from the front porch as I make my way up the sidewalk. When I'm close enough to the steps, he jumps into my arms, clinging to me like a spider monkey.

I hope they're not sitting outside already because Kate can't wait to get rid of him. Would she write her own version of Judith Viorst's classic book and rename it Kate and the Horrible, No Good, Very Bad Day? I didn't hear from her all day, not that I honestly expected to. Zach and Haylee seem to have faith in her to watch Emme from time to time, so I figured it would be okay. Deep down, I know I can trust her.

"Hey, buddy, I missed you today." I wrap my arms tightly around him as I walk up the steps and find Kate standing in front of the porch love seat, wiping crumbs off her lap. She gives me a warm smile, and I carefully glance over my shoulder to see who she could be smiling at because I can't imagine it's me on the receiving end of that beautiful and genuine smile.

"Hey there. I hope he wasn't too much trouble for you today."

"What?" she shrieks, and a piece of hair falls onto her face. "Of course not. We were just having a snack. I hope that's okay." She finally tucks it away, and my shoulders slump because my fingers itched to do it myself.

"We had peanut butter crackers. Miss Kate let me use the knife," Andy says as he rests his head on my shoulder. I can smell the peanut butter breath from here.

"I held the knife with him, and it was just one of those little cheese spreader knives, nothing sharp."

"And we had chocolate for breakfast." I chuckle at his honesty.

"It was just Reese's Puffs cereal," she clarifies again. She taps Andy's nose. "You're gonna get me in trouble, little dude. Those were our secrets."

He pretends to zip up his mouth and hands her a pretend key, and she winks at him when she dramatically places it in her pocket. Wow, she's such a natural with him.

"Anything else I should know?" I glance back and forth between the two of them. Kate shrugs, and Andy presses his lips together as if he really had locked his mouth shut. "Do you have your bag ready?"

Andy lifts his head and looks around, but we don't see it on the porch.

Kate claps her hands together. "Oh, it's over by the couch inside."

I pat his back and set him down on the floor. "Why don't you go get it, and then we can head home? I'm thinking pizza for dinner." Andy is out of sight inside before I can even tell him not to run.

I shove my hands into my pockets because I might do a crazy thing and touch her. "Thank you for today, seriously. It's going to be a long week."

"Were you able to figure something out?" Kate asks as she piles up their dishes on the table.

"Nah." I shake my head. "I brought work home with me, and I'll just have to wing it." *Just another day in the life of a single dad. It'll be fine.*

Kate looks lost in her thoughts for a moment and opens her mouth a few times as if she's conflicted.

"What if I watch him for you until Denise is better?"

Of course, at that exact moment, Andy's running out the front door. At least he didn't Kool-Aid Man right through the storm door.

"I don't know." I rub the back of my neck and feel sweat coating my skin. I'm unsure if that's from the sun shining or being this close to Kate. "I couldn't ask you to do that."

"I mean, you did last night when you called about today." She shrugs one shoulder as if it's no big deal, but her offering to watch my son *is* a big deal.

My stomach drops, and I must wince, feeling bad that I had. "But that was—" I stutter. "—that was different. That was one day."

"Calm down, I was only kidding. But it's not really all that different. Just one day versus multiple. Plus, you're not asking. I'm offering."

"Come on, Dad, please." Andy tugs on my arm.

"Jaxon, stop being a stubborn asshole and accept my help. You said it yourself that it's going to be a long week, so relax knowing I've got Andy under control while you work."

"Miss Kate," Andy gasps, and she throws her head back in laughter.

"Add it to my tab, kiddo." She winks and giggles.

I smirk, wondering how much, in fact, she owes him after today.

I don't know that this is a good idea. We went from complete avoidance to now wanting to see me every day—well, spend every day with my son, but she would at least have to see me when I drop him off and pick him up.

Andy rushes to her side as she kneels, both pouting with the bottom lips out. *Great, these two are ganging up on me.* I sigh, giving in. "All right, fine."

Mainly, I concede and agree because seeing her pout on her knees has me wanting to throw her over my knee and spank that plump bottom or have her sticking her lip out while she begs for my cock. I'd say anything for her to stand up again.

They both stand, and Andy dances around. I recognize some of those moves from Kate's performance this morning. It seems even after one day together, they've already formed a bond.

"Are you really sure it's not a bother?" I guess I'm just expecting her to pull the rug out from under me and say "gotcha." Or maybe, in a way, I'm hoping she does. It was easier to push my feelings aside when we rarely interacted, but seeing her every day? It may be good for my son, but what about my heart?

"Jaxon, will you calm down? It's fine." The seriousness of her tone tells me not to question it, that it's a done deal. "Do you prefer here at my house or over at yours?"

"Umm, here is fine. But I'll leave you the spare key tomorrow, just in case."

"Be careful. Kyler and Dani gave me a spare key, and I raided their food and booze when they were on their honeymoon." She laughs before realizing I didn't join in, and she grows serious. "I'm kidding, sort of."

"Well, we should get going." I reach down and grab the backpack that Andy had dropped by my feet moments earlier.

"Daddy, can Miss Kate have pizza with us?"

Kate's and my eyes lock, and I give her a weak smile. I know I should have seen this coming.

Kate swoops in to save the day, crouching down to his eye level. "Not tonight, little dude. You wore me out today. I need to rest up so we can do it all again tomorrow. How about you bring over that dinosaur coloring book you were telling me about tomorrow? Okay?"

Andy nods and puts his arms in front of her, nonverbally asking for her to pick him up, and she does. She stands, holding him tightly, and my throat grows thick, and my nerve endings tingle as I witness the motherly love in front of me.

I take a step back and cross my arms to keep the desire at bay, to move closer and touch her, pulling them both into my arms. I close my eyes and count to three as I will my racing heart to slow.

When she sets Andy down, she smiles at him with adoration in her eyes, and it shoots a direct line to my heart. *I'm in trouble.* But maybe this is going to lead us down a fresh path. Or maybe set the stage for a category 5 destruction. If only I could guarantee I won't self-destruct first.

After confirming for me to bring him over, I swoop Andy in my arms, and we head home. He continues to tell me all about his day at Miss Kate's that in his words was "awesomely epic," all through pizza, bath, and story time.

Chapter 20

Jaxon

The house is quiet when I arrive home. I had a late meeting that turned into dinner with the client. Thankfully, Kate said it wasn't an issue to stay later with Andy tonight. She's been watching him all week.

I look around the living room and see there's not one thing out of place—was the house this clean when I left earlier?

I make my way to the kitchen and stop in my tracks just in front of the fridge. I reach down and take Andy's latest artwork that Kate must have hung up there. The picture is a drawing of a little boy in the middle. On one side, a man holds one hand while a woman holds the one on the right. The woman has pink lines in her hair, so I assume that's Kate.

Speaking of Kate… I assumed she would have heard me come in. Where is she?

After sticking the drawing back to the fridge with the magnet, I make my way up the stairs to search for her. Andy should be long asleep by this time, but there's no sign of Kate anywhere.

I stop in the doorway of Andy's room, and my heart catches in my throat. I find Kate sound asleep beside Andy. She has him wrapped up in her arms, and his arm is draped over her. There is a book over her lap, so I assume she hadn't intended to fall asleep.

I watch them for a few moments, not wanting to disturb them. If I wake Kate up, she might stir and wake Andy, so I let them be.

I couldn't do this without her, honestly. We may have started off on the wrong foot and have been at each other's throats since then, but lately, she has been the rock holding me together. She didn't have to agree to help with Andy, but she stepped up. For the first time since Courtney passed, the house feels like home, and I feel at peace. Slowly, the guilt that threatened to pull me under many times has calmed.

I feel like I'm living someone else's life. A month ago, just kissing Kate sent me running for the hills, and now, seeing the bond that she has formed with my son, all I can think about is having her here every night, having dinner with us, helping with baths and bedtime, and permanently in my bed. Having those thoughts doesn't terrify me—in fact, it makes me want more.

After a quick rinse in the shower, I make my way back to Andy's room. I softly pad my way as quietly as I can to Kate's side and am at a crossroads—I could wake her up and send her home, or… I pick option number two and carefully remove the book from her and set it on the nightstand. I grab the blanket at the edge of the bed and pull it up, covering them both.

There is just enough room on the edge of the bed for me to slide up next to Andy. I watch them sleep for a few minutes, their chests rising and falling in unison. It's not long before my eyes grow heavy, and I drift off to sleep, feeling complete peace.

Kate

I'm jolted awake by a light snore. I open my eyes and realize this ceiling is not my own.

Oh shit, I fell asleep in Andy's bed.

Wait, that snoring is too loud to belong to a little boy. I recognize the scent that surrounds me. Jaxon.

I sit up and see Jaxon on the other side of Andy, both sound asleep. I bite back my laughter when I see Andy is currently curled up at his father's side with his little legs draped over his father's body.

I quietly and carefully scoot off the bed, however, I'm clearly not a ninja since the shift in the bed causes Jaxon to stir.

"Hey," he says, his voice full of sleep. He hasn't even opened his eyes yet. When he does, I'm met with blue eyes that look like the ocean, calm after a raging storm.

"Go back to sleep," I whisper, not wanting to disturb Andy. I step forward to cup his cheek but stop. *What am I doing?* "I'm just gonna go."

I finish scooting off the bed and walk around to the nightstand, where I left my phone.

"What time is it?" he asks in between yawns.

I glance down at the screen, and my eyes widen. *Holy shit.* "5:00 a.m. Wow, we slept all night. I'm sorry, I didn't mean to fall asleep. One minute I was reading Andy our third story, and the next, well." I extend my hands to mean this moment.

Jaxon carefully unwraps Andy's legs from his body and rises from the bed. I take a moment to appreciate the way Jaxon looks in the morning—a relaxed look in gym shorts and a T-shirt that clings to every muscle, but it's the tousled hair, as if it had still been wet when he lay down.

Why didn't he just wake me when he got home?

He adjusts Andy, covering him back up with his favorite *Toy Story* blanket, and I take a minute to remember the moment between father and son.

I make my way out of Andy's room. Jaxon follows me down the stairs. I'm sliding my shoes on, which I had left by the front door, and look up to see Jaxon standing there, staring out at nothing. I follow his gaze to make sure he doesn't actually see something but come up empty. Or maybe he fell asleep standing up with his eyes open?

"Jaxon." I stand. "Get your butt back to bed. Seriously, it's Saturday. Go sleep in."

"There's something I've been thinking about since Christmas."

I'm searching the table for my keys. "Yeah, what's that?"

I'm surprised when I spin around to see Jaxon stalking toward me like a wolf seeking its prey until I'm pressed up against the wall, and he lowers his mouth to mine.

Whereas our first kiss in the alley was fast and demanding, this kiss is anything but. He slowly explores my mouth with his tongue. Not like when you're young and unsure of what to do with your tongue, so you try to choke the other person by trying to kick their esophagus, but as if he wants to know what every part of my mouth tastes like.

I get lost in his kiss. *Am I dreaming this? Holy shit, Jaxon is kissing me in his living room.*

"If this is a dream, I sure as fuck don't want to wake up," he admits honestly.

I cringe that I had asked that aloud but don't get the chance to express that wasn't meant for him to hear because we're kissing again.

"Do you have plans today?" he asks, his voice raw and husky. It's sexy as fuck.

I open my eyes and stare deep into his blue eyes. They aren't full of hostility like they used to, nor the reluctant friendliness as of late. No, instead there is a vulnerability bleeding through.

All the words not said in his gaze send a shiver down my spine, and a direct line of goose bumps erupt on my arms.

"Umm, no plans that I know of."

"Do you want to spend the day with us?"

"Are you sure?"

He steps back and looks away, feeling my hesitancy. I reach up and cup his beard-covered cheek. "No, I just meant it's your day off. Don't you want to spend it with just Andy or maybe do stuff around the house or other adulting things you don't get to do during the week?"

"I'd like to spend it with you, too. When you're around, Andy lights up. He looks forward to spending time with you, and life is better when you're around him."

I feel brave, or maybe it's the fuzziness of my brain still reeling from that kiss, but I take a step closer to him and place my palm over his heart. I can feel it ready to beat out of his chest. "And what about you?"

He covers my hand with his. "What about me?"

"Is your life better when I'm around?"

He smiles, and I feel my nipples pucker, and my panties disintegrate into nothing. "I think you know that it has been recently. I would have been lost without you this week."

A breath away from my lips, I breathe him in. "Okay." His lips once again crash into mine. I could spend all day right here kissing this man. Just a few kisses and I'm already craving more.

He pulls back but not before placing a small kiss on my forehead, turning my insides to mush. I'm impressed that I haven't just melted on the floor. *What is so fucking sexy about forehead kisses?*

With his hands perched on my hips, he tightens his grip. It's as if he has to hold on to me in some way but stop himself from touching other places. It's pretty sexy, and I would love to see Jaxon lose control.

"Go home and get some more sleep or do whatever you need to do. We'll pick you up around eleven. That work?"

I nod, unsure if any words would even come out if I opened my mouth right now. I must be in shock. Am I agreeing to go on a date with Jaxon McAdams willingly? Well, a date with Jaxon and Andy—when dating a single dad, I assume that's what plenty of dates will look like, and I have no issue with that.

Somehow, during my week of watching Andy, my anger toward Jaxon slipped. I saw him in a different light—the man that does everything for everyone else and nothing for himself. He finally took something for himself—me.

I exit the front door, heading back toward my house, and decide at the last minute to take one last look at Jax's house over my shoulder and see him standing in the doorway, watching me leave. As I cross the street, I add a sway to my hips like I had on the first day we met. I heard his low-breathed curse before the door closes.

I pull my phone out and call my sister. I'm thankful I still have battery, even though I hadn't plugged it in all night.

"He—hello?" she answers on the third ring.

Oh shit, right, it's only five in the morning.

"Good morning," I say as I cross the street.

"It's five in the fucking morning on a Saturday, Katherine. You're clearly fucking dying if you're up and calling me this morning. So hang up and call 9-1-1."

"But I have an emergency," I whine.

"What is it?" Her voice is more awake at the moment than a minute ago.

"I kissed Jaxon."

She groans into the phone. "We already established that at Christmas. Goodbye."

"No, as in like right now."

"At 5:00 a.m.? I'm shocked you're even up, let alone kissing Jaxon, of all people."

There's some shuffling on the other end and hushed voices.

"Laur, you still there?"

"Kate," Finn's deep voice comes through the phone. "Look, I'm happy for you and my best friend finally getting your heads out of your asses. And I'm sure whatever it is you need from my sexy wife can wait until normal business hours. Until then, goodbye." *Click.* Someone is grumpy this early in the morning.

I pull the phone back, verifying that he hung up. I scoff. "I can't believe he fucking hung up on me."

Doesn't he know about twin code? I need her. He's lucky my sister loves him so much and I hate to see her upset, or I'd be hopping in my car, heading over to their house, and beating his ass, maybe even burying him alive. That way, he can have a peaceful sleep.

How am I supposed to go back to sleep now that I'm flying high from that kiss? I do the only thing I can think of to calm my nerves since my sister or, well, her husband ever so rudely hung up on me at this hour—I head to my studio and paint my heart out.

Chapter 21

Jaxon

I'm not sure what came over me this morning when I had Kate pressed up against the door. Andy could've woken up and walked down the stairs at any moment, but I just couldn't pass up the opportunity to kiss her.

Sleep lined her eyes, and her hair was a mess.

As I watched her head back to her house, all I could think about was when I could kiss her again. I saw a glimpse into a future I could have if I just grabbed it. The scariest part was that I didn't feel ridden with guilt. I know that my love for Courtney will never waver. Like Dani said, I carry her with my heart, but I'm tired of sitting back and watching life pass me by when everything I want is right in front of me.

When Andy woke up around seven thirty, I told him we would spend the day with Kate, and his smile lit up the room. I had to occupy him by putting on *Toy Story* on the TV so he would stop asking if it was time to go pick up Kate.

Andy and I knock on Kate's door promptly at eleven. She nearly knocks the wind right out of me when she opens the door. I openly admire her and have no shame in it. My eyes travel up her body, starting at her pink-and-black Chucks, the form-fitted denim that clings to her small curves, a black T-shirt tucked into the top of her jeans, and a maroon bomber jacket. Her signature aviator sunglasses rest on top of her head.

"Wow, you look pretty," Andy says first. The kid took the words right out of my mouth.

"I wasn't exactly sure what we were doing today, so I thought I'd dress comfortably. Is this okay? I can go change." She nibbles on her bottom lip as she takes in her outfit.

"It's perfect."

"Well, okay then." She tucks her house keys in her purse. "Shall we?"

Andy steps in front of me, and I stumble over my feet. He lifts his elbow to Kate for her to loop her arm with his. Because of their height difference, she wraps her hand around his arm. Thankfully, he doesn't know the difference. She giggles, covering her mouth with her other hand. *Where the heck did this kid learn this move?*

"So, Mr. Andy." She looks down and smiles at him. "Where are we going?" My eyes dip down to her ass and the way her jeans cling to it. I bite my fist to suppress a moan.

"Umm." He looks back at me. "Daddy." He waves his little hand for me to come closer. "Where are we going?" He attempts to whisper, but it seems much louder.

"Since it ended up being a gorgeous day, we thought we'd go check out Soundside Park."

I open the back door to the truck to help Andy into his booster. Kate attempts to walk around me, but I hold my arm out to stop her. She glares at me, and I want to kiss that scowl right off her face.

Once Andy is all buckled, I shut the door and move to the passenger door.

She throws her head back in laughter. "Seriously? This again?"

She reaches for the handle to lift herself up, but I steady her hips, stopping her, and lean in to her ear. "Babe, I told you, I'm a fucking gentleman."

"Oh yeah, quite the gentleman with that mouth," she retorts. This damn woman. I'll show her how gentlemanly I can be with my mouth.

"I know this probably isn't your ideal first date, huh?" We've been walking the trails for the past thirty minutes. Andy is walking in the middle, holding each of our hands.

"Is this a date?" She bunches her brows together. *Shit, I kind of thought that was obvious.*

"Umm—" I freeze.

"I'm only kidding. And what do you think my ideal first date would be?"

"Hmm, to be honest, I'm not really sure." I don't want to say I think she's a simple girl and she takes that the wrong way. What I mean is that

I don't think Kate is one for fancy dinners, but then again, she's always surprising me.

"This is perfect, honestly. I like simplicity." I do a double take and wonder if I'd said that aloud versus in my head. She looks around the park and smirks. "You know, it's funny. My brother actually brought Dani here for their first date. There had been a food truck festival on the other side of the park."

That sounds nice, especially as we get closer to lunchtime.

Andy pulls away from both of us to chase a group of ducks on the grass beside us.

"Be careful, buddy." This kid is always keeping me on my toes.

"I will, Daddy," he shouts over his shoulder. "Come on, little quackers," Andy laughs. And then he bends his knees and starts quacking like a duck, causing both me and Kate to crack up laughing.

We stand there watching my son laugh at his own jokes. When I look at him, it's amazing that I helped create him. He is the perfect part of his mother and me. There is an innocence to him I hope he keeps as long as possible. Children don't have a care in the world, leaving them free to enjoy themselves, like laughing at ducks.

Our fingertips brush, and the old me may have pulled away, grabbed Andy, and run in the opposite direction. But this Jaxon, the one whose inner monologue is telling him to *live a little, be adventurous. He* is taking the reins now.

I lace my fingers with hers, and the corners of my lips flick upward at how perfectly her hand fits in mine. Out of the corner of my eye, I see that while Kate is still looking straight forward at Andy laughing, there's a bigger smile reaching her eyes.

All this time, I've focused on Jaxon McAdams, the dad. Not Jaxon McAdams, the man.

I decide to take a shot in the dark and spin to face Kate. Her body instinctively turns to mine.

"What?"

"Nothing. I was just wondering something." With my free hand, I brush a stray hair out of her face and tuck it behind her ear.

Kate steps closer to me so that our chests are brushing against each other. "And what were you wondering?"

I glance over at Andy one last time before turning to face Kate and leaning down at the same time she pushes up on her toes.

"I was wondering, if I kissed you right now, would you kiss me back?"

She is just a breath away from my lips now. "Why don't you find out and see?"

I press my lips to hers in a chaste kiss but long enough to sample her minty taste. Before I allow myself to get completely swept up in the moment, I pull back and rest my forehead against her.

"Wow," she breathes.

I press a quick kiss to her forehead and savor this feeling of being content.

"Daddy! Daddy!" Andy shouts, and I take a step back. It's not that I plan to hide anything from Andy, but this is all new. I'm not sure what questions he might have, and right now is not the time for that. I will sit him down and talk to him soon.

Dating a single parent is much different than dating someone without kids. She wouldn't just be dating me, but in a way, she's dating Andy, too. We are a pair. I have to take this slow because there are more than two hearts on the line.

Andy comes up to us and begins jumping up and down. "Can we go to the playground now?"

"Yeah, let's go."

Andy runs off ahead, and when Kate follows, I reach out and relace our fingers together. She pauses, I guess in shock, so I take the lead and pull her along as Andy runs in front of us toward the playground. It's a gorgeous day; I am surprised the park isn't more crowded. There's only one other family playing over on the swings.

"Can I go down the slide?" Andy sticks out his bottom lip in a pout—as if I'd ever say no.

"Sure."

Andy carefully climbs the ladder and slides down, squealing.

"Miss Kate! Miss Kate! Come with me. It's so much fun."

Kate crouches down to Andy's height. "Oh, I don't know. That looks pretty high up there. I might be a little scared."

"You can do it. You just have to be brave. I'm very brave. I'll go with you."

She sighs with a smile on her face. Kate winks back at me as she lets Andy pull her over to the slide.

"Daddy, watch us," his high-pitched voice screams.

I pull my phone out from my back pocket and snap a few photos of Andy and Kate as they go down the slide.

After the slides, we move on to the swings. Kate takes the swing beside Andy. I try to sit down, but the link chains dig into my muscular thighs, so I stand behind them and softly push them both.

"Make sure you hold on tight, okay," Kate says as she picks up speed.

"Can I fly? You know, like how we used to?"

"You betcha." I move around the front of the swings, narrowly avoiding a kick to the junk.

Kate's gaze never wavers, and I give her a small smile as I remind Andy of what to do and hold out my hands, ready to catch him.

On three, he releases his hands and lands straight into my arms. I hoist him on my shoulder and spin him around as if he had just scored the winning run at the World Series.

Once I set him down, he bounces on his feet, yelling, "Now, Miss Kate, it's your turn. Come on, be brave." My heart swells at his enthusiasm.

She purses her lips together in a scowl. "Schooled by a four-year-old."

"Better get used to it." That kid could talk his way out of a grand larceny felony charge. I hold my hands up like I'm a catcher at a baseball game.

Andy counts down from three before yelling, "Blast off."

Kate soars through the air with a little too much force, and when I catch her, we tumble to the ground.

"Oh, my God. Jaxon, are you okay?"

I lie there for a moment and still my breath. With my eyes closed, I can't see her expression, but the shadow over my face blocking the sun tells me she's hovering over me.

When I can't take it anymore, I let out a deep belly laugh.

"Oh, you ass." She smacks me playfully. I rub the spot on my chest she just hit.

"Miss Kate, you said a potty word," Andy scolds. One day, I really need to find out what her bill is up to.

She rests her forehead on my chest, and her body vibrates from my rumbled laughter.

"You are so right. How about we go over to the stand over there and I buy you a pretzel and we call it even?"

"Yes!" Andy throws his arms up in the air.

Kate pushes off me and stands. She holds her hand out in front of me to help me up. I stand and brush the mulch off my shirt.

"Did I get it all?" I spin around.

"You missed a spot." I hear the playfulness of her tone and wonder if she's telling the truth.

"Did I really, or did you just want to touch my ass?" I quirk a brow, challenging her.

"Guess you'll never know." She shrugs and winks before taking Andy's hand and heading over to the snack shack.

Today was a good day. After spending another two hours at the park, we came back to the house, and I convinced Kate to allow me to whip up some burgers on the grill. Andy is now sound asleep upstairs, and there's some new show on Netflix playing on the TV, but it's mere background noise. My focus has been on Kate for most of the evening.

"So, today was all about being adventurous," I admit, breaking the silence.

"Huh, that was adventurous? Remind me not to ask you to go skydiving or bungee jumping."

"Oh, you think you're funny, huh?" I tease, cocking my head to the side, amusement dancing in my eyes.

"Yeah, I'd like to think so," she taunts with a sassy expression on her face. All that's missing is a finger snap in the air.

I lunge for her and tickle her sides.

Her laughter is the type that's infectious. When she does it, you can't help but join in. I'm not sure I've smiled as much as I have today.

I pull Kate upright so she is now straddling my thighs. My dick instantly hardens at her closeness. *Fuck! This was a bad idea.*

"What was it you were saying?" she asks me in a low tone as her hips rock back and forth. I groan and close my eyes, trying to gather composure before I rip these clothes from her and we continue this dance naked.

I grip her hips to keep them from moving. As much as I love the feel of her against me, all the blood is rushing from my head to my cock, and I can't get one coherent thought in.

Kate pouts when she realizes I'm stronger than her and she can't tease me anymore.

"Okay, fine. What was it you wanted to say so we can get back to that?"

"Right." I close my eyes. "Today was all about being adventurous," I repeat. "But there's one more thing I want to do."

She sits back on my knees, putting more space between us.

"You have my attention. What is it that you would like to do, Mr. McAdams?" I swallow thickly, and her eyes dip down, following the bob of my Adam's apple. The way she says Mr. McAdams reminds me of Marilyn Monroe saying Mr. President.

"Well, I would like to explore this thing."

She purses her lips together and tilts her head to the side. "I'm going to need you to be more specific."

I tickle her side again, and she jolts, nearly falling off my lap. Taking advantage of her guard down, I flip her so she is now on her back and I'm hovering over her. "I want to explore this thing with you, Kate."

She forms an O with her mouth, and oh shit, the things I want to do to that mouth right now. "As much as I enjoy fighting with you, I think I might like kissing you more."

"Just kissing me?" She pants as my lips trail over her goose-bumped flesh.

"For now."

I pull back and allow myself to drown in her warm chocolate eyes. There are golden specks in them that captivate me. "Look, I don't want to beat around the bush, but I need you to know that this is completely unfamiliar territory for me. And I let my guilt for moving on get in the way for quite a while. It was never you—it was always my issues, and I'm sorry if I ever made you feel otherwise. I've never dated someone while doing the whole single-parenting thing. So, I might not be very good at this, but I'd like to try."

She cups my cheek in her palm and runs her thumb over my stubble with a soft smile on her face. "You, Jaxon McAdams, are an amazing dad. And I will go any speed you need. I want to explore this with you, too. Somehow, you and that little boy of yours wiggled your way under my skin, and you're right, as much as I love bickering and fighting with you, I think I'll enjoy this more. Maybe all that arguing was just an awkward form of foreplay." She laughs before I capture her lips with mine.

And that's how we spend the rest of the evening, kissing and bickering like an actual couple.

Chapter 22

Kate

Poor Denise can't catch a break. Turns out Jaxon was right, and they diagnosed her with the flu. She had started feeling better but then came down with bronchitis. I offered to keep Andy until she felt better. It was no trouble at all since I'm right here.

Yesterday, we spent the day apart, and it wasn't until silence surrounded me that I realized the house lacked the energy that Andy brought into it. I'd bottle up his giggles and squeals if I could.

I've never been one to be excited about Mondays, but this morning couldn't come soon enough. Andy and I have had a busy morning. We played outside, and he picked the flowers that are now sitting in a glass on the dining room table. He even picked a bunch for his house. I didn't have the heart to tell him I didn't mind him picking them since they're technically weeds. He was doing me a favor. We also spent the morning drawing and coloring. He has a knack for art. Next time I swing by the art supply store, I might pick up a few more items for him. There is an endless amount of energy in him—I have no clue how my sister does this every day with about thirty students.

But he's finally settled on the couch, resting after filling his tummy with grilled cheese and tomato soup. Now that it's finally quiet, I think it's a good time to check in with Jaxon. Is there a rule for how soon you can text someone you went on a date with if they live across the street and you watch their kid?

I blow out a breath when I realize my life has turned into one of those romance novels Laur loves so much. She must love this.

Me: *Hey.*

My phone instantly buzzes with a response.

Jaxon: *Hey. Is everything okay? Is Andy all right?*
Me: *Everything's fine. Calm down, killer. I was just checking in.*
Jaxon: *Oh. I'm sorry for freaking out. You've never texted me before.*
Me: *It's okay. I probably should've started out with something more than just hey. Totally my bad.*
Jaxon: *No, it's fine. I'm just a little stressed out. Natasha fucked up some stuff this morning and so now I'm scrambling a little.*
Me: *Oh well, I won't keep you.*
Jaxon: *No, it's fine. I've actually been thinking about you.*

I nibble on my bottom lip as I decide what to respond with. Is *"So have I?"* too needy?

Me: *I had a lot of fun the other day.*
Jaxon: *Me too. I was thinking maybe I could take you out again, just the two of us.*
Me: *I'd like that, but I don't want you to think that I want you to do that. I know Andy is a priority, and I don't expect you to go out of your way. I love hanging out with that kid.*
Jaxon: *Good to know. I'll be sure to keep that in the vault.*

Soft snoring comes from the couch, and I look up to find Andy sound asleep with his lips parted. I snap a quick photo and send it to Jaxon.

Jaxon: *I'm jealous. Not only does he get to spend the day with you, but he gets to nap.*
Me: *Aww poor baby.*
Me: *How about I make dinner tonight for you and Andy? When you get home, shower or whatever, and then walk on over.*
Jaxon: *You don't have to do that.*
Me: *I know that, but I want to.*

I realize how domesticated that sounds and wonder for a moment if we're moving too fast. Have we jumped into the fast lane? But Jaxon's quick response sets my mind at ease.

Jaxon: *Sounds like a date. Looking forward to it.*

Jaxon: *I need to get to on a call. I'll see you later, though.*

I hop up from the chair and tiptoe out of the room to see what I have in the kitchen to cook.

"Wow, it smells amazing in here." I look up to see Jaxon standing in the doorway. He's changed out of his work clothes, and his hair is still slightly damp from a shower.

"Do you make it a habit of walking into people's houses unannounced?"

"Nah, not typically. But once again, I knocked before entering. And I wasn't fully unannounced because I even said hi to Andy."

"What do you have behind your back?" I arch my neck, trying to see what he's hiding, but he turns his body slightly away from me. I frown. *Jerk.*

He finally caves as he approaches, holding up a familiar bottle of wine in one hand—my favorite bottle of red. It's also the same bottle of red that he had bought the last of what feels like forever ago.

"I thought it was only fair to not show up empty-handed. Plus, I heard from a little birdie that it was your favorite and some dick took the last bottle of it at the store once. And I brought dessert." He reveals his other hand, holding a plastic container with three cupcakes from the bakery.

Emotion bubbles up in my throat as I meet his gaze. There are so many more layers to this man, and it's hard to believe I thought of him as anything more than a sweetheart.

I compose myself to keep myself from running into his arms. "You spoil me."

"That's the plan. I have some making up to do." He sets both items on the counter. "So, what's on the menu? Seriously, my stomach started growling as soon as I walked in the house."

I prop my hip against the counter. "See, my brother-in-law might be a beast in the kitchen with meatballs, but I am the master at shrimp scampi."

I'm grateful that Jaxon had left a spare booster seat so that Andy and I could run to the grocery store after he woke up from his nap. I close my eyes and inhale the delicious aroma of butter and garlic. When I open my eyes, I see the smile has fallen from his face into a solemn frown.

Oh, no. Did I fuck up?

"Wait, you're not allergic or anything, are you?" My voice is slightly higher than normal, laced with worry. I try to replay any meals in my mind where he might have declined seafood but am coming up empty. I'm berating myself for not paying attention more. Back then, though, had I learned that information, I might have used it more as information to use against him than thinking one day I might cook him dinner.

He barks out a laugh. "I'm only kidding. I love all seafood, and no known allergies." He walks up behind me and wraps his arms around me. It's strange not fighting with him, but I definitely don't hate it. His arms bring a comfort I wasn't sure I would ever find.

"While I can't wait to eat it, I'm not sure my picky little eater will." He twists his lips in apprehension.

I nudge him with my hip and point toward the oven. "I already got that covered. There's fish sticks for him."

"Look at you, being prepared and shit."

"Hey, Girl Scouts are always prepared."

Jaxon leans back against the counter, crossing his arms and ankles. "Were you a Girl Scout?"

I grin. "No, but Lauren was." Turning back to the stove, I drop the noodles into the pot of boiling water.

"What can I do to help?" His fingers fidget as if he needs to keep them occupied to keep from touching me. Not that I mind, but Andy is just in the other room, and I don't want to burn dinner. On Saturday, we didn't go further than kissing—lots and lots of kissing—but the heat in Jaxon's eyes right now has desire building in my core, and if we started something right now, I'm not sure I'd have the strength to stop.

"You can open that bottle of wine."

"You got it." He presses a quick kiss to my shoulder before backing away. "Where do you keep the opener?"

I point to the drawer in the corner. I watch as Jaxon moves with ease around my kitchen. Almost as if he was meant to be here.

I don't drink wine often, so I don't have the fancy wine openers like everyone else—just an old-fashioned corkscrew style. Now, I'm thanking all things Christmas presents that I never got one because I glance up after checking on Andy's dinner to find the corded muscles in Jaxon's forearms taut. I think the temperature in the kitchen just raised a few degrees.

"You're gawking," he teases playfully.

"What?" I gasp. The smirk on his face tells me I've been caught red-handed. I can feel my cheeks heat.

"I said you're gawking," he repeats, bringing over two glasses and handing one to me.

"No, I wasn't." I accept the glass and look away as I take a rather large swig of wine.

Jaxon tips my chin upward. "For the record, feel free to gawk at me anytime. But just know that if you look at me with those heated stares, I'm not responsible for what kind of savage it might turn me into." It's clear we're both on the same page. I kind of want to see the savage side of Jaxon McAdams. Would he hold me down? Would he fuck me ruthlessly?

A shiver runs down my spine at the combination of his proximity and his own heated gaze as he professes dirty promises.

He closes the distance and presses his lips gently against mine. I taste the lingering wine flavors on his tongue as it slips into my mouth. The dry tannins of the wine already make my mouth water, but with each swipe of his tongue, I'm craving more.

"Miss Kate, is dinner ready yet?"

We pull apart from Andy's voice ringing from the other room.

"Just about, kiddo," I shout over my shoulder. "Why don't you go in and keep him company so I can finish this? Otherwise, you might be too distracting."

He salutes me with a "Yes, ma'am" and swats me on the ass as he passes by.

After finishing our plates, Andy dramatically leans back and places his hands on his stomach before sighing, "I am stuffed."

We laugh at his exaggeration, but I feel the same way.

"Miss Kate, can we show Daddy what we made today?" Andy's smile is contagious.

"Umm, sure. Let's carry these dishes into the kitchen first." I back up from my seat to stand, but Jaxon holds out his hand.

"Let us clear this up. You cooked, so the least I can do is clean up."

I sit back down. "Won't see me complaining."

After he clears the table and loads the dishwasher, Jaxon follows us up to my studio. Andy rushes into the room, grabbing the canvas off the shelf where we left it to dry.

"Look, Daddy. Look what I did." Andy jumps up and down, shoving the canvas up and nearly hitting his dad in his face.

"You did this?"

He nods enthusiastically. "Yup, today Miss Kate and I painted together. I did this." He walks over the unfinished canvas on the easel. "And she worked on that."

"Wow, I could never do anything like that. I don't have the talent to draw."

"You're an architect that can't draw?"

He tilts his head side to side as if disagreeing with me. "Well, I can draw buildings and stuff. Those are precise lines and a concrete idea. This stuff, though—wow, it's fantastic, Kate."

I've received compliments on my art for years. Hell, I make a living off my artwork, but that simple compliment coming from him means more than any commission I've ever made.

"Did you always want to be an artist?" he asks, walking around the room, looking at the various pieces I have in there.

"For as long as I can remember. I've always loved art. My mom told me I've always had a pencil or paintbrush in my hand." My sister has been the same way but with books. I'm surprised she didn't become an author or a librarian, but she loves teaching too much to ever give it up.

When things went south with my parents' marriage, I focused on my art, channeling all my emotions I held inside when my father left to the canvas.

Boy would I love to rub it in his face that my "so-called hobby," as he called it, not only earned me a scholarship to art school, but in college, I sold quite a few pieces that allowed me to continue this as my dream and make a career out of it. One day, I want to have my own gallery, but right now, I work off my website and word of mouth.

"Well, you're extremely talented." He points to the one hanging just beside the window. "I think that one's my favorite."

I follow his gaze to the framed canvas I have hanging on the wall beside the window. Inspired by the beach house that Finn had rented for his and Lauren's wedding, one side of the canvas is the stormy seas and rough waves before they transition into calm waters after the storm. Their relationship weathered the storm, and even though they faced many rough seas during their ten years apart, their love was strong enough to survive and reach the shore of happiness.

"That's my favorite, too."

Andy yawns loudly, pulling our gaze from the piece. Turning around, we find Andy sitting on my stool, his eyes heavy.

"All right, mister, let's get you home and into the bath." Jax walks over to him and scoops him up. I can tell he's tired because he didn't put up any fight and instead settles against his dad. I follow him out of the room and down to the front door.

"Same time tomorrow?" he asks as I hand him Andy's backpack.

"You bet." We linger in the doorway, neither of us ready to end the evening but knowing we have to for Andy. I stand there for a moment, unsure of what happens next.

Is he going to kiss me?

Are we at that point where we are more than just sneaking touches and glances in front of Andy?

Does he want to do that in front of his son? We haven't actually discussed how to handle that. Now definitely isn't the time for that, so I decide on a simple kiss on the cheek like I would on other guys' cheeks like Finn or my brother. The stubble along his face tickles my lips as I pull back.

"Good night," I say, leaning against the front door.

"Good night." He smiles before walking out the door.

I'm pretty exhausted myself, so I head straight upstairs after locking up and turning the lights off. I go through my normal bedtime routine of brushing my teeth and washing my face. By the time I climb into bed, I see there is a text notification waiting for me on my phone.

Jaxon: *Thank you for dinner.*
Me: *Of course. Anytime. It was a nice evening.*
Jaxon: *Yeah, it was, but one thing could have made it better.*

I take the bait.

Me: *Oh yeah? My cooking and company that bad? Maybe next time you do it.*
Jaxon: *I'll cook anytime although I can't guarantee it will be as good as that scampi.*

I've had his cooking before, and he's a fantastic cook. I can't believe I ever thought to compare him to Haylee, who could probably figure out how to burn water.

Jaxon: *But I was thinking had I been able to give you a proper kiss good night.*

My fingers graze over my lips, imagining his lips on mine.

Me: *Yeah, that would have been nice.*
Jaxon: *Oh baby, it would have been a lot more than nice. :)*

I can feel my cheeks flush at his insinuation. I'm feeling suddenly awake, wondering where this conversation might be leading.

Me: *Don't start something you can't finish.*

No further messages appear, so I set the phone back on my nightstand and slump my shoulders, a little disappointed. I reach for my remote and bring up Netflix. As the home screen appears, there is a loud knock at the door.

Who the fuck is that?
My phone buzzes as I slide off the bed to peek out the blinds to see if there is a car outside.

Jaxon: *Open your door. I forgot something.*

I rush down the stairs and look toward the living room to see if there's anything obvious that he left before opening the front door.

"What did you forget," I huff, slightly out of breath and regretting running down the stairs.

He closes the distance and threads his fingers in my hair, holding my mouth to his. He holds nothing back, tugging slightly on the strands before pulling my bottom lip between his teeth, earning a moan from deep within me.

When he pulls back, we're both panting. "Told you it would be better than nice."

He winks and quickly rushes down the steps and across the street. I am left utterly speechless.

Did that seriously just happen? Maybe I should borrow one of my sister's books the next time I'm over for some pointers because I definitely feel like I'm getting in over my head with this, but I would gladly drown in Jaxon's blue eyes, especially if he can revive me back to life with kisses like that.

Chapter 23

Kate

Goose bumps coat my flesh as Jaxon circles his thumb on the top of my hand. Our fingers are laced together, resting on the back of the couch. I've spent my days with Andy at my house and the evenings with the two of them. Tonight, we watched the latest *Trolls* movie after making homemade pizzas together.

"Psst," I whisper.

Jaxon turns away from the screen and follows my gaze down between us, where Andy is out cold.

He gives my hand a squeeze before unlacing our fingers. Standing, Jaxon lifts his arms and stretches from side to side. His shirt rides up a smidge, exposing a dark happy trail that leads into his pants—his gray sweatpants. This man is seriously trying to kill me. *Sweet Jesus, those things should be illegal.*

Over the last few days, we haven't gone further than a few stolen kisses. With him being a single dad, there's not much time for sex, although when I go home at night, my little vibrating bestie works overtime. I thought my self-induced orgasms hit me hard with my fantasies of him—now they're on a whole new level. When we finally take this further, I'm not sure I'll survive it. But hey, death by orgasms seems like a pretty sweet way to go.

Jaxon effortlessly scoops a sleeping Andy in his arms and smirks at me. My face flushes, wondering if he knows what I'm thinking about.

"I'll be right back," he whispers before heading up the stairs.

I glance around the room, unsure of what to do. Deciding to help him clean up, I gather our snack bowls and cups and carry them into the kitchen. I'm currently rinsing them out when I feel his presence. I decide to have some fun and slowly bend down to load the dishes in the dishwasher, and I have to press my lips together to suppress my laughter when I hear a growl and throat clearing behind me. There's a hint of that savage man he referenced before.

I pretend not to notice him until his heavy footsteps come closer and strong arms wrap around my waist.

"You didn't have to clean up." He presses his face into the crevice of my neck and inhales.

"I know, but I just wanted to help."

"Well, thank you. You do so much for me. I don't know how to thank you, honestly."

Lick me, fuck me, own me, my inner slut screams.

"I'm gonna go" is what I mean to say, although I can't for sure confirm that because once I felt Jaxon's stubble rubbing against my skin, all coherent thoughts were running away, just like the big moment in *Independence Day*.

His hands explore at the same time his lips nip at my skin. They slowly drag up and down my sides and eventually slip under the fabric of my T-shirt. Jaxon teasingly drags his fingers over the waistline of my pants, and I relax back into him.

"I really should go," I say in a breathy tone.

"Or…"

When his thumb slips under my bra and brushes over my hardened nipple, I'm not even sure you could drag me out of this house or out of this man's arms.

"Or I could…" While one hand continues playing with my nipples, the other cups my pussy over my pants. He moves his fingers in a circular motion, and I know I would die if this man stopped touching me.

Has his restraint been struggling as much as mine has? I can feel his erection poking me where it's currently nestled between my ass cheeks. He brings me to the brink of an orgasm before he suddenly removes his hands from me. *What the fuck?*

"I'm sorry for getting carried away. You said you were leaving."

Is he serious? I spin around and narrow my eyes at him. My body is ready to explode. Need and desire leak from my pores. His smirk tells me that he knows exactly what he was doing. That bastard. Well, guess what, two can play that game.

"Or I could stay and you keep doing that." I drag my finger down the material of his cotton T-shirt to his cock, which right now, thanks to his pants, leaves nothing to the imagination. And trust me, I've imagined it a lot—in my hands, in my mouth, in my pussy.

Jax takes a few steps toward me and cages me in against the counter. "I like that idea better," he says as he cups my cheeks in his hands and kisses me with such a brutal force that if he hadn't been holding me with his hands, I would have melted straight to the floor.

He doesn't break contact once as he removes his hands from my face and hoists me up against him by the back of the thighs. I gasp in surprise, but all that does is make him plunge his tongue further into my mouth. *Holy shit, this man can kiss.*

I wrap my legs tightly around his waist when he moves, carrying me up the stairs as if I weigh nothing. By the time we're walking into what I assume is his bedroom, I'm practically clawing at the man and dry humping him to gain any form of friction. My body craves release and needs him to give it to me.

Jaxon drops me on the bed and hovers over me between my spread thighs.

"Now, Kate. My son is sleeping down the hall." Jaxon reaches his hands into my pants, and I jolt in surprise as his thick fingers drag over my clit. "Do you think you can stay quiet?"

When his finger dips inside me, a loud moan leaves my lips. Jaxon makes a tsking sound with his tongue as he removes his hand from my pants. I whimper at the loss of his touch.

"Okay, okay. I promise to be quiet. Please, I need you," I beg. *I need you like I've never needed anyone before.* That thought should absolutely terrify and send me running for the hills, but I'm spreading my legs wider.

A devilish smirk spreads across his lips, and in a flash, he yanks my pants and panties in one swoop from my body and tosses them somewhere in the room.

"Good, because I have a hunger only you can satisfy." Jaxon's eyes darken to a shade I've only dreamed of as he takes in my bare, wet pussy. "And I'm going to eat this cunt until I've had my fill. But if you make a noise, I'll need to stop. Understand?" I've never been a fan of the *see you next Tuesday* word, but hearing it on his lips sends a new pool of wetness to my opening.

"Yes," I pant. "Touch me, Jax—" He cuts me off when he suctions his lips to my clit. I feel a slight pinch when he nibbles on my sensitive skin. His strong fingers explore my thighs, which are wrapped around his head.

When his tongue dips into my center, my hand shoots out to the side and reaches for anything I can to keep from making noise. I grab the pillow he set me down on and shove it over my face as his tongue violently licks my slit. When he adds two fingers inside me, my body convulses, and I would gladly suffocate in order for him to keep going. I can't handle another missed opportunity of an orgasm, although maybe he gets off on edging me and making me so fucking hot that I'm ready to combust at the flick of his tongue.

"Mmm." He groans against my pussy. "I could eat this cunt for every meal and still never get enough of it." *Holy fuck.*

He continues to feast on me through the orgasm. He slips his hands under my ass and hoists me up to bury his tongue deeper inside me. After the second orgasm comes even faster than the first, my legs have lost all feeling.

"That's a good girl," he says, pulling the pillow from my face. My hair clings to the sweat on my forehead. "I should be mad that I couldn't see your face when you come. I bet it's even sexier than what I've imagined—" I am curious what all he has imagined. I want to bring every one of this man's fantasies to life. "—but I'm going to watch it now."

He does that amazing trick men do—pulling his shirt off with one hand—and shoves his pants and boxers down. *Holy dick size, Batman!*

Jaxon settles on the bed, switching our positions so I now sit upright, straddling his thighs. "I want you to ride me. Let me look in your eyes as I bottom out inside you. Take the pleasure you need from me."

Am I dead? Did I just die and go to heaven? No, not heaven. There's no way this man's mouth and cock would let him past the gates of heaven. It would be so worth it to burn in hell to savor a few moments with him.

"See something you like, Kate?" My name sounds like an addicting drug on his lips. I can't take my eyes off his cock as he moves his wrist with slow and steady strokes.

"Meh," I shrug. "It's all right."

"Oh, just all right, huh?" he taunts as his hands grip my sides and tug my hips forward.

"Yes," I scream as he spears me onto his cock. *Holy fuck! Take my breath away.*

"Shit, a condom." He lifts me off him quickly. His cock, still wet with my arousal, bobs on his abdomen. It gives me a moment to catch my breath. Before I can tell him he doesn't need it—though this isn't exactly the time to have that talk—he already has the foil packet in his teeth and is sheathing his cock. "Ride me, baby."

I grip the base of his cock and line the tip up at my entrance. He doesn't have to tell me twice. I slowly sink down on him, adjusting to his size once more. Once he's seated inside me, I throw my head back in pleasure at the fullness I feel in my core. My breaths come in quick pants as I slowly rock back and forth.

The view in front of me has my breath coming in quick pants as I watch the hardest part of him disappear into the softest part of me with every grind of my hips. It is better than any fantasy I've ever played out in my mind.

I press my palms down on his chest, picking up speed, bouncing up and down. My gaze never wavers from his as I feel his cock plunging deeper and deeper.

"God, you're fucking gorgeous like this. You like my cock inside you, don't you, sweetheart."

I nod, sinking my teeth into my bottom lip to suppress the moan from slipping from my lips. *He feels so fucking good.*

There are so many words not said in his eyes. Crossing this line between us, it feels so much more than sex. It feels like something bigger, the beginning of something more. My pulse thrums in my throat under his thumb when he places his hand at the base of my neck. Slowly dragging it down the valley between my breasts, he continues until he finds my clit. I need to come, but I also don't want this moment to end. As he alternates between circular movements and slight pinches, the pressure gets to be too much, and I know I can't hold off much longer.

His palm comes in contact with my ass with a smack. It jolts me slightly forward, and he growls when my pussy clenches around him.

"Come for me like a good girl," he commands, repeating the move, this time gripping my flesh harder. "Give it to me."

Jaxon grips the back of my neck and pulls me to his mouth, sealing our lips together. He swallows every one of my moans as the orgasm rips through me.

He groans with a few more deep thrusts, following me over the edge and spilling into his condom.

Both of our breaths are harsh.

"I thought you wanted to see my face," I tease.

"You're right. Guess we'll just have to do that again."

Chapter 24

Jaxon

The aroma of lavender and mint—a combination I will always associate with Kate—is the first thing I notice when I wake from one of the best sleeps in years. I'm not sure if that's thanks to the festivities that led into the early hours of the morning or the naked woman wrapped in my arms. Either way, I don't care.

Although I would think the former would have me completely exhausted, I find myself—and my dick—fully awake.

When she stirs, her bare ass pushes against me, and I groan. How easily I could slip right inside her. *Talk about a fantastic wake-up call.*

Kate stretches and pulls away. Whether she's trying to leave or just stretch, I'm not letting her go far. "No," I protest and quickly intertwine my legs with hers. I press my lips against the exposed skin, and she moans in appreciation. I do it again and trail my fingers along the front of her body, finding her pussy already wet for me. She arches her back, begging for more as I drag my fingers through her wetness.

"You miss this cock inside you, baby?" I whisper, and she shivers under my husky tone.

"Yes," she pants as she grinds against me.

"You want me to slide it inside you over and over, hitting that sweet spot?"

"Jaxon, stop teasing me and fuck me, please." Hearing that word—*please*—on her lips makes me want to give her whatever she wants.

I wrap my hand around the base of my cock to line up with her entrance when the door handle jiggles. *Cockblocked by my son.*

"Daddy," Andy shouts from the other side. "Why is the door not opening?" My son's voice is like my balls being dipped in ice water.

"Oh shit," Kate mumbles and lunges away from me with such a force she falls off the bed with a thump. "I'm okay," she whispers.

I groan and run my hands over my face. Grabbing my boxers off the floor, I quickly slip them on.

When I reach the door, I glance over my shoulder and no longer see Kate. I don't have time to look around more before Andy starts banging on the door.

I unlock the door and whip it open.

"Daddy! What took you so long? The door wouldn't open." He plants his hands on his hips, doing a great impression of me when he's about to be in trouble.

"I'm sorry, buddy. I was getting dressed. I didn't realize the door was locked."

"Daddy," he draws out. "You forgot clothes, silly." He shakes his head in amusement.

I look down to where he stares at my bare chest.

I throw my hand in the air goofily, and he giggles. "You're absolutely right. Why don't you head downstairs and you can watch something on your iPad. It's on the table. And I'll get dressed."

I wait to hear the pitter-patter of little footsteps down the stairs and close the door behind me.

"Kate? Kate?" I whisper loudly, looking around the room.

I hear movement on the floor by the side of the bed she was lying on, so I follow the sound.

I cover my mouth with my hand to suppress my loud laughter when I see Kate wrapped in the sheet but clearly still naked, worming her way out from under the bed.

"What the hell are you doing?" I ask, extending my hand to help her up.

"I'm sorry. I panicked." She brushes off the sheet wrapped around her body. "I hadn't realized that you had locked the door, and we haven't discussed when to tell Andy, so I went to the closest place I thought of."

I glance down at where she just came from. "Under the bed."

"Hey, don't judge," she scolds when she sees me struggling to hold off my laughter. "Also, you should probably clean under there. It's nasty."

I walk over to the dresser and grab a pair of gym shorts, sad that our morning plans are derailed, or should I say postponed, because I am counting down the hours till I can be back inside her. "Sorry, I don't typically hide women under there in the morning."

Kate drops the sheet and searches for her clothes, finding them scattered throughout the room. I walk up behind her and wrap my arms around her just as she pulls her shirt over her head. She fits perfectly against me.

"I'd much rather spend the morning continuing where we left off." I kiss her shoulder.

Spinning in my arms, she loops her hands around my neck. "Me too—but we're supposed to go to breakfast with Finn and Lauren."

"You sound more like a meal I'm craving." She squirms in my hold when I squeeze her ass in my hands.

"Keep it in your pants, McAdams," she laughs, shoving me away. She might be small, but she's mighty. "I'm going to go home to shower."

"Is there something wrong with the shower here?"

Kate's eyes darken, and she blinks them away. "Yeah, actually. I think it will be more of the opposite of getting clean."

I stalk toward her, and she retreats, holding her hand up. "Oh no, Mr. I'll see you soon."

Before I can reach her, she's already out the door and running down the stairs.

· ♥ · ♥ · ♥ · ♥ · ♥ ·

"You know, this living arrangement is pretty convenient for us. It's like a one-stop shop. Lauren can walk across the street to Kate's, and I can hang out here."

Finn continues talking, but I tune him out as my mind drifts to what it felt like to finally have Kate in my bed. It was more than I imagined each time my fist wrapped around my cock with thoughts of her swirling around my brain.

"Jax," he shouts and snaps his finger in my face.

"Huh?" I whip my head to the left to find Finn staring at me with furrowed brows.

"Did you hear me at all?"

I run my palm over the back of my neck. This woman is already consuming me, and that terrifies me, yet I'm too invested to stop now.

"Sorry, I'm just tired. Long night." I scrub my hands over my face.

"Hey, Daddy," Andy calls out from the couch. "Can Miss Kate sleep in my room next time?"

Finn quirks an eyebrow and turns to face Andy. "Did Miss Kate spend the night, buddy?" Finn tickles him, and giggles fill the room as Finn lifts him up to sit on his lap.

"Yeah, but she slept in Daddy's room. I heard her in there this morning, even though she thinks she was hiding. She's not very good at playing hide-and-seek. Maybe you can teach her. You're the best at it."

"Huh," Finn snorts. His eyes move to me, and he gives me a knowing smirk before diverting his attention back to his godson. "Maybe we will have to show Miss Kate how to hide better."

"Hey, Andy. Why don't you go get dressed and we can head out?" Anything to avoid little ears hearing the third degree I know I have in store for me at any moment.

"Be right back." Andy hops off Finn's lap and runs up the stairs. "Don't leave without me," he shouts.

"We won't," Finn and I reply in unison.

Just as Finn opens his mouth to interrogate me, the front door opens, and in walk the Lawson sisters. Kate looks freshly showered with her hair pulled up on top of her head in a messy bun.

Lauren goes straight to Finn's side, and he pulls her down into his lap.

Kate stands there hesitantly. If we're going to work whatever this is out between us, that's not going to work for me. I close the distance between us and swoop her into my arms. She gasps, surprised at my public display of affection, and I'd be lying if I didn't say it surprised me as well. I kiss her as if it's been days since her lips last touched mine—not a matter of hours.

"Well, good morning to you, too." Lauren's sassy tone causes a laugh from her sister. I tug Kate against my chest, wrapping my arms around her shoulders. "How come you don't say good morning like that to me?" Lauren jokes, turning to her husband.

Finn nuzzles into his wife's neck. "That's because I say good morning with my tongue in your pussy instead of in your mouth most days."

I shake my head at his abrasiveness. *Thank fuck Andy is still upstairs.*

"Ah la la la la," Kate singsongs with her fingers in her ear. *Hmm, that's not a bad way to wake Kate up.*

"Reynolds - 1, Lawson - 0," Finn teases and winks at Kate as she finally pulls her fingers free and settles back against my chest. My fingers dance along her back.

"And don't worry, babe. That's not good morning. It seems these two had a slumber party last night." Cupping his mouth as if he were playing a game of telephone, he whispers dramatically to his wife, "A naked one."

I choke on air, and Kate slaps my back while Lauren's eyes first go as wide as saucers, and then the same mischievous smile that is on her husband's lips appears on hers. Lord only knows what's going on in their heads right now.

The amount of rumbling coming down the stairs clearly sounds like a stampede headed our way and not just my four-year-old son running down them.

His smile widens as soon as he sees Lauren and Kate. "Miss Kate, you're back." A snicker from the peanut gallery behind me has me flipping Finn the middle finger behind my back.

"Auntie Lo!" Lauren slides off Finn's lap and crouches down to the floor, holding her arms out as Andy lunges straight for her. I think if her back wasn't partially resting against Finn's knee, she would probably topple over with Andy in her arms. She lifts him up with ease, and he wraps his arms around her neck, clinging to her.

"I missed you, little man."

"You just saw me," he giggles as she peppers kisses all over his face.

Lauren pulls back, with her face still toward him but her eyes wandering over to where her sister and I stand. "A lot can happen in just a few days. Hey, Andy, what do you say you ride with me and Uncle Finn to the restaurant and we give Daddy and Miss Kate some alone time?"

Anyone who's not a child could understand the innuendo in her voice when she says "alone time."

Andy thrashes his arms excitedly, and Lauren has to be quick on her feet to hold him tighter. Andy stops moving and waves his little hand for Lauren to come closer. He "whispers" in a tone that, unlike Finn's, he actually thinks is being quiet. "Can I pick the music?"

Kate shuffles in my arms, and my fingers tighten my hold on her instinctively.

"Of course, little dude. I always like your music choice better than Uncle Finn's," she teases back.

Finn scoffs as he rises from the couch and swoops Andy right out of his wife's arms. "Hey, I have great taste in music. Now, what do you say we go get some grub?"

"Yes!" Andy pumps his fist in the air as Finn carries him out the front door, and Lauren follows.

Kate shifts and follows her sister, but I quickly snatch her hand to stop her. I step up behind her and press my body against her back. "You look beautiful, by the way. Although I think I prefer the Kate Lawson freshly fucked look." She shivers in my arms, and my smile widens at my effect on her.

Kate spins in my arms and loops her arms around my neck. "Sorry, I reeked of sex."

I'm not sure I see a problem with that. My cock stiffens at not only the feeling of her in my arms but the memory of last night… and this morning.

"Well, I can arrange for that to be your new perfume."

I'm feeling like a teenage version of myself. I went from only having sex with myself to not being able to get enough of this woman. I'd bury myself inside her 24/7 if I could. I'm pretty sure all I need is to have someone say her name, and then I'd be hard as a rock.

I pull her flush against me and lean down to kiss her. Just as my tongue swipes hers, the sound of a car horn outside forces us apart.

"Come on, you two lovebirds," my best friend shouts.

"Yeah, come on, lovebirds," my son mimics. *Great. Maybe I should rethink how much time Finn and Andy spend together.* I sigh, dropping my head to Kate's shoulder, but her laughter causes my head to bob up and down.

"Come on." Kate laces her fingers with mine. "Before the entire neighborhood hears those two." We walk out the front door, locking it behind me just as Finn is fastening Andy into the car seat in Lauren's vehicle.

"It's about time you two emerged," Finn laughs as he shuts the back-seat door. "We'll meet you guys there."

They're already pulling off by the time we make it to my truck. Kate lets me help her up with no sassy remarks. Once settled in, I lean over the center console and grip Kate's chin, turning her to face me, and smash my lips to hers, picking up where we had left off. Being a parent, especially a single parent, you need to take advantage of being alone, and that's exactly what I want to do. Being a few minutes late won't hurt. I'm ready to pull her into my lap and sink my cock into her when my phone vibrates from the cup holder.

Kate is panting when we separate. A lustful glaze sparkles in her eyes. I groan, knowing exactly who it is, but I humor myself by opening it up. He knows I won't ignore them since he has my son with him.

Finn: *Tick tock motherfucker! *Kissy face emoji**

I bellow out a laugh and turn my phone to show Kate. She joins in my laughter as I set the phone back in the cup holder.

"Let's not leave the man waiting. Plus, I'm hungry. Someone used up all my energy last night," Kate says seductively.

And she's going to need plenty of energy for later. Months of tension between us finally exploded, and even though it's only been a few hours, I'm already needing to be back inside her.

"Yes, ma'am." I smile as I start the ignition and put the truck in reverse.

Chapter 25

Finn, Lauren, and Andy are already walking toward the front door of the diner when we pull in. It's not that we took our time or anything. I'm just pretty sure I hit *every single* red light. Usually it would have brought on serious road rage, but I didn't mind the longer alone time with Kate.

"See you guys inside," Finn shouts with a wave. Andy is on his shoulders, playing the top of his head like a bongo drum.

"He's good with him," Kate says from the passenger seat.

I prop my elbow on the center console and rest my chin on my fist. "You're good with him." I can't believe I ever doubted her ability. She's an absolute natural, and one day, she's going to be an amazing mother.

She matches my stance, wiggling her small arm against mine.

"He makes it pretty easy. In case anyone hasn't told you lately, you're an amazing dad." There's so much sincerity in her voice that it seeps from her pores where our skin lightly touches directly into the veins of my heart.

"Thank you," I manage just above a whisper.

I lean forward and press a chaste kiss against her lips. The warmth of her tongue is comforting, just like her words. I could get lost in the world, kissing her over and over. To think there was a time when I would have gladly found other ways to want to shut her up, like duct tape over her mouth, and now I can just shut her up sealing my lips to hers.

My stomach growls, overpowering my hunger for her.

Kate giggles when she pulls back.

"Hey." I wrap my fingers around her arm to stop her. "You know the drill."

"Seriously," she huffs.

I challenge her with my stare, and she sinks back into the seat while she waits for me to hop down and rush around to her side.

She grumbles as I help her down. "You and your fucking chivalry."

Kate pulls me into the diner, and we see everyone piled into a corner booth. "I'm learning there are other sides of you, Jaxon McAdams—the sweet and the spicy." Her voice is low enough so that other patrons of the diner can't hear, but I can.

My lips turn upward, and Kate stops halfway to the table. She turns to face me and presses up on her toes to reach my ear.

"But I think my favorite version of you is the not-so-gentleman version I met last night." She presses a quick kiss to my cheek before spinning around and heading to the table with a bit of pep to her step.

I exert a groan and narrow my eyes at her when she winks over her shoulder. *That little minx. I'll show her how gentlemanly I can be later.* Shit, that is not helping the situation.

That silly wench knew exactly what she was doing and, with just one sentence, has all the blood rushing to my dick. The last thing I need is to scare my child by walking up to the table with a raging boner.

Roadkill. Grandparents banging. Toenail clippings.

I shiver at the thoughts but breathe a sigh of relief when my pants feel less tight.

"Took you guys long enough," Andy teases when we finally join them at the table, obviously taking cues from Finn.

When the server delivers an abundance of plates in front of us, Andy has his focus honing in on one plate in front of Finn.

"What in the world is that?" Andy pinches his nose and grimaces. "Yuck!"

"Oh, little dude, you are in for a new experience. This is only one of the of the best breakfast foods ever made." Finn eyes the plate pretty close to the same way he stares at his wife, and I let a few chuckles slip.

I remember the first time Finn introduced me to scrapple after his parents had visited and brought him some. We were both hungover as shit, and he said the cure to a hangover was a scrapple, egg, and cheese sandwich. However, just the smell of it turned my stomach more than just the overabundance of booze left in my system.

"It doesn't look like bacon. And my daddy says that's the best breakfast food."

I correct him. "Best food in general, not just for breakfast."

"No, Andy, this isn't bacon. And your father is also wrong."

I smirk.

"Okay," Andy draws out and cocks his head to the side.

Finn holds up the plate as if he's offering a sacrifice to the gods. "This, my friend, is scrapple."

"Well, what is it?"

Finn, Lauren, and Kate share a knowing look, and I'm curious how they plan to explain what exactly scrapple is to a child. I'm pretty sure if he tells him the truth, that it's a mush of pork scraps and trimmings, he may just become a vegetarian or give up food completely.

When they all turn their heads toward me, I hold up my hands and shake my head. "Oh no, don't look at me like that. You weird East Coasters can handle this."

"You wanna try it?" Finn waves the plate in front of my son, and I wish I had a camera to watch that insta-replay of his grimacing face.

Kate scoots closer to him and leans down, resting her arms on the table. "You know, Andy, when I was little, I thought it was stinky, too."

"Yeah? Do you eat it now?" He's very skeptical about this whole situation.

"Yup," she says, making a popping sound with her lips. She reaches across and steals a piece from Finn's plate and takes a bite.

Finn's jaw drops.

"Wanna know a secret?" Kate asks Andy, ignoring the scowl on Finn's face.

He nods his head enthusiastically.

"I used to dip it in ketchup, and it covered up the smell but added to the delicious taste." Yeah, I call bullshit on that. I don't think anything can do that.

Andy eyes up the ketchup bottle curiously before twisting his lips.

My son is one of the pickiest eaters I've ever known. There is no way in hell he is going to try that.

With one last sniff over the plate, he lifts his gaze to his godfather's. "Uncle Finn, can I try a bite?"

Finn's eyes widen in shock, as do mine as my head draws back quickly in shock. I'm speechless. Rubbing my eyes, I verify I'm not dreaming.

"Of course, little dude." He turns his attention to Kate. "Maybe you could learn a thing or two from this kid who has manners and asks before just taking it."

Kate shrugs, and behind Andy's head, she lifts her middle finger to Finn. With the other hand, she squirts a bit of ketchup on the edge of his plate.

Andy hesitantly takes the piece from Finn, never taking his eyes off the mushy center. He swipes almost the entire sploosh of ketchup up with the piece of scrapple before bringing it to his lips.

"Mmm, that's yummy."

Andy reaches over to grab more, but Finn is too fast and grabs the plate and pushes it out of his reach. "Uh-uh, I'll order you your own plate." Finn looks up and flags the server down.

I can't believe that actually happened. I've been trying to get him to try new foods forever, and this one time, she gets him to try scrapple, of all things. I'm in complete shock.

I wrap my arm around her shoulders and pull her into my side, kissing her temple. "Thank you," I whisper in her hair.

She nods with a smile. She settles against my side, and I leave my arm resting against the back of the booth.

Kate turns back to the rest of the group and laughs at something her sister said.

I feel like I'm dreaming at the scene in front of me. What a difference from the last first family meal I shared with them. While that meal was filled with tension and made us feel like outsiders pretending to be a part of the family, this meal makes me believe that we truly are. And that's all I've ever wanted for Andy—to be surrounded by people who love him.

Chapter 26

"Oh man, did I tell you I was on the phone with Kyler earlier?" Lauren leans over the counter, laughing. When she lifts her gaze again, she has to wipe away the tears. "Poor Levi had explosive shits. Thank God there's no such thing as smell-a-vision. Based on Ky's expression alone, it did not smell good."

I grimace. "Oh shit." I realize my choice of words, and that only makes us laugh harder.

"Literally."

My brother and sister-in-law definitely have their hands full with Levi and Charli. Watching them juggle life with twins totally makes me want to go hug my mama and say thank you for not dropping Lauren and me off at the fire station. No wonder my parents waited six years to have Kyler.

Once we have ourselves semi-composed, I lift the tray of snacks.

"Hey, can you grab those?" I nod toward the box of graham crackers sitting on the counter.

Lauren grabs it and places it on top of the pile of items in her arms.

I use my elbow to open the sliding door open that leads to Jaxon's backyard.

After a few days of rain, everything has finally dried out, and Jaxon suggested having everyone over for a bonfire. Kyler, Dani, Zach, and Haylee all passed, being home with newborns, but Lauren, Finn, and Kelsey didn't have to think twice about it.

"Who's ready for s'mores?" I shout as we approach where the guys have set up the fire pit. Adirondack chairs and a few camping chairs surround the circle of stones that have bright orange flames already roaring.

"What's a 'more?" Andy asks as he takes in all the ingredients Lauren and I set down on the picnic table.

"What's a s'more?" I repeat, but with my voice an octave higher. *Did I just transform into* The Sandlot*?* I wonder if Andy is old enough to watch that. A smile graces my lips at the memory of Kyler quoting this movie for-eeevvvveeerrrrr after he first saw it and continued to quote it in his wedding vows.

"S'mores are life, kiddo." I ruffle his hair and walk over to one of the Adirondack chairs and pull it closer to the fire.

"But I thought you said cheese is life," Andy says as I take a seat.

I giggle and adjust in my seat. I pat my thigh for Andy to hop up on my lap. "You know, you're a very observant little dude."

"What's uhserbent?"

"Observant," I correct him. "It means you notice a lot of things and remember things that people say. It's a good habit to have. Now, let me show you how to make a s'more."

I hold my hand out to my sister, who is unpackaging the s'more sticks. Of course my sister has official "s'more sticks." Sticks off the ground would have worked just fine. "Stick me."

She passes me a stick and the open bag of marshmallows.

"Okay, Andy, the first thing about making a s'more is that we need to have the marshmallow be the perfect amount of doneness. Now, if you are like Auntie Lo here—" I tilt my head toward my sister but see that she has now moved beside where Finn and Jax stand. "—then she will tell you the perfect marshmallow is only lightly toasted." I adjust us in my seat, leaning forward so that the speared marshmallow is just inside the fire.

"It is," she shrieks.

"It's okay, babe." Finn wraps his arm around her shoulders and pulls her close to him to kiss her temple. "Nobody's perfect."

She mocks him before ducking out of his grasp and moving to stand next to where Kelsey sits with Liam on her lap.

"But to me—" I'm cut off when Andy flails in my arms, rocking side to side. I have to tighten my grip on the stick so that I don't drop it.

"Miss Kate! Miss Kate!" Andy shouts. "It's on fire! It's ruined."

He sticks his lip out in a pout, and I worry that he's about to get upset. I give his side a reassuring squeeze. "Oh, Andy, that's not ruined. That's utter perfection." I blow a chef's kiss in the air. I bring the stick up to my face, careful not to let any of the flame near Andy, and blow on the marshmallow to put the fire out, revealing the perfectly burned piece of sugar.

Andy looks thoroughly confused and tilts his head to examine it. "What do you do with it now?"

"Can you hand me one of each of those?" I point to the plate with the graham crackers and chocolate chunks. He hops off my lap and retrieves one of each before settling back on my lap.

"Thank you, sir. Now we assemble."

"Like the Avengers do?"

I laugh. "Umm, sure." Okay, if he knows the Avengers, he's probably old enough to meet the Beast and the gang. "Can you hold this for a second?"

He takes the stick and continues to inspect it, looking very unsure if this makes any sense. "Look, Daddy, I'm like the Statue of Liberty," he giggles as he holds the stick up and brings his arm to his chest.

"Yeah, buddy. Looking good."

I quickly glance over at Jaxon as he watches us with a smile on his face. Then I take the two crackers and place them on each side of the marshmallow and carefully drag it off the stick. Lifting one of the crackers, I place the chocolate on it and smash them together.

"Now what do we do?"

"Now we eat it. You want the first bite?" He nods enthusiastically, but I pause halfway to bringing it to his mouth. "Well, maybe we should ask your dad first."

"Please, Daddy? Pretty please? Can I has a 'more?" We both pout just to add some dramatics.

Jaxon is just about to take a sip from his beer when he pauses and nods. "Yeah, sure, but not too much sugar. Otherwise, you're going to be wired." Our gazes lock as he brings the bottle to his lips and takes a long pull. I've never been jealous of an inanimate object before.

Andy takes a big bite out of the snack, and the crunch of the cracker under his little teeth breaks our staring contest.

"What do you think? Does it have the Andy stamp of approval?"

"Dat's so good," he says with a mouthful, spraying crumbs everywhere.

I take a bite and let a soft moan slip as the sugary treat hits my taste buds.

"Can we make more?"

I nod. "But let's finish this one first."

･❤ ･ ❤ ･ ❤ ･ ❤ ･ ❤ ･

What's that phrase they say—what goes up must come down. After splitting three s'mores with me, much to Jax's dismay—hey, you're only young once and get to experience your first s'more… or two or three… one time. And since we split them, he technically only had the equivalent to one or one and a half—Andy is currently dead weight in my arms, snuggled up against my chest. Kelsey took Liam home not long ago, being well past his bedtime, leaving just the five of us.

Jaxon's gaze met mine several times over the course of the evening, mentally asking me if I wanted him to take Andy, and each time, I shook my head that we were fine.

The light from the fire fakes when Jaxon's tall form stands over us. He crouches down, resting his elbows on his knees. "Okay, time for bed, kiddo."

Andy stirs in my arms. He snuggles in closer to me, and the tightness of his grip on me is in no comparison to the vise around my heart. Somehow, without even trying, Andy has wiggled his way in there and held on so tight, I'm not sure I could even let him go if I tried.

"Could've fooled me," Jaxon jokes.

He doesn't even bother opening his eyes but yawns big, clearly giving up the fight. "Daddy, can Miss Kate put me to bed?"

His gaze bounces back and forth between us, and he looks unsure. Jaxon opens his mouth to say something, but I cut him off.

"I don't mind. Better than bouncing him around, which might fully wake him up."

"Are you sure?" Jaxon's gaze bounces between Andy and me. His eyes have an unspoken conversation.

I narrow my eyes at him. *I don't mind at all.* "Yes. Now, get out of my way, you big lug."

He pushes off his knees to stand, and I carefully hold Andy in my arms while I follow suit.

"I'll come with you." Lauren rises from where she was sitting and jogs by my side. She glances over her shoulder. "Give you boys time to gossip."

Loud chuckles behind me fade as we disappear into the house.

Chapter 27

Jaxon

I watch as Lauren, Kate, and Andy disappear into the house, but I can feel eyes boring into the back of my head.

"Whatever you're wanting to say, just spit it out, Reynolds." I turn to find my best friend observing my every move with his chin propped up on his elbow.

"Who, me?" He fakes shock, bringing his hand to his chest.

"Yeah, I can hear your thoughts all the way over here. They're so loud, I feel like I'm at a damn rock concert."

"It's nothing, really. It's just good to see you like this."

I cock my head to the side. What's he talking about? "Like what?" I'm still the same old me.

"Happy." I didn't realize how much weight just one word could hold.

"I've been happy," I snap back, yet my words don't hold much conviction. I try to hide my expression by taking a long pull of my beer. "Happy" isn't the word I would use to describe myself over the last few years, I know that. You could say that I was content. Content with the way things were that I wasn't going to push for more, but then Kate barreled into my life, and I realized what exactly was missing.

Finn snorts. "Yeah, okay, grumpy ass. And I'm the president of the United States."

"Mr. President," I tease, tipping my bottle in his direction.

I sit back in my chair and use my thumb to pick at the label on the bottle to distract me from what's going on inside.

I glance up over my shoulder, trying not to bring too much attention to myself, knowing it will only poke the bear, aka my best friend. *How are things going? Does she need help?*

I should have just put Andy to bed. He's not Kate's responsibility. She's gone above and beyond to help us out. I don't want her to think that I'm taking advantage of her and only using her to help with Andy. I mean, she knows that, but there's always lingering doubt swirling in my mind. I think watching her and the bond she has with Andy only adds to her attractiveness.

"Uh-huh." Well, so much for sneaking a glance past Finn. "I'm serious, man. It's about time I saw that smile on your face." Without a second thought, I run my palm over my mouth. Was I smiling at the thought of Andy and Kate?

Finn continues. "You know, I was thinking I might never see you actually happy again." He pauses. "Courtney would want you to be happy, you know."

I grip the back of my neck as I process the same words that my father-in-law said on our last visit. Of course, he didn't necessarily mean with another woman, just in general when he asked how I was settling in.

I don't really want to get all deep right now, so I just grunt out a nod.

"Funny how it all works out." He leans forward on his elbows and takes a sip from his beverage. "Me moving back here and getting the girl and you moving out here and moving across the street from a particular brunette that just so happens to share my girl's DNA. Maybe it was some higher power pulling some strings for us."

I cover my teeth with my lips and hold back a laugh. "I'm sorry. Are you trying to tell me you think my dead wife was behind the house fiasco when I moved here so I could end up here in this house?"

He shrugs. "I've heard of weirder shit happening."

I shake my head at him. "All right, crazy pants, I think that's enough out of you."

"Okay, okay." He holds his hands up in the air in surrender. "I love you both, you know that." The slider door opens and closes behind us. "And it's nice to see a genuine smile on her face, too."

He tips his head behind me, and I look up to see Lauren and Kate giggling over something.

Kate focuses on her sister when I grab her hand and pull her into my lap.

"Oh," she gasps. "Fancy meeting you here."

"I think I like the East Coast. There are beautiful women just falling into your lap here." My comment earns me an eye roll but also a smile.

"I know, right?" I look up to see Finn's pulled Lauren into a similar position on the other side of the fire.

Kate is wearing jeans with rips in them, so my thumb touches her skin when I place my hand on her thigh. I slide my thumb under the denim, and she gives me a seductive smile.

"Everything go okay?"

"Yeah, little man didn't even budge when I laid him down. Had he woken up, I would've given him a quick bath. Pretty sure his sheets will need to be washed tomorrow because they're going to smell of campfire."

I lean forward and press my nose into her hair, which resembles the same scent. I think it might be my new favorite scent because it will forever remind me of this moment. The moment I truly let Finn's words sink into my head—*I am happy.*

"Oh, and I brought the baby monitor out, just in case he wakes up." She reaches into the front pocket of her hoodie and retrieves the baby monitor I keep by my bed.

I accept the baby monitor and set it down on the table beside me. I see her motherly instincts kicking in. For a moment, I picture Kate standing before me with her stomach swollen with my child, and my heart beats faster. Woah, where the hell did that come from? An ache forms in my chest, and my stomach knots with anxiety. The last time someone I cared about was pregnant, I lost her. I blink and shake away the thoughts and tighten my hold on her leg.

"I see that's not the only thing you grabbed from my room, huh?" I pinch the material of the sweatshirt she's wearing that I now recognize as one from my closet.

"What?" she teases. "It was getting colder, and your closet was closer than mine."

"No, it's fine. You look good in my clothes." I tip her chin back toward me and press my lips to hers. The lingering sweetness of the burned marshmallows and rich chocolate still lingers on her tongue.

A clearing of throats breaks us apart. We keep our foreheads together for a moment, breathing in the moment. I reluctantly pull back to see Lauren and Finn both making a gagging face.

"There may not be children around anymore, and you two will act like two horny teenagers, but I don't need to rinse my eyes out with holy water," Finn jokes.

"Says the man who just had his hand up his wife's shirt, copping a feel." I don't know if Kate's comment is true since our focus was on each other, but sounds like something he would do. Finn doesn't deny the accusation but instead mocks her.

I could sit back with popcorn and watch these two banter for days.

Kate reaches for her drink and settles back on my lap. "Why don't you make good use of that mouth and tell us an embarrassing Jaxon story?"

"How about not and say we did? I'm sure you've heard plenty," I say, knowing there are plenty of ideas popping into Finn's head. I don't really need to be roasted tonight.

"I could always share some of Kate," Lauren chirps up, which piques my interest. Kate groans when she sees her sister has my attention.

"Or," Finn draws out, "we could just play Never Have I Ever. That way, we get embarrassing shit about everyone."

"What are we, still in college?" Lauren asks at the same time Kate says, "Works for me."

"Come on, babe, live a little." He nuzzles his head into his wife's neck before moving to her ear. Her expression tells me not to ask what he said to make her reluctantly agree.

"Are we doing the whole put a finger down thing?" Kate asks as she plays with the hair at the nape of my neck. Typically, I always keep my hair short, but with her doing this on the unruly ends, I might just need to put off going to a barber a little longer.

"Fuck that. We'll just go in a circle, and everyone says never have I ever with whatever—nothing is off-limits; we're all family here—and if someone has done it, then they need to take a drink."

Simple enough. We all nod in agreement.

"Who's starting," Lauren asks.

"Ooh," Kate laughs and fidgets in my arms. "Never have I ever worked for Reynolds Contracting."

"Cheers." Finn and I hold up our drinks.

"That was easy," I laugh as I bring the cold beer bottle down to the revealed skin on her thigh. She jumps at the dampness, and I only chuckle harder.

"Never have I ever been a twin," my best friend says before making a goofy face. *Take that, ladies.*

After enthusiastically holding up her drink toward her sister, Kate says, "Womb mates for life," after taking a quick sip. The key to this game is all about pacing yourself. "I think the world is a much better place without two Finn Reynolds. Lord help us."

We go back and forth a few rounds. Some simple things—like I learned that Kate once got smacked in the face with a spoon when Kyler was trying to break the world record for holding a spoon on his nose, but he sneezed and launched it toward his sister. But others were a little too extreme. Some things I don't need to know about my best friend and his wife behind closed doors.

When Kate brings her pointer finger to her pursed lips, tapping them lightly while she thinks, I want nothing more than to pull her bottom lip between my teeth and force those sexy little moans out of her mouth.

"Never have I ever had anal sex."

Her ass cheeks clench against my thigh. Is she thinking about me taking her back here because shit, I am now, and that's rushing all the blood in my body straight to my dick.

She gasps when she sees me lift the drink to my lips, and her head sharply moves back to where Lauren and Finn are also taking a sip.

"Oh my God. I'm surrounded by a bunch of freaks," she shrieks, shaking her head in amusement.

"Just to clarify, it's never been my ass." My statement causes Kate's body to shake with laughter.

"Oh yeah, it's only been Lo's butt, not mine."

Kate laughs louder. "Thanks for clarifying boys."

Finn tips his beer in her direction before leaning in to whisper something in Lauren's ear, and I take this opportunity to see how far I can push Kate. I move a stray piece of hair away from her face and tuck it behind her ear. "Would you ever let me fuck you there? Let me pop that cherry." Her breath hitches. "Slide my cock into that tight ring of muscle and feel you stretch around me." I groan when she lets out a soft whimper, and her ass cheeks clench again. That wasn't a no though.

I pull on the pant leg of my pants to adjust myself. It seems her plan to embarrass her sister backfired because I'm ready to slide my cock in her right now, not giving a damn who's around.

"My turn." Lauren leans forward, and there's an evil glint in her eyes. Something tells me I should brace myself, but I think it's going to be more payback for Kate, so without thinking, I bring my beer to my lips the exact moment she speaks.

"Never have I ever gone home with someone who ended up sleeping in a race car bed."

I didn't expect that and end up spraying my beer all over the chair beside me.

She twists in my lap. "Oh my God, Jaxon. Are you okay?" She jumps up from my lap, and I already miss her touch.

I wipe the liquid still dribbling from the corner of my mouth with the back of my hand when I manage a "mm-hmm."

"Well, are you going to drink or not?"

Kate flips her sister the middle finger but drinks anyway before settling back in my lap.

"Umm, that sounds like an interesting time." A million different scenarios play out in my head.

Kate avoids looking at me and focuses on the bright embers in the fire pit. "You probably think a little less of me right now."

I bellow out a laugh. "Seriously? You found out that minister caught me getting a blow job on my wedding day in the church before the ceremony, and you think your dating history is going to make me think less of you?"

Kate brings her bottom lip between her teeth, and I free it with the pad of my thumb, forcing her gaze to mine.

"We both have a past. I don't expect you to be pure, and I'm sure as shit not." We both laugh. I think we've established that if not before, then definitely after this game.

"Okay. I just feel like one-night stands differ from hearing about Courtney. I mean, she was your wife and Andy's mom, where those meant nothing to me. But you're right. Our pasts made us who we are."

And if it weren't for those fucking losers, you wouldn't be in my arms right now. But I keep that to myself, so I settle on the simple answer. "Exactly."

"Well, I don't know about you guys, but I think it's about time to call it a night. Don't need my wife to turn into a pumpkin or anything." Finn lifts Lauren off his lap to stand, however, she doesn't remain on her feet for too long.

He scoops her into his arms. She shrieks when he hoists her up over his shoulder, firefighter-style. "Finn, put me down, you caveman."

"No can do, baby doll." He spanks her bottom and laughs before twisting to face us. "Kate, I hope you don't mind, but before we leave, I'm gonna go fuck my wife in your driveway so that we can drink if someone ever brings that back up in the future when playing this game." Umm, never have I ever wanted to play this game again.

"So much for turning into a pumpkin." Kate puts her fingers in her ears and singsongs, "A la la la la."

That only makes Finn laugh harder and Lauren's body shake. "Reynolds – 1. Lawson – 0."

"You know what? It's fine. I'll be too busy with your best friend's dick in my mouth to notice." She wraps her arms around my shoulders and pretends to shoot him with her finger pistols. "That, my friend, makes it 1-1." Their banter is out of control, but hey, you won't see me complaining about her plan.

I settle us back in the chair as we hear Lauren's laughter fade as they walk away toward the front of the house. We watch the fire crackle and begin to fade.

"I had fun tonight," she finally says to fill the silence, snuggling closer. "Thank you."

My fingers find the holes in her jeans again.

"Who said the night was over?" I nuzzle into her neck, trailing soft kisses along her skin. "I'm pretty sure you said something about my dick in your mouth."

Chapter 28

Kate

After putting the fire out, Jaxon links his fingers with mine and leads me into the house.

He stops at the bottom of the stairs and turns to face me.

"I'm going to make sure everything is locked up down here. I want you to go upstairs and wait for me in my bed." His eyes are full of heat, while his voice is full of lust.

He lets go of my hand, and I head up the stairs.

I've only made it halfway up when he says, "Oh, and Kate." I pause and turn to him. "Lose the clothes." He walks off, and I rush up the stairs.

When I enter his bedroom, I remove the hoodie I had stolen from his closet earlier. A strong whiff of campfire assaults my senses.

As much as I love that scent, I need it gone. A quick shower is a must.

Hands wrap around my waist from behind as I'm leaning into the shower to check the water temperature.

"I thought I told you to be waiting for me in bed, naked." He sinks his teeth into the sensitive spot on my neck, and I slink back against him.

Strong hands wander, leaving goose bumps in their wake.

"I know that, but I reeked of campfire and needed to shower."

Jaxon groans against my skin as he pushes the strap of my bra down. "I guess you're right. At least I'll have you naked." With one quick flick of the wrist, the material falls to the ground, joining the rest of my clothes I had previously discarded.

When his fingers reach my nipples, he pinches one between thumb and forefinger, and a moan escapes my lips. The other hand travels south until he finds my clit. Jaxon moves in a circular direction.

"Mmm, are you sure you need a shower? You're already soaking wet, baby," he rasps against my skin.

"Yes," I pant, unsure if I'm responding to the question of needing a shower or encouraging him to keep going.

He must assume the first because he stops moving and removes his hand from my body. Before I can tell him to keep going, his palm comes in contact with my ass. It causes me to jolt forward, but his powerful hands steady me.

"Now, be a good girl and get in the shower."

I'm too turned on to challenge. The quicker we rinse off, the sooner we can get back to this.

Stepping into the shower, I lean back and let the hot water wash over me. Moments later, the curtain opens, and Jaxon joins me. I run my hands down my hair and open my eyes to see heat in Jaxon's eyes.

"Come here." He crooks his fingers. When I press up against him, he spins me so my back presses against the cold tile. Lowering his mouth to mine, he pulls my bottom lip between his teeth. We lose ourselves in the kisses and touches. My body responds to his touch. With a few swipes of his finger, he can have me falling apart, begging for more. Each calculated move brings more pleasure.

"Widen your legs, baby." I spread them a little further for him. "That's my girl." His fingers dance over my clit, and I shiver. "I've been thinking about this cunt all fucking night."

Even though I'm dying for him to touch me more, I want to taste him. "There's something I need first," I rasp.

I press my palms into his chest, putting a little distance between us before trailing them down the ripples of his stomach. Seriously, how the fuck does this man look like this?

I drop to my knees in front of him, his erection jutting out and standing proud. I wrap my fingers around his shaft. With slow and steady strokes, I move my hand back and forth. I add a little twist to my wrist when I reach the mushroom tip. Jaxon lets out a harsh, ragged breath.

I sit back on my heels and drag my tongue up the underside of his cock before sucking the tip between my lips.

"Fuck me," he pants, and I smile around his cock.

I pull off with a pop but continue moving my wrist up and down.

"Not yet. Let me enjoy this first."

Jaxon laces his fingers in my hair, and the pads of his fingers massage my scalp, encouraging me back down and I oblige. Hollowing my cheeks, I take him back in my mouth, deeper this time.

The noises he's making tell me that even though I'm the one on my knees, I could bring him to his.

"Sweetheart, if you keep doing that, I'm going to come down your pretty little throat, and I'd rather make a mess of your cunt."

"Mmm," I moan, the vibrations of my humming cause him to jolt, and I smile. As much as I want to fuck him, I need to make him come. Rotating my wrist, I stroke him in tandem with my mouth, suctioning my lips from root to tip.

His body tenses, and a harsh grunt and the tightened grip on my hair is the only warning I get before he releases in my mouth. He attempts to pull back, but I keep a firm hold on his lower back while I lick up every drop from the tip. He hisses at his sensitivity. I look up at him and smirk.

Yeah, not so fun when you're super sensitive postorgasm, huh, asshole?

"Stand up, sweetheart," he commands. He moves me to be in front of him with my back to the running water, which is definitely colder than it was originally.

"We need to get you clean," he says, reaching for the bottle of shampoo and squirting a dollop in his palms. He runs it together before applying it to my scalp, massaging it. "Then I'm going to take you back to bed and show you what happens when you don't listen to me."

If he's trying to convince me to listen to him more, then he shouldn't lace his voice with dirty promises that have my pussy dripping and ready to take any punishment he's ready to give.

Chapter 29

By the time Andy comes down in the morning, Kate and I are already working on breakfast. Well, I'm cooking at the stove while she sits on the counter beside me with a cup of coffee and feeds me fruit she had cut up this morning.

His eyes go wide when he sees Kate still here. Her hair is still wet on the top of her head from her shower this morning—one where we didn't get distracted by fooling around. I'm not sure I'll ever be able to be in that shower and not think of how talented her mouth is.

"Good morning, Miss Kate. Do you live here now?"

"No, buddy." She smiles as she sets her coffee mug down on the counter and hops to her feet. She carries the bowl of fruit over to where Andy sits at the table. "I need to go home today and get some work done."

"Can I come, too? I can paint, too."

I cut in as I flip the pancake. "Maybe another time, buddy. You and I have some errands to do."

"We do?"

"Yep. You need to get ready for your big night at Uncle Finn's."

Andy gasps. "I get to sleep at Uncle Finn's?"

"Yeah, that sound good to you? I mean, unless you don't want to," I tease. I plate the pancakes and carry it over to the table.

"What? No, I can't wait. I'm going to go pack now." He climbs out of his chair, but I hold up my hand to stop him.

"Slow down, slugger. You're not going over there till later. You've got plenty of time to pack. Let's sit and eat our breakfast first."

"My mom always made the best pancakes," Kate says, stabbing another bite of pancake on her fork. "But these are freaking amazing. Compliments to the chef." She tips her fork in my direction and winks before bringing it to her lips.

"What about your dad? Did he like pancakes?" Andy asks with a mouthful of food.

"Umm—" Kate pulls her bottom lip between her teeth, and I can tell this might be a sensitive subject. To be honest, I don't know much about her dad. She never talks about him, and I've only ever met Liz.

"Did he go to heaven like my mommy?"

Kate squares her shoulders and shakes her head. "No, sweetie. He didn't go to heaven. He lives in California with his family." Pieces come together as to why no one ever mentions him.

"But you're his family, and you live here."

She smiles, pressing her lips together, but it doesn't reach her eyes. I decide to save this conversation for later. We don't need such a sensitive subject this early in the morning, especially when things feel so perfect sitting here—just like a family.

"Once you're done, you can go watch some TV, and then we need to take a bath to wash off the campfire smell."

Andy stabs the last few remaining bites on his fork and shoves them into his mouth. "All done," he says. At least, that's what I'm pretty sure he says. There's food halfway hanging out of his mouth.

That boy is going to make some woman happy one day. I shake the terrifying thoughts from my mind. I'm not ready for him to grow up.

Andy rushes off to the living room, and Kate and I finish our breakfast. This is nice. It feels right, something I could definitely get used to. I can't believe I fought this for so long. We both rise and begin clearing the dishes.

"So, Andy has a sleepover tonight, huh?" Kate rinses the plates before handing them to me to load into the dishwasher.

I nod. "Yeah, I arranged it with Finn last night while you and Lauren were gathering s'more supplies early in the night."

"Any big plans?"

I smirk. "I've got something up my sleeve."

Kate pauses and lifts my arm and looks into my sleeve. I laugh and pull my arm out of her grasp. "What are you doing?"

"What?" She shrugs. "You're the one who said you had something up there, so I was just seeing what it might be."

"You're ridiculous, woman. So you have some work to do?"

"Yeah, I have to finish a commissioned piece. It's being shipped to Willow Creek, NY, soon."

I turn and rest my hip against the counter and cross my arms and ankles. "You think you can finish by five?"

Kate steps up to me, places her hands on my waist, and pushes up on her toes. "I think that can be arranged."

She presses her lips quickly against mine, but my hands wrap around her waist to match mine. "Good. I thought you and I could have some alone time."

"Huh," she smirks. "I thought we had alone time"—she winks—"last night in the shower and again this morning."

I throw my head back in laughter. "Not what I mean. Keep it in your pants, Lawson." I release her waist and bring my hand down to her ass and squeeze. Kate is currently wearing a pair of my gym shorts that are rolled at the waist multiple times so that they don't fall off her waist. "I want to take my girl out to dinner on a proper date. As much as I enjoy movie nights and sharing you with Andy… call me a selfish bastard because I want to take you out—just us."

"I like that." She pulls out of my arms. "I'll see you soon. Bye Andy," she yells as she walks out the front door. "Be good for your dad."

"Daddy, is Miss Kate your wife?" Andy asks from the back seat.

I gasp. "Umm, no, buddy. Miss Kate isn't my wife." Where in the world did he get an idea like that?

"Well, what is she?"

"She's, umm—" I think, unsure how to answer that. I guess we never had that official "talk." Shit, do people even have the "talk" at our age? Do you have to formally ask someone to be their girlfriend? I am kind of out of practice on that front. Never really imagined I would be in this position. "She's, umm, my friend." I stick with the safe word choice for four-year-old ears.

"Emme is my friend. Do I need to kiss her like you kiss Miss Kate?" Well, so much for *safe and simple*.

Oh boy. Maybe I should give Zach a call and warn him before their next playdate.

"Umm, friends don't just kiss each other. It's when feelings are involved that you, umm, kiss like that."

"And you feel Miss Kate?"

I chuckle at his choice of words. Yup, I feel her—feel her curves and how her pussy clings to my dick. *Fuck, this talk is going in the fucking wrong direction.*

"Yeah, buddy, I *have* feelings for her. I guess I could say that she's my girlfriend."

Andy doesn't react, and I worry this isn't a good thing.

"Would you be okay with that if that were the case? Would that be okay with you?"

"What does being a girlfriend mean?" Andy is just as curious as a little monkey named George. His brain is like a sponge, taking in everything around him.

"Well, Miss Kate and I would hang out and share meals, have movie nights with you." Among other things that I don't need to share with him.

"And kiss," he says but makes a grimace, scrunching his nose. I laugh again.

"And kiss," I repeat.

He purses his lips together as if he's actually thinking. "That's cool by me." Good to know I have the permission of a four-year-old. But in all honestly, a sense of relief passes through me. If Andy wasn't on board with this, I don't know that I could pursue more.

"But Daddy?"

"Yeah, son." I glance back at him through the rearview mirror.

"Could Miss Kate maybe sometime stay in my room instead of yours?"

"Maybe sometime." I smirk. Lord help me when he's older and figures out there's more to adult sleepovers than ghost stories and s'mores.

Well, now that I have the approval of a four-year-old, maybe I should actually talk it over with the person in question. I make a mental note to bring that up at dinner tonight.

Chapter 30

Kate

"A toast." Jaxon holds up his wineglass and waits for me to do the same. The heat in his gaze burns brighter than the flickering candle reflecting off my glass as I raise mine.

"To us." He smiles genuinely—a far cry from the scowl I was first graced with when we met.

I pinch my thigh under the table where the hem of my dress meets my bare thigh. My sisters all but fainted when Jaxon and I dropped Andy off at their house and she took in my outfit.

"I am shooketh," my sister mocked with her hand over her chest. "I never thought I would see the day where Kate Lawson willingly wore a dress like that." Her hand left her chest and moved up and down as she appraised my outfit.

I wanted to dress nicer than usual tonight, with it being a special occasion of sorts—our first date, just the two of us. After pulling out half of my closet in search of the perfect dress, I settled on a black lace-top long-sleeved skater dress and black suede peep-toe booties.

"I wear dresses," I retorted. "I wore a dress to the holiday party, and Kyler's wedding, and hey, your wedding for that matter."

Lauren rolled her eyes at my response. All events I mentioned were ones that required a dress. Tonight, I willingly put one on. I may or may not have worn a dress for easy access in case Jaxon's hands went exploring before we arrived back home—a perk of a no-kid outing.

I shoved my hands in the pockets of my dress and swayed side to side. "Plus, there's pockets. You know I love pockets." We both giggled. "And, you know, sometimes people surprise you." A wide smile spread across my lips when my eyes lifted and found Jaxon staring at me from his conversation with Finn and Andy on the other side of the room.

Lauren clicked her tongue as she followed my line of sight. She stepped up closer to me. "Have you told him yet?"

My smile faltered, and I turned my head to her, not that Jaxon could read my lips or hear the conversation. "I don't even know how to bring something like that up. What, over appetizers? 'Oh hey, by the way, I know we only just started dating, but I—'"

"Ready to go?" Jaxon interrupted and wrapped his arm around my shoulders.

I nodded. Lauren pulled me in for a hug goodbye and whispered, "Just tell him. It'll be okay. I promise." Easy for her to fucking say. It wasn't her life ready to implode.

"Hey, you okay?" Jaxon places his hand on top of mine.

I shake off the thoughts. "Sorry." I give him a smile and my full attention. "To us," I repeat and clink my glass with his. When I take a sip of the red liquid, the balance of sweet, sour, and bitter flavors explodes on my taste buds, and I can't help the moan that slips from my lips as I pull the glass away from my lips. When I open my eyes, there's a darkness in his eyes that tells me my moan wasn't as soft as I thought. I feel my cheeks flush under the heat of his stare.

He adjusts our hands so our fingers now interlock. "I'm thankful that Finn and Lauren agreed to babysit Andy tonight so I could take my girl out and spoil her."

I snicker. "Oh please. That boy has my brother-in-law and sister wrapped around his little fingers. I'm sure it wasn't that hard to convince them." We both know damn well they're not the only ones wrapped around his fingers. I pull my hand from his grasp and prop both elbows on the table, resting my chin on my hands. I'm thankful for the smaller size of the table so that I can cross my legs underneath it, caressing his leg with my foot. "But feel free to elaborate on the whole spoiling your girl thing," I say in a flirtatious tone.

"Behave," he growls.

"You started it." I hide my smile behind my wineglass, and I take a quick sip, never breaking our eye contact.

A throat clearing beside us breaks the trance between us. "Are you two ready to order?"

"Yes, I believe we are," Jaxon says, as if he wasn't just giving me a look that told me he wasn't thinking about climbing under the table and eating his dessert first. Once we place our orders and the waiter leaves us, Jaxon leans forward on his forearms.

"So, a funny thing happened today in the car with Andy." He pauses. "He asked if you were my wife."

I choke on air, thankful that I hadn't chosen that moment to take another sip. Otherwise, I would have painted the area with red wine.

"Umm, what did you say to that?" I observe his body language to see how he reacted, but he gives nothing away. My leg bounces under the table in anticipation.

"Well, I told him no, but then he asked what you were."

"And what exactly am I?" I ask, just above a whisper.

"One thing's for sure—no matter what we call this, I can only think of one word to describe you." He leans closer, closing the distance between us.

"Which is?" I place my elbows on the table and push up the remainder of the distance.

"Mine."

"Yours," I repeat against his lips before pressing mine to his. I love the sound of that.

♥ ・ ♥ ・ ♥ ・ ♥ ・ ♥

"You need to try this," I say, stabbing a bite of food with my fork and holding it in front of him. He presses up from his chair and leans forward to capture the bite.

"Mmm, that is delicious," he says mid-bite. I was torn between the filet with the peppercorn cream sauce and the Tuscan sausage pasta. Nine times out of ten, if pasta is on the menu, I'm ordering it. *Give me carbs or give me death.* I've never tasted anything more heavenly between my lips before. Italian sausage, baby spinach, sun-dried tomatoes, and basil all nestled into the most amazing garlic cream sauce.

"Aren't you going to let me try yours?" My eyes dip down to the half-eaten filet on his plate.

Jaxon laughs and shakes his head. "Nope, I'm not sharing. This is too damn good."

I gasp in shock. "You're such a dick."

"Never claimed I wasn't, baby," he taunts back before taking another bite of his meal, making sure his groans of delight tell me how good it is.

Naturally, I roll my eyes at him, with a smile on my lips, of course.

I set my fork down and relax back into my chair. I'm pretty sure the zipper on my dress might burst if I even try to eat another bite.

"Are you ready for Andy to start school in the fall?" Jaxon had recently made an appointment to tour the kindergarten class at Central Academy, the school where Lauren teaches.

Jaxon's fork drops with a loud clank against the plate as his eyes go wide. "What? Why would you say that?"

"Umm, sorry?" I question, my voice raising an octave higher. I thought it was a simple question to ask, so I'm unsure of why he responded that way.

"No, it's just with kids—you want them to stay as little as possible, but then you also want to watch them grow up." Jaxon swirls his wineglass around and stares at it like it holds all the answers. "You'll understand what I'm talking about when you have kids of your own one day."

I regret having taken a sip of my own wine at that moment because I sputter the wine back into the glass. I set the glass down and reach for my napkin to clean the liquid dribbling down my chin.

"I'm sorry, did talking about something so heavy freak you out? I guess I'm not up-to-date on what's appropriate first-date talk." He laughs nervously.

"No, it just went down the wrong pipe." I let the lie slip from my lips before reaching for the glass of water in front of me. "Is that something you want?" I ask as my heart beats in my throat, waiting in anticipation for his answer. "More kids?" I clarify when he arches a brow, unsure what I was asking.

He brings his napkin up from his lap and wipes his mouth, then sets it on the table beside his plate.

"Ya know, I never thought I'd want more kids after…" He trails off. "I don't know, though. That was all before."

My throat becomes as dry as the Sahara. "Before what?" I can feel my heart racing, and if I'm not careful, it may jump right out of my chest and onto the plate at the table beside us and be served as an entrée.

Jaxon leans forward and reaches for my hand. He links his fingers with mine and squeezes tight. His eyes lock on me, and my mouth goes dry. "You."

Who knew one word could hold so much power and weight? I guess, of all people, my sister would understand. One word changed her life, just like it has me.

I swallow thickly as the world disappears around us as he slides his thumb back and forth. The touch alone sends a trail of goose bumps up my arm and straight to my nipples, which are now hard and pushing against the material of my bra. The intensity of Jaxon's stare has me believing the temperature in the restaurant rose.

Is this some sort of sign? First, my sister brings it up, and now it's been worked into the conversation. If that's not the world telling me I need to be open and honest with him, well, I'm not sure what is.

I take in this man in front of me, one who was still putting the broken pieces of his life back together but admits for the first time in years, he sees his life moving forward from the pain and loss he's endured, and here I am about to stomp all over it. This is going to change everything.

I know I should tell him.

I know I need to tell him.

"Jaxon, I, umm…" I begin to say. I pull my bottom lip between my teeth, biting down so hard I'm surprised I don't taste copper. "There's something I need to tell you."

He leans forward, and I take a deep breath.

Just as I open my mouth to speak, he reaches into his pocket and retrieves his phone, which is buzzing in his hand. He presses a button on the side and sets it down on the table face down.

"What were you saying?"

"I, umm—" The phone begins buzzing again. "You should probably answer that."

"I'll call him right back." He ignores the phone and focuses his blue eyes on me.

Just spit it out, Kate. That way, you get just get it over with. Rip the fucking Band-Aid off. Maybe Lauren was right, and it will all be okay.

"I—"

This time, it's my phone vibrating. *What the fuck?* I look down to see my sister calling. I hold my finger to pause this conversation.

"Hello?"

"Kate," Finn's voice shouts. "I tried calling Jax, but he didn't answer. Where is he?"

"Umm, he's right here." I look up to Jaxon, confused, and wonder what's going on.

"Please hand him the phone. I need to talk to him, now," he barks.

"Okay, hold on." Something is clearly wrong, and I shakily hold the phone out in front of me.

"What's going on?" Jaxon stares at my phone for a moment before accepting it.

"Finn. He needs to talk to you."

"Hey, man, sorry I didn't answer. Is everything okay?" he asks as he brings the phone to his ear. I take a moment to catch my breath. As I watch his smile fall and the color drain from his face, I know my news will have to wait. Everything happens so fast that I nearly get whiplash.

"We'll meet you there." Jaxon quickly rises to his feet, nearly knocking over the chair. "We have to go." He reaches into his wallet and throws some bills on the table.

I'm grabbing my bag from the back of the chair and look up to see Jaxon all the way by the front door.

I double my pace to catch up with him by his truck. By the time I make it there, he's hunched over with his palm on the driver's-side door. I rush to his side and move my hand in circular motions on his back.

"Jaxon, breathe. Breathe, baby. What is it? Tell me what's wrong?" My voice breaks, but whatever it is, I need to be strong for him.

He looks over, his dark eyes shimmering with unshed tears, and it shatters my heart into a million pieces.

"It's Andy. They're headed to the hospital."

Chapter 31

Jaxon

My truck wasn't fully turned off before I had exited the vehicle and ran toward the main entrance to the emergency room. I know it may have been an asshole move, but I didn't even look back to make sure Kate had kept up with me. My sole focus was on my son—I should have been there. I shouldn't have been out. If I had been there, this wouldn't have happened.

I race through the doors and straight up to the desk. "My son, where is he?" I demand. The nurse sitting at the desk jumps back, startled at my tone.

"Sir, how can I help you?"

"My son. Where is he? His godfather brought him in, and I need to see him." I slam my fist on the desk, and she flinches.

"Sir, I really need you to calm down. Otherwise, I'm going to need you to leave."

I run my palms over my face and grunt before gripping the edge of the counter. Kate's hand covers mine, her thumb rubbing back and forth, trying to soothe me. While yes, it is comforting, it's getting us nowhere. *I need to see Andy.*

I jerk my hand out of hers, not wanting to get distracted. Out of the corner of my eye, I see a security guard approaching the counter to investigate the commotion.

I take a few calming breaths to avoid being hauled away in handcuffs. "Ma'am, my son was brought in earlier. I need to know that he's okay. His name is Andrew McAdams." I plead, my voice on the edge of breaking.

"Okay, sir. Give me just a moment to find something out for you." She focuses her attention on her computer screen, and I rapidly tap my fingers on the counter.

"Jax," someone calls out from my right. I turn to see my best friend running toward me.

"Finn, what's going on? Where's Andy? Is he okay?" I brace myself, gripping onto his shoulders. My chest is tightening. I've already lost his mother. I can't lose him, too. He's all I have.

"He's okay. We were outside playing after dinner, and he fell. He broke his arm, but Jax, he's fine."

I should have been there.

"Where is he? I need to see him." I try to steady my nerves.

Finn's attention turns next to me, and he gives a weak smile. "Come on, he's back here. Lauren is sitting with him." The double doors swing open, and I race back there, not even caring that Finn and Kate are behind me. I look around as I race to the next desk.

"Andrew McAdams," I shout to the nurse.

She points to the corner room with the curtain pulled. I don't bother announcing myself before entering. I pull the curtain back to find Lauren lying on the bed with Andy in her arms. Her eyes open and meet mine. Those eyes are so similar to the ones I stared into tonight when I wasn't there for my son.

There's a moment just before a tsunami hits that the waterline recedes from the shore as the wave gathers. When it finally has enough momentum, it crashes along the shore, uncaring of the destruction it causes in its wake. That's what my guilt feels like.

She leans down and says softly, "Hey, look who's here."

Andy stirs, only slightly opening his eyes. "Daddy?" His voice is so quiet.

"Hey, buddy, I'm here."

I walk over to the bed and take Lauren's place. She squeezes my arm as she gets out of the way. I maneuver myself onto the bed—these things are definitely not made for men my size.

I gently gather Andy into my arms, avoiding his arm that is currently wrapped in an Ace bandage. I kiss the top of his head and feel the tear slide down my cheek. I can't believe I wasn't there for him. I have never *not* been there for him.

There are soft voices floating through the room. While I can't tell what they're saying, I recognize the voices to be Kate, Lauren, and Finn. Eventually they step outside, leaving Andy and I alone. I lie there with my eyes closed, feeling the evening out of Andy's breathing and syncing it with my own. The chaotic noise of a bustling emergency room reminds me I'm lying in a hospital bed with my son instead of in my bed at home.

I press a kiss to the top of his head and quietly get up. Once on my feet, I stretch from side to side. Those beds really are shit. I hope we're not here much longer, wanting to get him home. Andy looks so small and frail in this bed. My shoulders slump in defeat.

I slip past the curtain and squint while my eyes adjust to the bright lights. The lights were softer and dimmer in Andy's room to allow him to rest. Arms wrap around my waist, and I stiffen.

"How is he? Is he okay? What did the doctor say?" I look down and meet Kate's brown eyes. The redness and glassy glaze tell me she had been crying. I grip her wrists and pull them off me before taking a step back. Lauren and Finn have since joined us.

"The doctor hasn't been in yet." My voice is flat.

Kate takes a step closer, concern laced on her features, and I take another step back.

"I think it's best you go home."

The concern turns to hurt. "What?" She takes a step closer to me, gripping onto my forearms. "I'm not leaving you. I'm staying right here till he can go home."

"No." I yank my arms from her grasp. "I want you to go. There's nothing else you can do here."

I glance at Finn for help. He nods. "Baby, here, take my keys. Why don't you drive Kate back to the house? I'll stay here with Jax and Andy." He presses a kiss to his wife's forehead before handing her his car keys.

Lauren's shoulders sink. "Okay." She places her hand on Kate's shoulder. "Come on. I'll drive."

Kate holds my gaze as tears stream down her cheeks, but I'm the first to break it. I exhale, looking down at the floor, and put my hands in my pockets to keep from reaching for her. I can't look at her anymore. Distracted by her once before, I let my own happiness distract me from my number one priority—my son. I won't allow myself to do it again.

Lauren gives me a brief smile and wraps her arm around her sister's shoulder before leading her down the hallway. Finn steps up beside me. "Come on, Jax. Let's go back inside and wait for the doctor."

Chapter 32

Kate

I've nearly worn a hole in the floor of Jaxon's living room by the time headlights shine through the front window, letting us know they're finally home.

After we left the hospital and made a pit stop at Lauren's house to grab Andy's things, I used the spare key Jaxon had given me to let us into his house. I've been a mess of nerves waiting for news. Thankfully, Finn has been keeping Lauren in the loop. Andy's arm has a small hairline fracture and will need to be put in a cast for eight weeks. I know Jaxon has his hands full at the moment, which is why I didn't take his radio silence personally.

I rush to the front door, letting out a sigh of relief as I open the door to find Finn propping the storm door open for Jaxon. Andy is asleep in his arms with a temporary cast on his left arm.

Finn gives me a weak smile, but Jaxon brushes past me and heads for the stairs.

"Hey, I swapped the sheets for Andy's favorite on his bed and have it all ready for him."

Jaxon freezes and glances over his shoulder but doesn't meet my gaze. "He's going to be with me in my bed."

"Oh, of course." I watch Jaxon retreat up the stairs and out of view. *Should I follow him and help? Does he even want my help?* I've felt helpless for hours.

A hand on my shoulder breaks my train of thought. I turn to find Finn. "Hey, it's okay. He'll be back down in a few. Come on." He tilts his head toward the kitchen, and I nod before watching him lead Lauren that way, hand in hand.

I'm about to follow them when I remember I left Andy's stuffed animal in the car. I swipe Lauren's keys from the coffee table and run out, grabbing it from the back seat. After depositing the keys back where I found them, I jog up the stairs, expecting to run into Jaxon, but when I enter his room, it's empty sans Andy, who is curled up on his dad's side of the bed with his arm resting on top of a pillow.

I softly pad my way over to the side of the bed and take a seat, careful not to disturb his arm. Finn had told Lauren that they gave Andy some pain medicine before they left that would help him sleep for a while, so he doesn't even stir with the dip of the bed.

I brush a few stray hairs off his forehead. When my eyes dip down to his arm, I press my lips together to suppress a sob. I hate this for him. "Don't worry, little dude. I'll be sure to draw all your favorite things once you get your cast on." I'm thinking maybe dinosaurs wearing capes. Andy is so brave, the bravest kid I know. Leaning forward, I kiss his forehead. "I'll be back up soon. I love you."

Raised voices come from the kitchen as I approach.

"Jaxon, you have no idea how sorry I am that this happened on my watch," my sister says. Her voice is shaky, and I know she's crying. I'm not sure who was more of a mess the past few hours—her for her guilt that this happened while she and Finn were watching him or me worried about him and Jaxon.

"No, it's not your fault. Andy is my responsibility. I shouldn't have been distracted." His voice is strained. I know he blames himself for this, but that word "distracted" and the way he says it… I see the undertone of his words.

I step into the kitchen. "I'm sorry I was such a distraction to you. In case you forgot, tonight was your idea. In fact, I wasn't the one to pursue you. It was always you."

He sighs heavily. "That's not what I meant." He holds his hand up and shakes his head. "You know what? When you have kids of your own, you'll understand."

"There's that line again." He's used that exact phrase twice tonight now. What, because I didn't give birth to the child means I can't care about them and love them as if they were my own?

"It's nothing personal, Kate." The way he says my name sends the same feeling through my veins as it did in our first meeting, full of disdain and annoyance. "Until you have kids of your own, you will never fully understand what I'm going through right now."

"Well, I guess the joke's on you, asshole." There's no more hiding the hurt and the anger. Jaxon looks confused, of course, because we were interrupted just as I was about to tell him. "I can't have kids, so I guess I never have to worry about feeling like that."

"What?" He gasps and takes a step toward me, but I retreat. I wince when I back directly into the corner of the counter, but the pain radiating through my back is nothing compared to the pain in my heart.

This wasn't how I wanted to tell him. But then again, life doesn't always go as we planned. We don't ever expect change or loss to disrupt our lives, but I learned long ago to just accept it.

People will pity me if they find out, so I've always just pretended I didn't want kids than tell them the truth. And that fear I've had is written all over Jaxon's face. My worst nightmare come true.

"No, I don't want your sympathy." I use his own words against him.

"Kate," he pleads. I've never hated my name more than hearing it on his lips. Sorrow swirls in his eyes.

"What, now that you know my deep dark secret, is that supposed to change what you just said? Change how you feel? No, you put those words out there, and now you have to deal with its consequences. It was a mistake to get involved with you—to think that this wouldn't blow up in our faces, especially when we're connected in so many ways. I might be forced to see you around, but I'm choosing to end this and walk away. I'm done."

I storm out of the house without a second glance, leaving the pieces of my broken heart behind.

I'm lost in my thoughts as I stare out the front window at the house across the street. Memories replay in my mind—chasing Andy around, watching Jaxon do yard work, and squaring off in the road numerous times.

There's been no movement there lately. The blinds are still drawn, giving no sign of life. I sigh and cross my arms as a chill washes over me.

Warm, strong arms wrap around my waist, and the sadness I felt moments ago vanishes.

"I'm sorry," his deep voice whispers in my ear.

I close my eyes and will the tears away.

"Look at me," he pleads.

I spin to face him—those blue eyes I've fallen so deeply in love with draw me in with a gentle but hesitant smile.

He knows he took it too far.

I only give a weak smile in return before looking away. Jaxon pinches my chin with his thumb and forefinger, lifting it so my gaze can't waver.

"Hey, I said I'm sorry. Can you ever forgive me?"

My mind reels over our fight. I can't just let him off the hook that easily. What he did hurt me.

Jaxon pouts, and his expression is identical to Andy's—no DNA test needed.

"I don't know that I can." My voice is void of emotion.

"Baby," he pleads.

"Jaxon." My voice raises. "You ate the last of the Reese's Puffs cereal, knowing that it's all I crave these days."

My hormones have been a raging mess lately. This is clearly karma for all the times I laughed at Dani and Haylee crying while watching coffee commercials while pregnant. I know I owe them a sincere apology.

"Well then, I hope you're in a forgiving mood because…" He reaches behind him and grabs a bag on the coffee table I hadn't noticed before to reveal a fresh box of cereal.

Emotions threaten to choke me. Fuck off, hormones—crying over fucking cereal.

Jaxon sets the box back on the table before dropping to his knees and pressing his lips against my swollen stomach.

"Hey, little one in there. I know Daddy upset Mommy earlier, and you've been giving her some trouble ever since." True story—this little one has been practicing karate all morning. "But I promise I made it up to her." He lifts his gaze back to mine, his eyes darkening to my favorite shade of midnight blue. "And if she's still mad…" He rises to his feet. " I promise to make it up after bedtime using my tongue on her sensitive parts to communicate just how sorry I am." He breathes the last four words against my neck in between kisses.

Goose bumps pepper my flesh, and I can feel my cheeks flush. If I wasn't already seven months pregnant, I'm pretty sure I would be from his words alone.

I gasp, waking up. My hand flies to my stomach, which is still flat, not swollen with a child like in the dream. Sweat coats my skin, and I brush the fallen strands from my messy bun off my forehead.

It was just a dream. It was only a dream. The pain in my heart was gone, and the fluttering in my stomach felt so real.

I glance beside me to find my sister sleeping peacefully, a stark reminder of last night's events. She followed me to my house and refused to leave my side. Sometime around two in the morning, I let the mental, emotional, and physical take over, and I passed out, only to let my emotions get the better of me in my dreams.

Sleep evades me the rest of the night, leaving me in the silence. If only my mind were that quiet. It's in the silence that my thoughts consume me. The what-ifs that forever haunt me.

When the sun shines through the cracks in the blinds, I carefully slip out of bed so as not to disturb my sister. When my mind is racing like this, there is only one place I can think of to go. After a quick shower and throwing on a fresh pair of clothes, I grab my keys and am out the door. Eventually, Lauren will figure it out, but I need a moment to myself to process it all.

Chapter 33

I'm not sure which weighed heavier on my chest—the dad guilt of my son getting hurt while not on my watch or Kate's words: *I can't have kids.* Either way, I spent the entire night restless. The one time I calmed my mind enough to close my eyes, Andy had woken up ready for his next dose of medicine.

When I hear shuffling downstairs, I decide it's time to stop hiding and get out of bed.

Last night, after Kate ran out and Lauren chased after her—something I should've done, but I was still in such shock, processing what she said—Finn had said that he was staying in case I needed help.

I walk downstairs, completely in a daze and exhausted. I scrub my hands down my face as I enter the kitchen. A figure out of the corner of my eye forces me to stop in my tracks. She's standing in front of the sink, staring out at the backyard. Her hair is in a messy bun on top of her head and that oversized hoodie she always wears. Is my mind playing tricks on me? Had I actually fallen asleep and this was all a dream?

My heart catches in my throat. I want to run to her, swoop her into my arms, and never let her go.

"Kate," I whisper.

Slowly, she turns around, but then reality hits me like an eighteen-wheeler—it's not Kate; it's Lauren. I press my hand to my chest, trying to relieve that pang in my heart. *Did I really just confuse the two of them? Wait, when did she get here? Is Kate here, too?*

Blinking hard, I shake the thoughts from my mind. "Sorry, I just thought—" No need to finish the sentence. I look around to see if she's here, but of course, I come up empty. Why would she be here? She made it very clear last night that she was done with me. I hang my head, avoiding her gaze.

"No, it's my fault. I didn't have anything else to change into from last night's clothes, so I stole these from her closet." She glances down at her outfit, and she pulls her bottom lip between her teeth nervously. "I'm sorry to barge in. I just came over to get my purse and keys. I ran out of here last night and didn't think to grab them."

I nod. There were other things on her mind, like her sister.

I walk over to the coffee maker. I don't know if it was Finn or Lauren who brewed an entire pot already, but I could kiss whoever did it in thanks.

How is she? is on the tip of my tongue, but before I can ask it, Finn strolls into the kitchen.

"Good morning." He stalks over and kisses Lauren's temple. "By the way, remind me to buy you a better couch. I slept like shit." He cranes his neck from side to side and sighs when a loud pop cracks.

"Do you plan on sleeping on my couch often?" I reply.

He holds his finger up. "Touché. It's still shit."

I try not to impose on their private conversation, even though they're standing in *my kitchen.* When he cups her cheek with his palm, she leans into his touch. I turn back toward the counter and grip the surface, looking down at the ground. Was it really only twenty-four hours ago that Kate and I were in a similar position?

God, this is so fucked-up. I wish I could go back in time and savor that moment. No, that's not where I would go back in time. I would rewind it to last night and tell her I needed her by my side at the hospital, watch as she comforted my son in my bed and stood here with me this morning.

"Well, I should go. I'll see you guys later." Lauren gives a weak smile in my direction and rushes out the door.

"Did you know?" I ask after taking a long sip of my coffee. I don't even bother with cream and sugar this morning, just needing the strong, bitter taste as an additional umph to wake me up.

Finn stares off into nowhere, so I repeat the question.

He shakes his head and presses his lips together. "I knew she had issues when we were younger, like late high school/early college age, but I did not know the extent of it."

I let out a harsh breath and close my eyes. I can't even put into words the pain I feel for her. Why did she not tell me? Here I was going on last night, telling her that when she has kids of her own and that I saw one day having more kids with her. The pieces all fall into place from last night before everything went to shit. What a whirlwind twenty-four hours it's been.

"Hey, take all the time you need. I can figure things out at work. You just focus on my godson, okay?"

"No. It's fine. I mean, we have an appointment tomorrow to get his cast set, but I called Court's parents last night at the hospital when you stepped out of the room. They're moving their trip up sooner and arriving tomorrow evening. So I should be able to be back in the office on Tuesday."

"Well, take all the time you need."

"Daddy," Andy calls out behind us. I look up to find Andy standing in the hallway.

"What are you doing out of bed, buddy?" I set my mug down behind me and walk over, scooping him carefully up in my arms, avoiding his wrapped arm.

"I woke up, and you weren't there." His lip sticks out, and tears fill his eyes.

"I'm sorry, Andy. I'm so sorry." My voice breaks as I hold him tightly. Once again, I let him down. "Are you hungry or thirsty? Anything you want and it's yours."

"Anything?" His eyebrows raise to the ceiling. *Oh boy.* I nod. "Could I have ice cream?" His voice gets higher when he says ice cream, as if he thinks I will say no but just wants to test the waters. I'd make him a whole ice cream buffet now if it meant he felt better.

I carry Andy over to his seat at the table and set him down. "One bowl of ice cream coming up."

"Where's Miss Kate?"

I freeze, leaning into the freezer to grab the carton. "Umm, she's not here."

"Why not? I had a crazy dream, and I wanted to tell her all about it."

Finn takes a seat beside him. "She had some things she needed to take care of this morning with Auntie Lo." Where was she when Lauren was here this morning? Was she home? "Can you tell me about it?"

He gives a small smile in my direction as I mouth, *Thank you.*

"There were dancing paintbrushes and singing brooms." He is so animated as he tells Finn about the story. His face lights up the room.

"What kind of meds did the doctor give him?" Finn chuckles.

I set the bowl of ice cream with an additional scoop than normal in front of Andy.

"Wow." As Andy is still in awe of the bowl in front of him, Finn swoops in and steals a spoonful. "Hey," Andy shouts, pouting.

"Sorry, little man. It looked too good. You're one lucky boy. Auntie Lo would never let me have ice cream for breakfast."

His frown transforms into a smug smile and, with his healthy arm, pats Finn on the arm. "Don't worry, Uncle Finn, I'll talk to her. She loves me." Where did this confidence come from in my son? Watching my best friend get schooled by a four-year-old is a pleasant distraction from my thoughts, but I know I can't avoid them for forever.

Chapter 34

Kate

Each time the ball releases from the machine, I channel my emotions through the bat as it comes into contact with the ball. I've been here at the batting cage since before it even opened. I was sitting in the parking lot already when Trevor pulled his old Chevy into the spot beside me. One look at my face and he told me to take all the time I needed today.

I'm angry for the children who have to grow up without a parent like Andy.

Clink.

I'm angry for the women who miss out on raising their children like Courtney.

Clink.

I'm angry for the women who dreamed of one day holding their child, of feeling them kick, but never get the chance to, like me.

Clink.

No one prepares you for the anger and emotions that sink in as you process at only nineteen that you'll never have kids. You're supposed to be living life and making stupid decisions. As a teenager, I suffered from severe pain and cramping during my periods. One day in college, I was doubled over in pain so fierce I could barely breathe. It felt as if my insides were being ripped out like in some cheap horror film. When I started bleeding, my mom insisted I get rushed to the emergency room. By the time I arrived, a fever had spiked.

We learned I had severe endometriosis with fibroids lining my uterus. One of the fibroids ruptured, causing the bleeding. It was rare to happen, but I guess I'm just lucky like that. My mom and sister held my hands as the doctors informed me an emergency total hysterectomy needed to be performed to stop the bleeding. I watched the dreams my sister and I talked about as kids of being pregnant together slip through my fingers. It took years to process it. Hell, I still don't even understand it. But I learned to stop asking *why* to questions I would never get answered.

I know there are plenty of options out there—adoption or surrogacy in some form—but there's something about being told as a woman you can never bear your own child that makes you feel broken in ways you never imagined.

For years, I've watched everyone around me move forward in their life—marriage, babies, their happily ever after. I was honest and truly happy for them. I have enough love to give my nieces and nephews to last a lifetime.

For the first time, I saw that for myself, though. And it was all ripped out from under me. There was something about Jaxon that made me believe, but I was a fool.

I've lost count of the number of times the bat has come in contact with the ball. Since I arrived, I've only missed six. Maybe if art doesn't work out, I have an excellent shot at the minor leagues.

"I figured this was where I'd find you," my sister calls out. I quickly glance over my shoulder to see her leaning forward against the fence, a tray with two fresh coffees in one hand from my favorite coffeehouse.

Clink.

"Hey, Baby Ruth," Lauren shouts, making a *Sandlot* joke, but it just makes my heart hurt, thinking of Andy. "Why don't you take a break for a minute?"

"Nah, I'm good," I call back.

Clink.

I'm angry as I play out last night's events.

Clink.

Clink

Clink.

Time feels like it slows down while my heartbeat increases to a rate that has me panting as if I ran a marathon. My skin feels clammy, and my grip on the bat loosens. My throat is so dry it's hard to swallow as I gasp for air. I run my hand over my chest and try to even out my breathing. I took my focus off the machine for a split second, and that second was too long. The ball releases, and before I can move out of the way, it hits me right on my back.

I wince at the sharp pain that vibrates through my body and drop the bat, dropping to my knees.

"Shit, fuck," Lauren shouts as she opens the gate and presses the red emergency shutoff button to turn the machine off before rushing to my side.

"Oh my God, are you okay?"

The tears fall, and I can't stop them. "It hurts, Laur."

"Let me look at it." She attempts to lift my shirt in the back, but I pull out of her grasp.

"No, not that." The pain on the inside is far worse than any superficial wound. It feels like I'm grieving all over again. This time, not only am I grieving the loss I endured, I'm grieving their loss, our loss. It's all just too much. Lauren comforts me as I let it all out. After a few minutes, my breathing calms slightly.

"Come on." She pushes up to her feet and reaches a hand out to help me up. "Let's go sit and talk."

"I'm not really up for talking."

"Well, I'm not asking." Her voice is stern.

I stand and let her lead me over to a picnic table that sits just off to the side of the cages. I wipe my sleeve under my eye as the tears continue to fall.

"I don't know what's wrong with me—it's not like we were together all that long."

"Don't you dare do that," Lauren scolds as she sets her drink back down.

"Do what?"

"Don't downplay your feelings like they don't matter."

I throw my head back and let out a harsh, awkward laugh. "Why? He did."

A somber cloud hangs between us. Lauren reaches over and squeezes my hand. I avoid looking at her, staring off into the sky as if it holds all the answers.

"He's scared and hurting. His son was in the hospital."

"Jesus, Lauren, whose side are you on?"

"Yours, dumbass, always yours. But what I'm saying is he feels guilty over something that he had no control over." I know she's only trying to play devil's advocate. This entire situation can't be easy on her or Finn. I don't want either of them to feel like they need to take sides and create a rift in their relationship.

"No control over? He may not have controlled the situation itself, but he *did* have control over his reaction. God," I scream, no longer caring if I cause a scene. "I fucking hate this."

"If it makes you feel better, he's a fucking mess. I had to go over there this morning to grab my purse, and he actually thought I was you because I was wearing that stupid hoodie of yours." She presses her lips together as if she's deciding to say more. "There was a moment of hope and regret in his eyes before he realized it was me, and then he just looked so dejected."

Good. He should feel like shit for how he acted.

"No, it doesn't make me feel better. I don't care."

Lauren slams her hand down on the table, nearly knocking over her drink. "You know you can lie to everyone and even lie to yourself, but you can't lie to me. You forget, we are basically the same person. When you hurt, I hurt." She gets up and walks around to sit beside me.

"If you think this is easy on me to see you feeling this way, it's not. It doesn't matter who the other person is—Finn's best friend or the damn king of England. I know him pushing you away hurt when all you wanted to do was be there for him and Andy. I know his words were a stark reminder of everything you've been through. But you also can't hold that against him because he didn't know.

"I know how bad you are hurting because I feel it right here." She presses a hand over her heart. "Remember, it wasn't long ago that you reminded me that when I love, I love with everything in my heart. You won't show it, and I get why you always keep yourself so guarded, but I know you are the same way. You didn't need to be there for that little boy. After the way Jax acted since you guys met, you could have left him to figure shit out on his own. You let them in that little black heart of yours—both of them. And it fucking terrifies you."

"Of course it does. Look where it got me."

"Do you think love is easy?" she snaps, and my eyes widen at the word—*love*. "Look at Finn and me. Shit, look at Dani and Kyler and Zach and Haylee. Look at what we've all been through, and we came out on the other side. Opening up to someone makes you vulnerable and realizing that you always risk losing them, and sometimes it's fully out of your control—whether it's a miscommunication, loss, or pure stubbornness.

"And don't tell me you don't love that man. And you know how I know it?"

I shake my head, afraid that if I open my mouth, I'll admit she's right. I don't exactly know the moment I fell in love with Jaxon. Maybe it's been festering for a while. But I knew that if I hadn't loved him, I wouldn't have wanted to tell him about me last night.

"Because if you didn't love him, you wouldn't feel this way. Think of all those dumbasses in the past. You never thought of opening up to them about this. The past few weeks, Finn and I have both watched our best friends turn into the best version of themselves. Plus, I think if love was easy, then Paloma Faith wouldn't have that hit song."

I groan, but a smile graces my lips. "You're so stupid."

"Hey, but one, it got you to smile, and two, you didn't deny it."

"I don't need to."

"Don't you have that painting being shipped up north?" I nod. "I know you typically just ship them, but maybe it would be a good idea to—"

I interject. "I'm not running away." She raises a brow, challenging my comment. Yeah, so I ran away last night, but that was different. I can't run away and avoid this forever. I love my house too much to move out of my house, and I can't exactly put out an ad for a new best friend for my brother-in-law.

"I know you're not. But maybe it wouldn't hurt to deliver it yourself. Give you a few days to just clear your head."

"Yeah, maybe."

Lauren wraps her arms around me and squeezes tightly. "I love you, Kate. You are stronger than you even realize."

Lauren's words replay in my mind as we sit in silence. But am I strong enough to live across the street from the man I love and the future I dreamed of but can never have? I guess only time will tell.

Chapter 35

Jaxon

"**I**s Miss Kate coming over soon? I want her to meet Grammy and Pop and show her my cool cast." He holds his arm up in the air, which is now wrapped in bright red material. *Let's see if he still thinks it's cool once his arm itches under there.*

Courtney's parents, Victor and Sidney, arrived just after we got back from the doctors. It had been a long day for everyone, so we voted on ordering takeout for dinner. Since they arrived, Andy has talked their ears off, showing them everything there is to see, including where we keep the spare toilet paper and where the trash cans are. Victor joked on the tour that, hopefully, there wouldn't be a quiz later. I was thankful that their arrival kept him busy so that he didn't ask for Kate once again. He's asked three more times since yesterday morning. I guess my luck has run out.

"Who's Kate?" Victor says beside Andy.

"That's Daddy's girlfriend." I freeze, and my eyes bounce back and forth between Sid and Victor to see their reaction. This wasn't exactly how I planned to tell them I was seeing someone. Although shit, after everything, can I even still call her mine?

"Is she nice?" Victor leans on his elbow closer to Andy.

"Oh yes, she's the best. She looks just like Auntie Lo. She likes to dance and taught me how to draw. She even got me to try scrapple. It's yummy. Pop, do you like scrapple?"

I chuckle at Victor's reaction. "Can't say that I've ever had it."

"Daddy, can we get some at the store? Miss Kate knows how to make it."

Victor must be able to sense the growing tension in the room with my lack of response.

"Andy, why don't we go into the living room and put on some TV? I need you to help me with it. You know us old guys can't figure out technology," Victor teases, helping Andy out of his chair.

"Pop, you're not that old," Andy giggles, and my father-in-law glances over his shoulder, giving his wife a knowing look.

"That kid is good for his ego," Sidney laughs once they're out of view. She then turns to me. "So a girlfriend, huh? Seems like a lot has changed since the last time we spoke."

"I'm sorry. This wasn't exactly how I wanted you to find out." My hand cups my mouth, rubbing back and forth over my stubble.

"What are you apologizing for?" she asks.

I let out an awkward laugh. *What exactly am I apologizing for?* "Well, I'm honestly not that sure."

"It's been almost five years since my daughter left us. Not a day goes by that I don't miss her, and I know it's the same for you. I've watched you keep yourself closed off. It's okay to move on—to open yourself up to the idea of loving someone again. I watched you love my daughter for years. I know how much love you have in you. Someone deserves to receive that love. Is it new?"

"Umm, not exactly. Well, sort of." I grip the back of my neck and feel a fresh wave of guilt wash over me. It appears as if I had been keeping Kate as my dirty little secret. But that's not the case at all.

"Jaxon Everett McAdams! You better not be hiding her—that girl deserves better."

I nod because there's no contest there. She does deserve better than me.

"Now, tell me about her. Andy said she looks like Auntie Lo? That's Finn's wife, right?"

"Yes, she's actually Lauren's twin sister."

"Oh, I see. Well then, I guess I don't have to ask where you two met. So tell me all about her."

I start from the beginning, telling her everything, from the first meeting to just the other day. Well, not everything—I leave out certain X-rated details that no mother-in-law needs to hear about.

She's engaged, and never once does she judge me. She gasps in surprise every so often and even laughs. Seeing her so interested to know more makes me wonder why I ever doubted telling her about Kate and me in the first place.

"Kate sounds wonderful. Why don't you invite her to join us for dinner tomorrow? I would love to meet her."

"That's the thing. I'm not sure I can call her my girlfriend anymore. I sort of fucked up."

"Well, you're a man. You're bound to fuck up now and then." I nearly choke on air at her words. "What?" She shrugs with a smile. "I've been married to that jackass in there"—she points to the living room—"for forty years. Now, tell me what happened. Maybe a fresh pair of ears can offer perspective."

I fill her in on our fight.

"Raising a child is scary and hard, and I'll never understand why my daughter was taken from this world too soon, but that boy in there deserves a mother. Someone to be there for him, teach him, hold him, comfort him, and love him as if he were her own. I've only spent a short time hearing about this woman, first from Andy and now from you, but I can already tell she's special."

"How can you tell?"

"Well, for one, she's the first woman you have ever entertained something with." She reaches over and places her hand over mine. "It's okay to be scared, Jax. Nothing worth having and fighting for comes easy."

"What if I can't do it?"

"That's the thing, Jax. You won't have to do it alone anymore. You two become a team; you communicate. But you have to let her in. It's clear that she loves that child, and I'm thinking she loves you, too."

"It's too soon, though, right?"

"There's no timetable for falling in love, just as it is the same with grief. I can recall numerous times that my daughter said she fell in love with you the moment she saw you."

It was the same for me.

"And just like you said, you saw a future with her. Will you do me a favor?"

I nod.

"Close your eyes." Is she serious? She arches her brow, challenging me. "Just do it." I close my eyes. "Now, picture your life five years from now. Can you imagine your life without her?"

"No." One word has so much weight to it. When I open my eyes, Sidney is smiling.

"That's what I thought." She rises from her seat. "You need to talk to her and fix this between the two of you. Because think about it this way: your friendship with Finn will tie the two of you together for the rest of your lives. Unless you plan on losing your friendship with him, are you willing to let her walk away and find someone else who is going to swoop in and steal her heart?"

At the thought, my fists flexed. My mind goes back to New Year's when I watched that douchebag kissing her. My blood boils all over again—Kate Lawson is mine. "What if she won't talk to me?"

"She might not, but you'll never know until you try." She double pats my shoulder as she leaves the room, leaving me to my thoughts.

Chapter 36

Kate

I focus on my hands as I rinse the lathered soap off them. After drying them on the hand towel beside me, I bring my hands up to my nose and inhale the sweet aroma of vanilla cupcakes and frosting.

I close my eyes and fight back the tears as a memory of Andy and his love of this soap comes to the forefront of my mind.

I heard the bathroom door open as I waited for Andy on the couch. His loud sobs rang out as he rushed into my open arms. I scooped him into my arms and tried to calm his tears.

"Andy, what's wrong? Did you hurt yourself? Did you burn yourself with hot water?" I looked over every inch of him with worry. I didn't see any visible marks, but I knew that didn't mean shit.

Andy wiped his nose with his sleeve while I brushed his hair off his face and dried a few fallen tears. He held on to me tightly, and in between his sobs, he finally spoke.

"You have the best-smelling soap, just like the kind Auntie Lo buys. And I thought—" Oh boy. I covered my teeth with my lips to hide my growing smile. I didn't want him to think I was laughing at him and to get even more upset. I had a feeling I knew exactly where this conversation was leading. "—I thought that maybe if it smelled so sweet that it tasted sweet, too."

A small giggle slipped from my lips, and I quickly tried to hide it by holding him closer to my chest. I ran my hand in a circular motion on his back to try to soothe him.

"Aww, Andy." I remembered being a little kid, and when one of us wouldn't listen, we got soap in the mouth. Of course, me being the mouthier of all of us, I got it the most. My parents used that nasty generic Dial soap. I couldn't imagine that even if the soap had smelled much better, it wouldn't even come close to tasting decent.

"You know, I think there might be a box of cupcake mix in the pantry. What do you say we whip up a batch? If you don't tell your dad, I'll even let you be the taste tester and bet that will help get that gross taste out of your mouth."

Andy's eyes lit up as if I hung the moon, and, well, right about now, he hung mine. "Can we add sprinkles on top?"

The smile on his face made me laugh. Clearly, the mention of cupcakes had taken the soap incident far from his mind. "I think we might be able to work out a deal with the sprinkles." I winked.

Andy hopped off my lap in a flash and did a little happy dance. His tears were clearly a thing of the past.

I don't even remember picking up the soap bottle, but here I am staring at the shiny pink label with the hand-drawn cupcake in the center. I hover it over the trash can, deciding whether or not to throw the bottle out, even though it isn't near empty in the least.

Will everything in this house be a constant reminder?

I set the soap back on the sink and walk out of the room, heading back to my bedroom. With a bit of convincing from my sister, I decided to deliver the painting to just get away to clear my head.

Searching in my closet for a bag to take, I find the blue gift bag on the top shelf—Andy's birthday present.

What is Andy doing? How is he coping? What did Jaxon tell him as to why I haven't been around?

I don't want him to think I abandoned him. I grab the bag from the top of my closet and set it down on my bag. After I finish stuffing the clothes in my suitcase, I glance out the window and see the driveway is empty. I could rush it across the street and leave it on the front porch before my sister arrives to pick me up after she gets done with her day to drop me off at the airport. Now is my chance to drop this off without running into Jaxon.

My hands are shaky as I cross the street. Just as I'm setting the bag down, the front door opens. *Oh shit.* I jump back, nearly tripping over my own two feet.

The front door fully opens to reveal an older woman with ashy blonde hair. "I'm sorry, dear. I didn't mean to frighten you."

"No, I'm sorry. I didn't realize anyone was home. There weren't any vehicles in the driveway." I glance over my shoulder to make sure I hadn't made that up and come up empty.

"Jaxon is at work, and my husband took Andy for some ice cream to get him out of the house. It's Kate, right?" *How does she know my name?*

"Yes…"

She must sense my hesitation. "I'm sorry, where are my manners—I'm Sidney, Andy's grandmother."

"Of course." I shake her hand. That's why she looked so familiar. I had seen her photo on the wall. "It's nice to meet you."

"You too. I've heard a lot about you."

"Oh." My eyes widen slightly. *She has?*

"Would you like to come inside? I just made a fresh batch of lemonade and some brownies." Sidney gestures with her hand to the front door, and anxiety soars through my veins. I wouldn't feel right being inside Jaxon's house without his consent. I know I was when I watched Andy, but that was under different circumstances.

"I don't think that's a good idea. I just wanted to drop this off." I hold up the gift bag toward her. "For Andy. It was supposed to be for his birthday, but I wanted him to have it now. Could you make sure that he gets it?"

Sidney accepts the bag and holds it close to her chest. "Of course."

"Thank you." I turn to head back home, but she speaks up.

"I was actually hoping to get the chance to talk to you."

"You were?" *What could she possibly want to talk to me about? She just met me.*

She nods. "I hope this doesn't sound stalker-like, but I've been watching out the front window, deciding if I should walk over, but then I saw you walking over here, so I took this as a sign."

I laugh softly at her honesty.

"Why don't we have a seat." She holds her hand out toward the porch chairs. I glance back at my house. I guess I have a few more minutes. I'll be able to see when Lauren pulls up. "I promise it won't take long." I turn back to find her giving a hopeful smile. I see glimpses of Andy in that expression, and I already know within moments of meeting her I can't refuse her.

"Sure." I follow her and take a seat.

She takes a few minutes to talk. "The day Courtney and Jax told us they were expecting was one of the happiest days of our lives. Nine months later, she was gone. Jax not only had to learn how to be a parent, but to do it while grieving his loss." Every time I hear this story, my heart breaks more and more for him.

"I hope you don't think I'm trying to replace your daughter," I admit. Sidney's head whips toward me, and she presses her lips together sadly. There's a look in her eyes that I recognize. I've seen it in Haylee's mom Natalie's eyes when I know she is thinking of her late son, Emmett. "All I want is to be there for him and Andy, but things aren't that simple."

"I don't think that at all, dear." She places her hand over mine reassuringly. "Can I ask you a question?" I nod. "Do you love him?"

I nod, afraid of saying the words aloud. Plus, I'm not sure it's fair to say those words to someone other than the person they are for. Not that it really matters anymore. But I love them both very much.

"Then why are you letting him just get away? My son-in-law is stubborn as an ox." I chuckle because I'm not sure that is a big enough analogy. "But he has a big heart. Why not go after him?"

"It's just—it's just—" I stumble over my words and take a calming breath. "It's just complicated. He wants a future I can't give him." After all these years, he said that he finally saw having more kids with someone. If he could develop those thoughts for me, then he can do it for someone else.

"Sweetheart, I don't think he needs whatever you think he needs. He's a pretty simple man. I think there's only one thing that he needs—well, two if you include Andy—and

that's you."

My sister's SUV pulls up in my driveway, and I'm feeling both happy and sad to end this conversation, but at least I have a little more clarity. My head is still a mess. I wish it was as simple as just making one decision. But my decision will be like a domino effect. One wrong move could send everything we've built toppling over.

"Well, that's my cue to go. That's my sister, Lauren, here to pick me up." I rise.

"It was wonderful to meet you, Kate." She pulls me into her arms before I can protest. I'm not sure who needs the hug more, me or her.

After a moment, we pull back, and I turn to head home when she calls my name.

"Don't give up on him just yet, okay?"

I nod and give her a small smile. It's not about me giving up on him. It's about him willing to let me in. I understand the struggles of being a single parent. I may have been a teenager when my parents divorced, but Kyler was still young, so I saw what my mother went through.

Lauren has exited her vehicle and is standing beside it when I approach. "What was that about?"

"It's nothing. I just have to grab my bag." I rush inside to grab my bag by the door and lock up behind me.

"All set?" she asks as I hop in the passenger seat.

"Yep." As Lauren backs up out of the driveway, I replay my conversation with Sidney. Before we reach the airport, I've made up my mind and open my last text message thread with Jaxon.

Me: *I have to go out of town for a few days, but when I get back, we need to talk.*

Once I hit Send, I don't wait for a reply and just toss my phone back in my bag. Maybe he can sweat it out a little more since I used those famous four words every man fears—*we need to talk.*

Chapter 37

We need to talk. Those four words have replayed over and over in my mind since Kate sent them this morning. I had been in a meeting with Finn and asked him where she was headed, and all he said was she was delivering a painting. I have a few days to figure out what I'm going to say to her. I'm not sure what her reaction is going to be. If she kicks me to the curb, I need to have a plan to not let her and fight for her. And if she welcomes me back with open arms—well, I don't really expect that to happen because she's not that simple of a girl.

"Daddy, is Miss Kate going to leave us like Mommy did?" Andy's question catches me off guard as I tuck him into bed.

"Umm, no, buddy." The unshed tears in his eyes nearly split my heart in two.

"Well then, why haven't we seen her? Does she not like us anymore?"

I sigh heavily. *Fuck!* This is another reason I was hesitant to get involved. It's not just me that feels her absence but Andy, too. Kate has been a sort of mother figure to him—the only one he's ever known.

"Things are a little complicated right now." I try to figure out the best way to explain this to a child. "Daddy said some things that made her mad."

"You should tell her you're sorry. When Emme was mad at me because I took her favorite truck, I said sorry, and we went back to playing. Now we're best friends again." *If only it were that easy.* Actually, it is that easy—had I not fucked up in the first place, then all this wouldn't have happened. Where's Doc Brown with a time machine when I need him?

"Uncle Finn said girls are simple. Say sorry and tell them they're pretty."

I let out a loud laugh. *Thank Finn for your words of wisdom, spoken through the eyes of a four-year-old.* "Thanks for the sage advice. I'll keep that in mind."

"Oh, and tell her you love her." He pauses. "Do you love her?"

"Is it okay with you if I do?"

He nods enthusiastically. "Yeah, because I love her, too."

I wrap my arms around Andy. "We'll see her soon, okay?"

Andy smiles. "Great. I need to give her the thank-you card Grammy helped me make today. Maybe she can help you make a card that says I'm sorry."

"A thank-you card?"

"For my present." I'm surprised there wasn't a "duh' said at the end because his tone tells me I should know what present he's referring to.

I furrow my brows. "What present?"

"My book. When I got back from ice cream with Pop, Grammy said she had a present for me from Miss Kate. That she had dropped it off while I was gone."

"Can I see it?" A million questions race through my mind.

Andy throws off the covers and jumps out of bed.

"Be careful," I warn. He's been managing his cast much better than I had. He's only knocked me in the head three times since getting it on. Not even the cast is getting him to slow down, though.

"It's the coolest," Andy says as he rushes back from his bookshelf with a spiral book in hand. He crawls back up under the covers and hands it to me. "Grammy read it all afternoon, but you can read it again. It's my favorite."

I wonder if she had bought this with the plan of reading it to him at bedtime. The image of them curled up reading on the couch comes to the forefront of my mind.

"Look, Daddy, that's me." I read the title, *Andy the Little Dinosaur*, before he flips the pages.

"Oh, his name is Andy. That's pretty neat."

"No, it's me. As a dinosaur. Grammy said that Miss Kate made it." His eyes sparkle with excitement.

She made it? I take the book out of his hands and flip it back to the cover and see the name at the bottom. My heart seems to freeze for a split second as I read, "Written and illustrated by Kate Lawson."

"Daddy, read it to me," he begs.

"All right, all right." I open the first page and laugh when the picture is of a little red dinosaur standing by a tree, peeing. I'm not sure Andy gets the reference, but I do.

"Look, she drew the dinosaur. She was teaching me how to draw. And he went on a walk in the park, down the slide, and even has a tire swing." We turn the pages, each one with a hand-drawn picture of a small red dinosaur doing different activities that we all did.

I cover my mouth with my palm, trying to fight back the emotion. The hard work that she put into this. The love she clearly has for my son right here, staring in front of me.

"Daddy, why are you crying? The story has a happy ending." I flip to the last page to find Andy the dinosaur hugging his mommy and daddy dinosaur.

"I see that. This book is wonderful." I wipe under my eyes, not realizing I had even let the tears fall. "Can I see your thank-you card?"

"Yup, it's right there." He points to the folded-up piece of paper on his nightstand. I reach over and grab it.

"Grammy drew the letters, and I colored them." Bold rainbow letters spell out *Thank you* on the front of the card. When I open it up, *I love you* is spelled in block letters. There are two stick figures holding hands.

An idea comes to mind, one that is going to sweep her off her damn feet right into my arms where she belongs. "Hey, buddy. This card is great. I think she's going to love it. How would you like to help me win Miss Kate's heart back?"

"Yes." He throws his hands up, nearly missing my cheek with his hand.

"Awesome. You get some sleep, and I think Daddy might call Uncle Finn and stay home from work. We have our work cut out for us. Sounds good?"

Andy lies back and closes his eyes. "Good night, Daddy."

"Hey, don't I get a kiss good night?" I mock offense.

"Oopsie." He pops up and kisses me with a loud smack. "Now, go to bed, too, Daddy. Tomorrow, we have to go get our girl."

I laugh at his excitement, but when he lies back down and closes his eyes, I'm pretty sure he's asleep before I even walk out of the room.

I've got my work cut out for me.

I need to make a list of items to get in the morning, but first things first. Before I head back downstairs, I pull my phone from my back pocket. I scroll through my contacts, and my thumb hovers over Kate's name, dying to press it, but I keep scrolling and press Send.

"Hello," the female voice answers.

"Hey, it's Jaxon. I need your help with something." I have to hope that this will work.

"Hey, it's Jaxon. I need your help with something." I have to hope that this will work.

Chapter 38

Kate

I watch the bags pass on the conveyor belt in baggage claim. I knew I shouldn't have checked a bag. With such a quick trip, I should have shoved everything in my carry-on. *You live and you learn.*

Getting away was just what I needed. I may have put distance between Jaxon and me, but he was never far from my mind. But by going on this trip, I got to speak with the client's wife, and she commissioned a dozen more pieces to fill the new building their media company had just purchased. She also said she was going to pass my information to all of her friends, too.

Finally. I sigh and grab my bag from the belt. I make my way out of the terminal to meet my sister.

I let out a loud laugh, scaring the people walking beside me, when I find Lauren standing there holding a sign that reads, "Welcome home from prison, Kate!" Written in large glittery letters, there is definitely no missing this sign. I watch people turn their heads as they pass, reading it and following her line of sight, landing directly on me. It takes a lot for me to be embarrassed, and yep, I can feel my cheeks heat. *Well played, Reynolds.*

Lauren's playful smile only makes me laugh harder. I didn't think it could get any worse, and then she flips the sign over where it reads, "We knew you didn't kill and eat those people. You're a vegetarian."

Oh, for fuck's sake. I let out a frustrated little groan at her shenanigans, dropping my head back. I will definitely need an amazing form of payback.

After an enthusiastic, happy dance, she drops the sign to her sign and makes a show of closing the distance between us. She runs to hug me as if it had years since she last saw me and not just a few days.

"Ahh, I'm so glad to hug you finally. I'm sorry—they never should have convicted you, even if the evidence was plain as day. I knew you didn't do it." Her volume is about three decibels higher than normal.

She sways us side to side with her overdramatic hug. "Really playing this whole thing up, huh?" I laugh, welcoming her embrace.

"You bet your ass I am," she laughs as she pulls back. "Now, what do you say we get you home?"

She leads us to the parking garage with eyes on us the whole way. One woman even pulled her son closer to her as we passed. *I'm going to kill you, Laur.* After refusing my money to cover the fee for the garage, she pays the attendant, and we are on our way.

I pull my aviators down over my eyes as Lauren maneuvers her way onto the highway.

"Umm, Laur, did you forget where I live?" I interrupt our singing performance when she passes the exit to my house.

She giggles and turns the music down a notch. "Oh shit, sorry. No, I didn't forget," she retorts. "But I *did* forget that I need to make a stop."

"You forgot till now?"

She shrugs. "Yeah, sorry. Hope you don't mind."

"Well, since I'm in the passenger seat of *your* vehicle and you already passed my exit, I think it's safe to say I don't really have a choice in the matter now, do I?"

"Nope," she says with a loud popping noise. She winks and turns the music back up, letting Walker Hayes fill the vehicle and focus back on the road.

I sink back into my seat, feeling a little like a hostage, and prop my elbow on the window as my sister taps the steering wheel to the beat.

I should have just taken an Uber home, but I guess I can't complain about the slight detour. The town passes by as I stare out the window. Further and further away from home. Further and further away from Jaxon.

I waited with bated breath for a response that never came. I guess I shouldn't really have expected one. This isn't a conversation to have over text. But the longer the silence went on, the more the anxieties circled in my mind.

What if this wasn't what he wanted?

What if he realized that the need to father more children was more important than the need to be with me?

I also wondered if Sidney had given Andy the book I made. I hope she did and that he loved it. I wish I could have seen his smiling face as he went through each page and recalled our memories together.

Lauren veers off the exit ramp and turns right, heading into downtown.

She pulls in front of a brick building. *Where the fuck are we?*

"Should I be concerned? What is this place? Was there some sort of truth to your ridiculous sign?"

She giggles as she turns the car off and unbuckles her seat belt. "No, it's totally fine. I just have to run inside real fast."

I don't know what this place is and why we're here. I don't see a sign with the name or anything.

"Okay, whatever. I'm just gonna wait here." I pull my phone from my bag.

"All right, I'll just be a minute. Here are the keys." She drops them in the cup holder beside me, and I nod as she gets out of the car.

While I wait, I decide to cyber stalk my sister-in-law's Instagram to see the latest photos of the twins. I'll call them later and see if I can stop by for some baby snuggles soon. I've missed them so much.

Fifteen minutes later, I realize my sister still hasn't returned. *What the hell, Lauren?* I shoot her a text.

Me: *Just checking in….*
Me: *Are you okay?*

I was for those three little dots to appear, letting me know she's writing a response, but they never appear.

While I meant it as a joke that murder might take place here, her radio silence is worrying me a little. We may be downtown, but anything is possible, especially when I don't recognize the building she disappeared into and, more importantly, why we're here. Why didn't I think to push further on why we were here? And what's even more worrisome to me is when Lauren says she'll be right back, I assume she's true to her word and will be right back.

She couldn't have deserted me since I have the car keys. My eyes drop to where they're still sitting in the cup holder. Well, she wouldn't have deserted me willingly, at least. *Damnit, Dani, for making me watch all that true crime shit with her.*

Another five minutes pass. I try calling her, but it goes straight to voicemail. Okay, enough is enough. *Lauren, I'm coming in.*

Exiting the car and locking it up behind me, I take in my surroundings as I walk up to the entrance. I wrap my arms around my waist as the hairs on the back of my neck rise and a chill goes up my spine. *That can't be good.*

What the actual fuck?

When I open the door, the building is empty. It's a gorgeous open space—wood floors and bare white walls—but it's fucking empty. This was the building that Lauren had walked into, right? I look back out the front door and see her SUV right out front. Yeah, she walked around the vehicle and straight into the door.

"Hello," I shout. "Lauren?"

There's no answer, and I know something is off. I hear soft music playing somewhere. Okay, so maybe if someone was attacking my sister, they wouldn't be playing music, unless they would be to cover up her screams.

I quicken my steps. "Lauren, this isn't fucking funny. You're scaring the shit out of me." Again, no answer.

I jog up the few stairs and around the corner and gasp, dropping my phone to the ground with a loud clank.

Chapter 39

The wait for her to arrive nearly killed me. Lauren had texted when they were leaving the airport to give me some idea of how much time Finn and I had to finish setting this all up.

When I hear Kate yelling for Lauren, I have to press my lips together to suppress my laughter. Her clipped tone is full of annoyance. Little does she know, her sister snuck out the back and left already with her husband.

My pulse races the closer she gets. When I hear her coming up the stairs, I worry I might pass out.

It's now or never, but I'm hoping for forever.

She knocks the breath right out of me when she turns the corner and gasps. The only sound in the room is the clinking of her phone hitting the floor.

"Oh my God, Jaxon, what the fuck are you doing here?"

It may have been only a few days since I've seen her in person—staring at the photos of her on my phone don't count—but God, she's just as fucking beautiful as she was the first day I saw her.

"Jaxon?" she questions as she approaches hesitantly.

"Hey, baby." Her body tenses at the nickname, but I don't let that deter me.

"What are you doing here?" She bunches her brows, and I want to smooth the wrinkles away that have formed as she takes in the room. "Where's my sister? Did I fall asleep in the car and this is all a dream?" She then looks to the ground and lowers her tone, clearly talking more aloud to herself than to me. "Or maybe the plane went down and I'm actually living in an episode of *Lost*. Yeah, that's it."

I take that time that she focuses on the ground to close the distance between us. When I place my hands on her arms, jolts of electricity bring life to my veins, instantly shocking my heart like a defibrillator would.

"Does this feel real?" My voice is soft but steady.

She nods.

"Does this feel real?" I cup her cheek with one hand, running my thumb back and forth over her supple skin, and she nods again, this time bringing her bottom lip between her teeth. I free it with my thumb.

I repeat the question one more time after closing the distance and breathing those four words against her lips.

"Yes," she exhales as I press my lips to hers. Kissing Kate Lawson is like coming home. I would die a thousand deaths just to savor her lips one last time.

She sinks into my kiss, but I feel the moment her body tenses and she realizes what she's doing. With her palms flat on my chest, she pushes me away.

Her stance goes defensive, crossing her arms over her body as if she were protecting herself from me. I hate I made her feel that way. "I'm still so mad at you." She points her finger at me as if she hoped lasers would shoot out of them.

"I know. I had a sound plan in place, but as soon as I saw you, everything I had planned left my mind, and all I could think about was touching you and kissing you." This woman consumes me, mind, body, and soul.

"Well, you haven't earned the right to kiss me," she adds.

"Fair enough. You said you wanted to talk, so here I am." It killed me to not respond, but I knew as soon as I opened up to her, I'd never stop, and this was *not* the conversation to have via text messages. She needed to see how much I mean these words.

"Where is here exactly?" She finally takes the time to look around the room. Her eyes widen in shock, and that makes me smile harder as she takes in the rows and rows of cards Andy and I made today. There's two hundred and twenty-five, to be exact. One for every day since I met her. My hand is still sore and cramped from writing, but I hope the end result is totally worth it.

She walks over and looks at the cards. I follow her but keep enough distance for her not to bolt.

"I love your dimples on your lower back," she reads aloud and giggles, but I can tell she is confused. "I love how patient you are with Andy." She flips open another card. "I'm sorry for not telling you the moment I saw you how beautiful that dress was and that I imagined ripping it right off you." She glances over her shoulder and arches a brow, and I shrug.

Okay, so some of my cards, I'm grateful my son didn't know how to read or ask what they said.

"What are these?" She circles her finger toward the rows and rows of handmade cards inspired by Andy's thank-you card.

"Well, there are two hundred and twenty-five. One hundred and twelve things I love about you and one hundred and thirteen apologies. I'm sure there should have been a lot more moments I should apologize for, but I figured this was a start."

Kate's jaw drops, and I think for the first time since meeting, she is speechless. I should mark this down in history as the day Kate Lawson doesn't have anything to say.

"I never should have let you walk away from me, and when I did, I should have run after you. I shouldn't have waited to tell you all of this."

"Tell me what?" I watch her throat bob as she swallows.

"If you would stop interrupting me, I could finish." I pretend to be annoyed, but I know on one of the hanging cards reads one that says, "I love how you have so much to say that you always have to interrupt me before your brain forgets the thought."

"Kate, a long time ago, I fell in love, and I fell hard. Life was perfect—until it wasn't. One moment, we were laughing and waiting impatiently on the arrival of our son, and the next, I was a new father, holding my newborn as I watched my wife's body being lowered into the ground. What was supposed to be the best day of my life turned into the worst. I was alone to raise a son, and I know I had others, and I am forever thankful for the help from Finn and my in-laws, but in my mind, I was still alone. They could help me, but they had their own lives to live.

"I preferred it that way so I could give Andy the life that he deserved. I had to love him enough for two. There wasn't time for distractions."

I wince at my choice of words, remembering that was the word that hurt us to begin with.

"I'm sorry. I shouldn't have called you a distraction. There's a card somewhere up there saying that. You were—no, you *are* far from it. When I lost Court, I closed that part of my heart to anyone, because how could I possibly have enough room in my heart for more than just Andy in it? That was until you. I was a dick to you at first, because from the first moment I saw you, I knew you were trouble."

"My mom said the same thing," she jokes. Jokes and laughter are good. It means all hope isn't fully lost yet.

"I knew I was in trouble. And to be honest, the feelings that I felt in that moment scared the shit out of me. How could I feel something so powerful before I even knew you? It was easier to make you hate me than to take the chance to open up to love for a future with someone else.

"And then I finally let you in. And I fell hard and fast, baby. Thoughts of you consumed me. It wasn't until almost losing you I realized how much I—" I pause and swallow, ready to say it aloud for the first time.

"How much what?" Her voice is low and shaky, almost as if she is bracing herself for what comes next.

"How much I love you. I know it might seem fast, and maybe it is. But I love you, I do. Maybe all those months of fighting were just our version of foreplay. But I want it all with you, the good and bad times, the fights and making up, the growing old together."

"But what about—" I smirk at her continued interruptions. It's just part of who she is.

I cut her off. "Yes, I meant what I said the other night at dinner. Because of you, I finally thought about having a bigger family." Her expression falls, and I'm not going to let her insecurities slip through the cracks. "But there's only one thing that matters to me. And that's having you in my life. If that means it's just me, you, and Andy for the rest of our lives, then so be it. That is enough for me. You are enough for me.

"I know you think of this as a weakness, but do you realize how strong that makes you? You truly are amazing, and I will spend every single day until my last breath proving that to you."

At some point in my speech, our bodies have come together like magnets, and my hands are resting on her hips.

"How's that for apologies?" I joke, breaking the intensity of our stare.

"I'd say you've definitely improved," she laughs.

"Well, I'm bound to fuck up again, so I'm sure I'll only get better," I vow, causing us both to smirk, knowing that it's the truth.

Before she can respond, I grab the back of her neck and seal her lips to mine. She doesn't resist when I push my tongue into her mouth, deepening the kiss.

"But there's one part in all of that you forgot to mention," she says, pulling back reluctantly.

"Yeah, what's that?"

"I love you, too." Four words never sounded so perfect on her lips. I kiss her again. I will never stop kissing this woman. I pull her body against mine, and I'll be damned if I ever put another inch of space between us again.

When we finally pull back, breathless, tears are flowing down her cheeks. I swipe a few away with my thumb. "Please don't cry anymore. I don't ever want to be the reason for your tears again."

She shakes her head. "No, these are happy tears. I just can't believe you did all of this." Kate looks around the room, taking in more than just our little corner. "What even is this place?"

"Well, that's the second part of the surprise." In my best infomercial voice, I say, "But wait, there's more."

I link my fingers with Kate's and walk around the room. "This building belongs to one of our clients. It was actually him who I was meeting with the day you first watched Andy. We recently remodeled it, and he's now looking for a tenant."

"It's a beautiful space. It would make for an amazing art gallery."

The corners of my lips grow into an even bigger smile. "I'm glad you think so." I pull her toward the front entrance. She must have walked right past this on her way in. Although, I'm not surprised she walked in like a woman on a mission.

When she stops abruptly, I turn to find her mouth gaped open. "Umm, Jaxon, why is my art on the wall over there?"

"Well, because this gallery is for you." I wait with bated breath for her response.

"You can't buy me a gallery."

"Well, I didn't buy it, but I took care of the first three months of rent already. So even if you hate the idea, you can still have it for three months without issue. You are so talented, Kate, and deserve to have a place of your own for others to fall in love with you and your art just like I have."

I step up behind her and wrap my arms around her waist and rest my head against the top of hers. Our breathing syncs as one, and my body vibrates with each hiccup.

"What do you say, Kate? Just say yes."

One day, I hope she will say yes to another question, but I'm not in a rush for that.

"Yes," she breathes. Before she can say anything else, I lift her in my arms and spin her around. She squeals and holds me tighter.

"I love you." I smile into her hair as I spin her around

"I love you, too," she replies once I set her back on her feet. "And I hope you feel that way again when I tell you there is already an opening show booked for two weeks from now."

Her smile transforms into a scowl. "Jaxon McAdams," she shrieks, and it echoes throughout the building. I chuckle at how red her face has grown. "Two weeks." Kate clutches to her chest as she takes in the size of the surrounding space. "Oh my God, I can't be ready in two weeks."

"Hey, baby. Take a breath," I cup her cheeks and turn her focus on me. I get her to take a few calming breaths with me. "You can. Do you know how I know that?"

She shakes her head, but because of the way my hands are holding her cheeks, she ends up making a funny face.

"Because I'm going to be right by your side every step of the way."

Chapter 40

Kate

What a night. Tonight was the opening of the gallery. It still feels just so surreal to me that not only was all of my art hanging in there, but Jaxon was behind all of it. My entire family and group of friends were in attendance.

I'd spent the past two weeks preparing new pieces and gathering old pieces from storage. We filled the entire gallery with Kate Lawson originals.

Andy has long since passed out upstairs in his bed. No surprise he fell asleep on the ride home. He was the life of the party, schmoozing many folks.

Jaxon walks into the living room and hands me a glass of red wine before taking a seat beside me. He extends his arm along the back of the couch and pulls me closer. I sink back against his chest and take a long exhale.

As I take a long swig of my drink, I feel Jax's lips against my temple.

"I am so proud of you, baby." The amount of elation in his voice makes my heart swell. I feel like there's nothing I couldn't do with Jaxon by my side.

"I couldn't have done it without you."

"Hey." He leans forward and takes my wineglass and sets both our drinks on the coffee table. Jaxon tilts my chin to his face. His blue eyes stare directly into my soul. "Let's get one thing straight. You are the reason behind this—those people were there to see *your* art, *your* talent, *your* passion. I just helped acquire the space. So, get that through your pretty little head." He presses his lips against my forehead, and I close my eyes, relishing in the moment.

When he pulls back, I lift my gaze to him. It's hard to believe that the same man who looked at me with such hatred the moment we met is the same man who is looking at me with such love and pride. I spin in his arms and throw my leg over his, now straddling him.

I run my finger through his hair and grind my hips against his. "Well, I don't know that I've fully shown my appreciation for you doing that, have I." His cock hardens underneath me as I play with the buttons on his dress shirt.

"You know, I don't think you have." His voice is straining to keep composure as he pushes his erection against my clothed pussy.

"Then please allow me to show you, Mr. McAdams." I kiss my way down his neck.

Before things can escalate more, there is a knock at the door. We both quickly turn to look at the door as if making sure there was actually someone there.

"Expecting someone?" I ask, looking back at him.

He shakes his head. He double taps my thigh to hop off him, and I do. I pull my feet under me on the couch and laugh as Jax stands as he adjusts his erection.

My laughter causes him to look over his shoulder at me with a glare. There is a second knock at the door, and Jax yells, "I'm coming!"

"Well, not anymore," I mutter loud enough for him to hear me but hide my smile behind the wineglass.

"You're killing me," he breathes as he looks out the peephole and swings open the front door.

"Hey, sorry for showing up so late and unannounced. I hope we aren't interrupting anything." I recognize my sister's voice, and I turn to see Lauren and Finn standing in the doorway.

Jax and I share a knowing look before he steps to the side and grunts.

He grunts. "No, it's fine. Come on in." He ushers them inside.

I jump off the couch and run my hands down my dress. "Is everything okay?" My gaze bounces between my sister and brother-in-law.

"Yeah, everything is fine." Lauren waves her hand for me to take a seat, and I do, curling my legs underneath me.

"Can we get you guys something to drink?" Jaxon offers as he approaches.

Finn shakes his hand. "Nah, we're good. Thank you."

Jaxon takes his seat back beside me and rests his hand on my knee while Lauren and Finn settle on the love seat across from us. "So what's going on?"

Lauren looks up at Finn, and he nods. *Okay, I'm confused.* She turns her attention back to me, gentle smile on her lips. "I know this is still very early, but Finn and I have talked this over, and I want to give you something."

I expect her to pull a present out of her purse, but she remains still, so my confusion only increases. "I don't understand."

"We're identical twins," she states matter-of-factly.

"Yeah, I kind of know that," I respond sarcastically. *What does that have to do with anything?*

"Which means our DNA is the same. When the time is right, and you're ready…" Her gaze bounces between Jaxon and me. "I want to donate my eggs to you and even be your surrogate."

"What?" I shriek. "Lauren, I can't ask you to do that." *She can't be serious right now.*

"You didn't. I want to. I know it's obviously still early, and you two still have lots to work out and all, but when the time comes, I want to give you the life you always dreamed of. The life we stayed up late talking about as kids."

"We're so not ready for kids right now. We haven't even been back together all that long, and we still have so much to talk about." I glance over at Jaxon, who has remained silent. *Does this completely freak him out? Is he ready to run for the hills?* He must be able to sense my racing thoughts because he places his hand over mine reassuringly.

"I know. That's why I said *one day*." She and Finn share a sweet secretive look, as if they're having a nonverbal conversation. "Plus, there is one condition to me agreeing to this, anyway. I have to wait at least nine months."

I fly off the couch, bringing my hands to cover my mouth in shock. "Oh my God, are you—"

I don't get the chance to say pregnant before Lauren nods with the biggest smile on her face. I jump over Jax's feet and can't get to my sister fast enough to pull her into my arms and hold her tightly. "I am so happy for you." My voice cracks.

I can hear Finn and Jaxon talking and doing their manly hug with back slapping behind me, but I continue holding on to my sister. When I pull back, we both have to wipe tears from our eyes.

"Hey, you know I was there, too," Finn teases. I crinkle my nose, cringing before I let a giggle slip. I might know where babies come from, but I don't need the visual of how it happened.

"You're so needy, you know that?" I turn to Finn and wrap my arms around his shoulders. "But I'm so happy for you guys."

We all settle back in our seats, and a memory from this evening comes to the forefront of my mind. "That's why you turned down a glass of champagne tonight."

Lauren's hands rest on her flat stomach, and she nods.

"I knew something was up, but then you said you were driving tonight. So it made sense, and I didn't think more of it. But then when I saw you guys leaving, Finn got in the driver's seat. I can't believe I didn't put that together. Plus, your girls"—I wave my finger back and forth at her chest—"are looking pretty perky."

"Anyway, maybe let's not all stare at my wife's tits, 'kay?" He laughs, and we all follow.

"Getting back to being a surrogate, there is also a plan B in place. This isn't something we just thought about at a moment's notice."

I tilt my head to the side. "What do you mean? I'm not sure I can handle any more news tonight."

"Dani and I have spoken it over already, and she decided that if for whatever reason I can't do this, she and Kyler have agreed that she will do it, but I will still donate my egg."

"What?" My voice reaches a high pitch loud enough to wake Andy upstairs. "That's crazy." I shake my head in disbelief.

I'm still shaking my head when my sister walks over to me and takes a seat on the other side of me.

"Kate." Her voice is stern. "It's not up for discussion." She takes my hands in hers. "Let us do this for you."

How can I even argue with her? This is all just so much, so all I can do is nod.

Lauren and Finn stay just a little longer and talk about what they know so far about her pregnancy and her due date before we say our goodbyes.

Jaxon and I stand at the front door, waving as they leave.

As Jaxon closes and locks the door, I pace the floor, trying to fully process the events of the evening.

"I don't even know what to say. There are so many emotions going through my head. I think I'm still in shock."

Closing the distance between us, he cups my cheeks and silences my rambling with his lips.

I grip the front of his shirt and deepen the kiss, channeling all my love for this man into this kiss.

Jaxon pulls back, and I whine, chasing his lips. Chuckling, he places a quick peck on my lips. He takes my hands from his shirt and loops them around his neck before resting his hands just above my ass. "So, Ms. Lawson, you have everything you ever dreamed of. What more could you possibly want?"

I feel like this is the moment a reporter interviews a football player who just won the Super Bowl and he responds with "I'm going to Disney World."

I twist my lips in thought. "Hmm, what more could I want?"

Jaxon leans down and places kisses along the column of my neck. "Mmm," he groans against my skin.

"I was thinking more like something I need," I say, emphasizing the last word.

"Yeah, what's that?" he breathes against my skin.

"I need your cock inside me," I demand.

Before I can even blink, Jaxon has led me over to the couch, him sitting on the edge with his legs spread. I step up between them, leaving my breasts directly in his face. He leans forward, capturing my nipple with his teeth through my shirt and bra. Fingers slowly dance up the back of my thighs and slip under my skirt. Bunching the skirt around my waist, he discards the sorry excuse for panties. They are so wet in just a short about of time—that's how much Jaxon turns me on—I'm surprised they didn't make a sound when he tosses them aside.

Jaxon quickly removes his pants and boxers and sinks back against the couch.

His eyes burn with desire as I rub my thighs together in anticipation.

"Are you going to just stand there and watch me, or are you going to be a good girl and sink that cunt down on my cock? Look how hard you make me." I watch him slowly stroke his shaft. *God, I could get off just watching this man touch himself.*

I grasp onto his shoulders as I straddle him. His hands instinctively go to my ass, where he presses his fingers deep, massaging the skin.

"Good girl," he pants. I never knew I had a slight praise kink until the first time he used those two words. Now each time he says them, I'm ready to do anything he says.

Jaxon drags the tip of his cock through my slit, gathering my arousal. My pussy clenches at his teasing. "You know the best part about all this?" I shake my head. I slowly sink down on him until my pelvis rests against his. "And they lived happily ever after."

Epilogue

Kate

Three years later…

"You ready for this?" Jaxon pauses in front of the solid wood door and pulls me into his arms. My chest heaves up and down. Anxiety and excitement flood my veins. He cups my cheeks and brushes the few tears I let slip away.

"Ready as I'll ever be." I sigh and lean into his touch.

He leans in, hovering his mouth over mine. "I love you," he whispers before pressing his lips to mine.

"I love you, too," I reply once we break apart.

He kisses the tip of my nose, and I can't hold back my smile. "Now, go help bring our daughter into the world." I can't believe it. The day is finally here that we get to meet our daughter.

I nod and press up on my toes and kiss him once more before opening the hospital room door. I find Finn standing next to the hospital bed, where my sister lies. Lauren's eyes are closed as Finn dabs her forehead with a washcloth and whispers words of encouragement.

"Hey, sis." I smile because how could I not be at this moment?

Lauren turns to me, and I cringe. Woah, the look on her face is fucking terrifying. "Next time I come up with a brilliant idea, tell me to keep my mouth shut. I thought they said labor the second time round was much easier. Labor with Nathan was nothing like this."

"Well, maybe don't listen to Haylee since she claims she can cook, too, and we all know that's far from the truth."

A contraction hits before she can continue. Lauren sits up quickly, reminding me of the childhood game Don't Wake Daddy and grabs Finn's hand.

"You're doing great, Lo. Just breathe, baby," her husband sweetly coos to her.

She ignores the gesture, gritting her teeth and tightening her grip on his hand. He winces in pain, and all color drains from his face, heading to his hand, which has now turned from a bright shade of red to a deep blue. *Damn, who knew my sister was so strong?*

"Stop staring and come over and help," my sister shouts. "I'm doing this for you, Katherine Renee McAdams."

Oh shit, she means business with the use of my full name. But I must admit, as much shit as I gave both Dani and Lauren over the years for smiling every time they heard their married name, I know that as I rush to my sister's side, there is no match for the smile on my lips.

It's still weird to not officially be a Lawson anymore. Obviously, I will always be one, but now I am officially a McAdams. Last Christmas morning, Jaxon, along with the help of Andy, proposed.

We had just finished opening Christmas presents, surrounded by mountains of wrapping paper. A fresh layer of snow fell the night before, and Andy was so excited to go outside and play. Jaxon had told him he had to wait until after we opened presents.

"Daddy, is it time? Is it time?" Andy jumped up and down, tugging on his dad's hand while we sat on the couch.

"Yeah, buddy, it's time." He winked and kissed my temple.

"Yes," Andy hissed and pumped his arms excitedly in the air.

"Come on, Ms. Kate." Andy grabbed my hand and pulled me to my feet. He pulled me up with such a force I had to steady myself on my feet.

"All right, little dude, how about we get you changed?" I suggested once I caught my balance.

"Already done," he exclaimed as he untied his robe and discarded it on the floor. He was no longer wearing the Christmas pajama top he wore last night. When on Earth did he change?

I expected him to take off running up the stairs, but he turned around to face me.

I gasped, bringing both of my hands to cover my mouth when I looked down and read the writing on his T-shirt. In bold red letters read, "Will you be my mom?"

"Oh my God," I breathed and followed Andy's gaze behind me. As I slowly turned, I found Jaxon no longer on the couch but down on one knee.

"What do you say, babe? Want to be stuck with us forever?"

I choked on my tears at his choice of words. "How romantic. Well, when you put it that way, how can a girl resist?"

He opened a small black velvet box to reveal a gorgeous diamond ring. Beside the ring was a smaller stone—Andy's birthstone.

I nodded. "Yes."

While our engagement may not have been as short as Lauren and Finn's, we didn't wait all that long. By Valentine's Day, we were married in a small courthouse ceremony. Jaxon, Andy, and I officially became a family in front of just our families. Not long after, Lauren had been inseminated with the eggs that had been mixed with Jaxon's sperm, and we must have had some higher power on our side because on the first try, a miracle had happened—*we were expecting.*

"Come on, Lauren, one last push. You're almost there." I will every ounce of strength into my sister as I encourage her to keep going. If I could trade places with her, I would, but watching her go through this makes me love her that much more.

She screeches like a banshee during her push, but my sister's sounds of horror are quickly replaced by the first wails of my child. The breath is literally ripped from my body as I watch the doctor hold her up.

"Congrats, it's a girl," the doctor says.

The tears are flowing as I lay my eyes on my daughter for the first time, and there is no stopping it.

The doctors are tending to my sister as another set of nurses cleans up my daughter. One walks over to me, carrying a wrapped-up bundle of joy—*my bundle of joy.*

"What do you say, Mom? Would you like to hold your daughter?" As if the answer is anything but fuck yes.

"Yes," I say, barely above a whisper. The hospital was aware of our situation, obviously not the first to go through this, and had brought in a second hospital bed so that I could lie with the baby to bond.

I slip out of my T-shirt, leaving me in a camisole, and settle into the bed next to my sister.

"Here she is, Mom. Meet your baby girl."

Oh my God. She is beautiful and all mine. Movement continues to happen around us, but all I can focus on is my daughter. Her beautiful brown eyes match mine and are wide as she takes in the new world around her.

Moments pass when there is a knock on the door.

"Come in," Lauren announces. The doctors have finished cleaning her up and are allowing her to rest before getting moved to the recovery room.

My gaze leaves my daughter's for just a moment to meet the gorgeous eyes of my husband. He's going to be jealous that she has my brown eyes versus his blue.

"Jaxon," I whimper through my tears. "You want to come meet your daughter?" I'm impressed that I somehow choked that question out and he could understand me.

His hand covers his mouth, trying to hide his emotions. I know he has been extremely anxious about this moment, especially after what happened with Courtney, but I had hope and faith that she was looking down on us as we brought our baby girl into this world.

Jaxon joins me on the bed. "Baby, meet our daughter, Hope Elizabeth McAdams." I adjust myself carefully and place her in her daddy's arms. Giving my daughter my sister's middle name doesn't even begin the express the gratitude we have for her. It's because of Lauren and her selflessness that we can have this moment right now. We had discussed if this hadn't worked, we could always try adoption, but Lauren was stubborn as hell and wanted to at least give this a shot.

He presses his lips against mine before pressing a tender kiss to Hope's forehead.

"Hi, baby girl. I'm your daddy."

I didn't think I could fall any more in love with this man, but at that very moment, witnessing him with our daughter, I fall head over heels in love with him all over again.

At some point, Finn slips out of the room, and we relish in the moment as a family together, completely forgetting that Lauren is resting on the bed beside us.

My sister is seriously a rock star for doing what she did today. I have no clue how Dani did that twice at once.

There is another knock at the door before it opens. Finn enters the room, carrying their son, Nathan—a spitting image of Finn—in his arms, one hand around Andy as he escorts him into the room. He gives Andy's shoulder a gentle squeeze before walking over and kissing Lauren on the forehead. "You did so good, Lo."

My nephew reaches for his mama, and she eagerly accepts him into her arms. "Mama!"

"Carefully, baby. Mommy is a little sore." Lauren winces as she hugs Nathan tightly.

Lauren looks up and smiles at me as I mouth, "Thank you."

When I turn back to my family, Andy is still standing at the edge of the bed, looking hesitant and nervous. Jaxon carefully stands, still holding Hope in his arms. I'm pretty sure I might need to pry her out of his arms to ever hold her again.

He walks over to our son—yes, *our* son. The paperwork officially went through not long after our marriage for me to adopt Andy.

"Andy, this is your little sister, Hope." Jaxon leans down so that Andy can see her cute little face shown under the pink hat with a bow.

His face lights up, and I'm pretty sure I hear, "Aww," from where my sister and her family are.

"Can I hold her?" Andy asks, looking up at Jaxon.

"Sure, buddy." He nods over to the bed. "Come sit in bed next to Mom."

I'm not sure I'll ever get over the fact that I'm a mom—a dream that a little girl once had ripped away, now a reality with a stepson and now a daughter. I was never going to push for Andy to call me Mom because, well, he already has one. We've never shied away from talking about Courtney when he asked. There were more questions about his mom as he got older—more so he wanted to hear Jaxon tell him stories about her and if they had the same mannerisms. But the first time he called me Mom, I nearly fell over. I hadn't realized how much I had actually craved motherhood until that moment. It felt like my heart was finally complete then—that is, until this very moment.

Andy climbs in the bed beside me, gives me a brief hug, and smiles. Jaxon comes up beside us and gently places Hope in Andy's arms. "Hold her head, okay? Just like you do with your cousins." Andy is a natural with Nathan and was amazing when the twins and Harper were babies.

Andy stares at her for a moment before opening his mouth.

"Hi, Hope. I'm Andy, your big brother. I'm going to always be there for you, I promise." My heart is overflowing with love as he presses a kiss to her little cheek. "And my other mom will look out for you when I can't."

THE END

Also By

What's Next...

Scars

An emotional, angsty, second chance romance
Coming Fall 2022

Returning to my hometown of Meadows Ridge, I'm just as broken as the day I left.
I'm no longer the teenager who had everything at his fingertips. All it took was one moment to turn the world as we knew it into a painful memory.
I deserve the nightmares plaguing me.
Then there's her, Riley Parker—the woman I left behind, my bleeding heart still in her hands. The hurt and anger in her doe eyes is justified. But I'm determined to prove to her that deep down, I'm still the same Cooper Graham she once loved.
Will I be able to get off this path of destruction, or am I doomed to live with the scars branded on my soul forever?

Playlist

A Mother's Prayer – Celine Dion
 To Build A Home – The Cinematic Orchestra
 Silent Night – Mariah Carey
 You Outta Know – Alanis Morissette
 Fade Into You – Mazzy Star
 What's Left of Me – Nick Lachey
 Waves – Dean Lewis
 All I Need – Within Temptation
 Hard to Say I'm Sorry – Chicago
 Fantasy – Mariah Carey
 Only Love Can Hurt Like This – Paloma Faith
 Oh Holy Night - Cary Brothers
 Slipped Away - Avril Lavigne
 Boogie Shoes – KC & The Sunshine Band
 Let Them Be Little – Billy Dean
 You Were Supposed to Be Different – Aron Wright
 Bad Liar - Imagine Dragons

Acknowledgments

I swear I dread writing this page more than I do the book itself. There are so many people to thank so I apologize if I have forgotten anyone.

The Reader: Well I should start with saying, your tears have been extra tasty haha I went back to my more emotional roots to finish off this series. If this is your first book of mine or your eighth, thank you for taking a chance on my words—these pages are literally my blood, sweat and my own tears for you. Ya'll have waited two years for this book, well some longer because you fell in love with Kate in book 1. I hope I did it justice.

Ethel: ETHEL!!! I'm not really sure there are words for what you've done to stick by myside during the shitstorm that was writing this book. Thank you for making me laugh and giving me a swift kick in the butt when I needed.

J & J: Thank you for dangling books in my face to get me to accomplish my writing goals. And the ocassional alien peen smacking.

Claudia: Thank you for telling me that the Lawson twins needed to have their story told. And just so I can make sure the world knows—Daddy Jax is all yours.

Amanda: Almost three years ago, we chatted about what my plans were for this series just days after typing the end on Zach and Haylee. When I told you the ringer I had planned for Kate, you were the one to convince me that her story should be the big finale. There were moments writing the twins books that I heavily cursed that decision but in the end, you were right. And I hope I karatekicked you in the feels with that final line. Thank you for your never ending support.

To my author friends: There are just too many to name so thank you for your constant support.

Peachy Keen Author Services: Thank you for handling everything with the review tour of the I Never Series.

Kate with Ya'll That Graphic: We've sat on this cover for over two years. Thank you for taking my silly drawing and bringing the covers of this series to life.

Sandra with One Love Editing: Thank you for dealing with my crazy ass even if I make you ugly cry on page 4. (Get ready for the next one *winkface*)

My Street Team: I couldn't do this without you. Thank You!

My facebook reader group: Ya'll haven't left me even when I let these crazy characters takeover the group and tell you what they are up to in life, which is quite often. I love you guys more than life.

Lindee Robinson, Andrew & Alyse: Lindee, thank you for taking my character description and helping me find the perfect images for this cover. And of course Andrew and Alyse for matching the vision of Kate and Jaxon in my head.

While the I Never Series may be finally finished, this may or may not be the last you see of this crew. Just saying…

About Author

Stefanie Jenkins is a contemporary romance author and stay at home mom. Born and raised in Maryland, she has called Surf City, NC home since 2018 with her husband, two sons and black lab. When not bringing the characters to life in her head, Stefanie enjoys reading, watching cooking shows, listening to true crime podcasts and collecting coffee mugs with funny sayings. You can always put a smile on her face with a Dunkin Donuts iced coffee, photos of Grant Gustin and inappropriate memes.

For exclusive content, join Stefanie's Facebook Reader Group-
https://www.facebook.com/groups/sjtalkwordytome

You can also connect with Stefanie through:
Facebook: Author Stefanie Jenkins
Instagram: @authorstefaniejenkins
TikTok: @authorstefaniejenkins

Amazon

Goodreads